THE
NIGHT
OF
MANY
ENDINGS

ALSO BY MELISSA PAYNE

The Secrets of Lost Stones

Memories in the Drift

THE
NIGHT
OF
MANY
ENDINGS

MELISSA PAYNE

LAKE UNION
PUBLISHING

Published by Lake Union Publishing, Seattle

www.apub.com

Amazon, the Amazon logo, and Lake Union Publishing are trademarks of Amazon.com, Inc., or its affiliates.

ISBN-13: 9781542029254
ISBN-10: 1542029252

Cover design by David Drummond

Printed in the United States of America

To Sean, my study buddy potato, my friend, my boyfriend, and my husband. This life is infinitely better with you by my side.

CHAPTER ONE

NORA

Nora Martinez stood in an empty parking lot on the edge of town, with its sun-burned asphalt rippled and cracked, weeds clawing up from the earth like zombified hands from a grave. She held a shopping bag of food in her hands, her nerves an electric tangle that poked against her skin.

The last she'd heard, her brother may have been couch-surfing with friends in Denver sometime last year. She only knew this through his loose collection of friends. The ones who'd partied with him in their twenties but who were able to stop when it was time to grow up. It hadn't taken long for Mario to grow apart from them, occasionally showing up for help or a place to sleep when he was more sober than not. And they took him in every time, motivated by guilt over anything else.

Nora understood guilt and how it had long arms that circled and squeezed and made it hard to breathe. But she also knew that guilt had a purpose too. And it was a driving force that shaped her life, gave it dimension and meaning. She had survived the accident, but in many ways, Mario had not.

The late-afternoon sun was a buttery yellow. In its warmth, even the shattered windows and broken bay doors of the old factory seemed less sad. But then, like it does in early spring, the light retreated when the sun slipped behind the trees, and the abandoned factory that rose before her became what it was—a rusted blight against the easy green of the pine trees and the angular peaks of the mountains.

She was here because of what Nonnie had said during a game of checkers about the homeless man who'd set up camp out by the old factory. Nora volunteered at the shelter once or twice a week, preparing food or setting up cots and sometimes just hanging out. She'd become a fixture over the years, and many of the regulars were comfortable with her. Nonnie was in her midfifties, with a pronounced lisp due to her two missing front teeth that, she'd once told Nora, had been punched out by a man, and why she'd rather be homeless than live with him for another damn minute. She had said this with a lift of her chin and a hardness in her eyes, and Nora had agreed. It had been a very brave thing indeed to leave him.

She felt comfortable talking to someone like Nonnie about Mario; she was one of the few people Nora had told about him who understood and didn't judge or tell her what she should or shouldn't do.

Nonnie had jumped two of Nora's checkers when she casually mentioned the man she'd seen, said he'd had a really bad limp. *Doesn't your brother have a bad limp?*

Nora's pulse had thumped so hard she felt it in her neck. A familiar sensation came over her, and she'd tried to push it away, but a wave of hope had crashed around her heart. There had been so many false alarms over the years, each one followed by a terrible desperation and a sinking feeling that he was lost forever. So she'd tried to stay calm, remind herself that it was more than likely someone else. Mario had always stayed in and around Denver anyway; he'd never come back to

Silver Ridge. Not since that horrible day when Nora was nine and she screamed at him to leave.

Nonnie had cleared the board, a triumphant smile on her lips, and Nora, grateful that the game was over, tried to be casual when she asked, *Did you talk to him? Was his name Mario?*

He only just came into town. Nonnie's gray eyebrows came together and she shrugged. *Didn't catch his name.*

Nora had already picked up her bag, her legs itching to sprint from the shelter and to her car. It was probably a false alarm, but there was always the chance it wasn't.

He seemed too young to be so bad off, Nonnie added. *'Course I was young once, too, you know.*

Nora had nodded her agreement before hurrying out the door and driving straight here.

But now she hesitated, her feet stuck to the warped pavement, the empty factory before her, wanting to enjoy the moment, when finding him seemed possible, before it all came crashing down, like it had too many times to count. A breeze brushed across her face, cooling the heat in her cheeks.

Her phone buzzed with a text, and she rubbed the back of her neck, grateful for the distraction. She cringed when she saw a message from Amanda.

Hey, we ate without you. I hope you're okay, but you probably just forgot.

She was supposed to meet her friend for dinner at six tonight. It was almost seven. She'd forgotten.

Joshua was looking forward to meeting you. Whatever.

3

Who was Joshua? She had a vague recollection of Amanda mentioning someone on the phone yesterday, but it had been while Nora was at Walmart with the phone pressed between her shoulder and her ear. Amanda's voice had been pleasant background chatter to Nora quietly counting the cans and boxes of food she'd loaded into her cart for a food drive at the elementary school.

Sorry A. I heard some news today. Her hands shook when she typed the next line. I think Mario might be in Silver Ridge. Out looking for him now.

Of all people, Amanda would understand. They'd shared a small apartment in college, and an easy friendship had grown between them, made stronger by a shared love of old rom-coms, hiking, and a desire to travel. They'd both wanted to take a few months after college to see the world, so Amanda had pinned a map to the wall of their tiny living room, pulled out a slim case of darts, and with a smile, said, *Let the darts decide.* The only dart that actually stuck into the hard wall had landed on Kansas. So Amanda had declared that the darts had no soul.

Then Mario had come back into Nora's life, and Amanda had gotten to know him during the few sober years he'd lived with Nora. In between her own travels abroad, her friend had stuck by Nora during the rehabs, relapses, and homelessness that came later. Nora loved to flip through her pictures and hear Amanda tell her in detail what the pyramids looked like and how the crystal-clear water in the Caribbean teemed with fish of every color and size.

Maybe Amanda had carried the load of their friendship these last few years, but her friend always seemed to understand. Amanda had known Mario when he was sober and working so hard to stay that way, so surely she saw what Nora always had: a man so damaged by the past he was frozen into the boy who had driven his family off a cliff. And if Nora couldn't be the ideal friend now, she would eventually—once Mario was safe and back on the road to recovery.

Nora typed fast. I'm really sorry.

Dots blinked in return, then went away before words sprang across her screen. You always are.

An anxious feeling pressed into her chest. The idea that Amanda might give up on her or drift away like so many people in her life made Nora bite her nail. I'll make it up to you, A. Promise. I'll text Joseph and explain, k?

It's Joshua, you dunce ☺, and I gave him your number. He's going to call you. You're welcome. Be safe and text me later.

Nora snorted. She could hardly maintain a friendship, much less date; his call would go straight to voice mail. But at least Amanda didn't seem mad anymore.

A link popped up on their text chain to a podcast called *Tales from the Flip*.

I wasn't sure if I should send this to you but you need to listen to it. Call me when you do. Love you, girl.

Nora breathed out and dropped the phone in her purse. Amanda was a good friend. Nora would check out her latest recommendation later, maybe even drop by after work tomorrow, bring dinner, and watch one of their favorites, *When Harry Met Sally*. Like old times. She rolled her shoulders. One day she'd be the friend that Amanda deserved, and they could finally travel somewhere together, maybe even take that trip to Kansas. Nora smiled to herself. Ha!

Cool air kicked up, and she crossed her arms, wishing she'd remembered a sweater. But it had been a warm March day, the cruel kind that teases with the promise of tiny aspen leaves and melting snow, and she'd been fooled into optimism. A stiffer breeze picked up her hair, whirled it around her face, and she glanced at the clouds that swarmed above her. There was a storm moving in tomorrow, a winter one with historic levels of snow predicted. But it was spring and a famously inaccurate time to try to predict the weather. It would fizzle, most suspected, leaving the weather people to shake their heads, shrug, and comment on the fickleness of Colorado storms.

The sound of fabric snapping against the wind set her pulse beating fast. Across the lot, she saw the edge of an orange tent, the unzipped door flapping open and closed. She gripped the handles of the shopping bag and started to pick her way across the uneven lot and toward the tent. Her uncle had worked at this factory. Right up until it shut its doors, leaving him and her aunt with twin baby girls, plus Nora, and no income. Mario had been long gone by this point, his recovery no longer a financial burden—just the emotional kind that built up like a brick wall between Nora and Aunt Sophie and Uncle Victor. She'd felt stranded and alone, a tireless advocate for her brother. Her throat grew tight with memory. It had been a hard time for all of them.

Her phone buzzed again, this time a call from a number she didn't recognize, and she groaned. Must be Jacob/Joseph/John. She pressed "Ignore" and kept walking.

Around the side of the building, the one closer to the forest, and set against the concrete wall of the factory was the tent, its unzipped opening snapping back and forth in the wind.

"Hello?" she called, and the sound of her voice against the vacantness of the building made her feel the sharp edges of loneliness that saturated the threadbare tent, so out of place against concrete and brick.

The shelter flapped, and from where she stood, it looked empty. She moved closer and her breath knotted in her chest, stuck within a lump of hope. "Hello? Mario?" Saying his name out loud felt every bit the foolish wish it was. She dug her fingers into her palms, straightened her back. Whoever camped here was someone like Mario, someone down on their luck, chewed up and spit out and doing the best they could to survive.

She knelt down and peered inside. A greasy sleeping bag—torn in spots, the stuffing pulled out of the holes like gunshot wounds—was balled up against one side of the tent. In the middle was a roll of toilet paper unspooled into a long white tail. Puffs of air sent it skittering across the vinyl tent bottom, where it danced with wrappers and plastic bags, used needles, and other trash. The campsite looked abandoned. Nora shivered, sat back on her heels. For a moment she didn't know if she felt relief or disappointment, but her heart broke for whoever had called this tent home. It was difficult to see anyone reduced to living in these conditions, harder still to know that her brother often had.

Mario wasn't here. She felt sure of it because whoever had been staying here was gone. There was a staleness to the space inside the tent, a feeling that it had been abandoned.

She stood up, rubbed her arms, and looked around, feeling vulnerable in the empty lot. Nonnie had said that most of the homeless people in town would be going to the shelters ahead of the storm. If her brother had been here, that's what he would do—Mario didn't mess with winter storms, not after that night so long ago. But in case the person who'd camped here hadn't left, she set the shopping bag of food—chips, water, Gatorade, energy bars, and a couple of apples—inside the tent and backed away.

In the shadow of the building above her, surrounded by forest and beat-up asphalt, she felt futility nip at her efforts, and for the briefest of moments, she wondered if it was all for nothing: her volunteering to help others in his same situation; donating clothes and money and all the time to shelters and programs that helped the homeless; the weekend hours spent searching, asking questions about a man with a terrible limp and kind eyes and with the deep voice he once used to sing her past the nightmares.

She shook her head, clearing it of the doubts that hung in the shadows, waiting for moments just like this, and added a business card to the bag of groceries that listed the local shelters and included one word she'd scribbled before in the car. *Peaches.* Because if her brother was here, he'd know she had come to find him. Squinting at the sky, she hugged her arms across her body and hurried back to her car. In the span of a few minutes, the clouds had piled on top of each other, layers of fast-moving wisps and grayish-black denseness. Now it was just plain cold. She slid into her car, grateful to find it held on to the early warmth of the day, and with one last glance at the tent, she pulled away.

~

On the way back through town, Nora called the few local shelters and asked if a man with a limp had come in. Most of the volunteers knew her by name and were happy to help, but nobody fitting Mario's description had arrived yet. Pine trees loomed over the curved road, bowing from an onslaught of wind that pressed against her car and sent brittle aspen leaves skipping across the yellow line. She just hoped that the poor soul out by the factory had found her bag of food and would eventually make his way to somewhere safe and warm, if he hadn't already.

Darkness had fallen when she drove through town and past the library. Her library, she thought with a smile, but only to herself because she believed it was a space for everybody. She'd once heard a librarian describe it perfectly on a podcast—that libraries were one of the last places someone could go where they didn't have to buy or believe in anything to come in. She thought it was so perfect she'd printed it out on a piece of paper that she laminated—a skill she'd honed to near perfection at the library—and kept it on her desk to let anyone who walked through the library doors know that all were welcome here.

The small lamppost at the end of the walkway to the library was lit, a beacon in the dark, and in the half-moon glow, a figure in a black coat huddled against the increasing cold. She knew this man. He'd been in the library to use the bathroom last week, and she'd made him take a library card even though he insisted he just wanted to piss and leave. She wasn't supposed to issue library cards to folks if they didn't have a permanent address, so she used a shelter address and had decided long ago that if the board had a problem with it, they could fire her. To date, they had left her alone, largely because one of the board members, Charlie, had been a fierce advocate for Nora and her unorthodox ways.

She glanced at the passenger seat and the remaining small bags of food and drinks. Nora made sure to have a few on hand every day in case she ran into anybody who needed to eat or hear a kind word. The temperature had dropped even more, and the cold tips of Nora's fingers made her worry for the man, who would likely spend the entire night outside, so she pulled her car into one of the slanted street parking spots in front of the library.

From the way the weather had turned so fast, she knew from experience that something big was coming, and she had to ignore an uneasiness that pulled at the muscles across her back. When she was six years old, a winter storm took everything from her. If she could, she would have moved like her aunt and uncle did, to a warmer climate where she'd never have to feel the cold sting of snow ever again. But she was her brother's only link to the family they'd once had, and she'd never abandon him. She'd done that once before: pushed him away, thinking it would be good for him; thinking that if she told him to get better, he would and everything would go back to normal. Instead, she'd found him sprawled on the front lawn, his skin blue, eyes sunken inside his head, foamy spit running from the corners of his mouth and onto the dead blades of grass.

"Hello!" She walked toward the man huddled inside his coat with the bag held out in front of her, shivering from the cold. The wind was biting, and her nose had already started to run. "I think we met the other day. I'm Nora." The man turned his head into his coat collar, mumbled something she couldn't hear. "You're, um—" She searched her memory for his name. "Lewis, right?"

The man hunched his shoulders and sat down with his back against the metal pole of the lamppost. "You can't make me leave," he said.

He wouldn't look her in the eye, and his voice was indignant and cautious, the tone of someone wary and mistrustful. She saw Mario in the protective curve of this man's back, the tatters of his coat, the weathered skin of his cheeks. He wasn't her brother, but he was somebody's brother or husband or father. Someone out there must lie awake worrying about him, their heart breaking just like her own.

She put the bag onto the sidewalk and took a few steps backward toward her car. "There's some food, water, and a Gatorade in there and—" She pointed up to the sky. "I think it might snow tomorrow. There's a card in there with the few shelters we have in town. You're, um, kinda new around here, right?"

He huddled into a tighter ball and didn't answer.

"Anyway, take care of yourself, okay, Lewis?" She had volunteered enough to know that sometimes less was more, so she walked back to her car, and as she drove away, she saw Lewis come out of his huddle and grab the bag of food.

From the console came a ding and a buzz and a voice mail banner stretched across her phone's screen. She picked it up, her eyes darting from the road to her phone, driving slowly enough to keep from drifting onto the sidewalk. She opened her phone and glanced quickly at the screen. Two voice messages, both from unfamiliar numbers. She groaned. The first was from an hour ago and must be from the guy Amanda was trying to set her up with. But the other one came in last week. Somehow she'd missed it. Her pulse sped up with a familiar worry. What if it was Mario?

She pushed "Play." At first there was only silence, and she relaxed her grip on the wheel. Probably just another robocall. She was about to hit "Delete" when a man spoke. "Hey, Nora, it's Mario."

Her face went numb, and her thoughts jammed up, making the road ahead blurry. She pulled the car over, sliding into a spot in front of Elk Falls Middle School, and suddenly she was twelve years old and sitting in class, staring at her phone and hoping her brother would call and explain why he hadn't shown up. Again.

"I'm sorry to call like this; I know it's been a while, but I just needed to hear your voice," he said.

It had been over a year since she'd last heard from him, and then it had been for only a few minutes when he'd called to tell her he was getting an apartment with a friend. He'd never called back, and the number he'd used to phone her had been disconnected soon after. Nora had assumed it hadn't worked out, like so many plans Mario had had over the years.

She pressed the phone to her ear, wanting to hear every word, trying not to breathe or move or miss anything. A snowflake hit her windshield, melting quickly.

"My roommate, Adam—you don't know him; he's been sober for five years, Nora, five fucking whole years." And then he started to cry—quiet, muffled sobs—and she pictured him on the other end of the phone, holding a fist to his mouth, like he had once as a teenager when he thought he was alone in his room: doubled over with an arm pressed into his stomach like he was going to be sick and his back shaking silently. The door had been open, and seven-year-old Nora had pressed her eye to the crack and watched, frozen. Then she tiptoed back to her bed and pulled the covers over her head, scrunching her eyes closed, sucking on her thumb, and trying to forget how sad he sounded, how alone he looked with his missing leg and tears.

"He died, Nora. Right here, in his own bed. He overdosed. I—I found him this morning, and then I had to call his dad. Oh God, Nora, his dad." His deep voice broke over the word, cracking like a rock split in two. Her aunt used to say that Mario's voice was perfect for radio, deep and velvet smooth, even when he was a teenager. She used to try to encourage him like that, in small ways, hoping that something would stick, that something would motivate him to try. It was one of the reasons Nora had loved Aunt Sophie so much.

"Oh, Mario, I'm so sorry," she said into the phone, wishing he could hear it.

"I never want you to have to get a phone call like that. Ever." He sniffled, seemed to regroup, because when he spoke again, his voice was calmer.

She stared out the window and blinked hard against a pressure behind her eyes. Outside, the first floor of the school was lit up, and a scattered few individuals hustled up the steps, heads down against the wind, past the bronzed statue of an elk and into the front doors of the school. For most of his life, Mario had tried on sobriety like a new sweater, but it just never seemed to fit, and each failed attempt had sent him into a tailspin of depression where he'd disappear for months, sometimes longer. It hurt to see him struggle, hurt to see him fail.

"Listen, I just—I'm afraid, Nora. Adam's dad is here and I"—his voice shook—"I don't think I can do this alone. I might check into rehab, maybe." There was a loud noise, like he'd punched something. "Five fucking years, Nora! What's the point?"

Silence, and Nora pressed the phone to her ear, heart in her throat.

"Listen, I just wanted to hear your voice, but I was wrong. I shouldn't have called." He sniffed. "Yeah, so, I hope you're doing good and living life the way you should. Have you been to the Great Wall of China yet, Peaches?"

She nearly smiled. It had been a childhood dream after she'd read about it in a book at the library. When she was eight, she'd started a fifty-cents-a-day fund and told Mario it was so she could go see the

Great Wall of China. She'd begged her aunt for odd jobs around the house and loved the plink of a coin when it landed in her piggy bank.

By the time she was nine, Nora had saved eighty-nine dollars and sixteen cents. Every night before she went to bed, she'd tapped the piggy bank and smiled, already picturing herself standing on the Wall and looking out over the vast emerald-green mountains. Until the morning of Thanksgiving, when she'd found it smashed to pieces, the money gone and her dream along with it.

"Life's too fucking short, Nora." There was another long silence. "I shouldn't have called. Don't call back. I'll be fine, okay? Bye, Peaches."

The message ended, and something in the way he said goodbye left her cold. Immediately she went to her call list; the number had an unfamiliar area code. She pressed the callback button, her leg jiggling while it rang straight to voice mail.

"You've reached Ed. Leave a message."

The unfamiliar voice threw her. "Um, oh—hi, this is Nora Martinez. I received a message from this number from my brother, Mario. Do you know him? I'm really worried about him, so please call me back right away, okay? Thanks." She added her phone number and started to push "End" but instead pressed the phone back to her ear. "Anytime day or night, it doesn't matter, okay? Thanks again and please call me back as soon as you can."

The phone dropped to her lap, and her shoulders slumped. Mario was out there somewhere, hurting and alone and scared, and she sat here, powerless, with no idea how to help or where to look. Suddenly the car felt stuffy and hot, and she turned on the air. It stung her wet cheeks. The phone call had left her jittery and unsure, plagued by her own mistakes and haunted by the past. As soon as she got home, she'd call some of the rehab places she knew Mario had gone before. Maybe a few of his old friends too.

~

Nora threw her keys in a dish by the door and changed into pajama pants and a sweatshirt. In the kitchen, she drank coffee and sat at the table with her legs crisscrossed on the chair. She made a list of places to call, including hospitals, and worked down the list, crossing each one off as she went. She chewed on a nail and paced her kitchen, making a new list, this one of Mario's friends and a couple of ex-girlfriends, most of whom had cut contact with him years ago. She called anyway. Nobody had seen or heard from him.

Her growling stomach reminded her that she needed to eat, so she made a pile of her notes and contact lists and started dinner.

She opened the pantry and sighed. A few cans of beans, some tortillas, cereal, a dried soup mix, and chips. The refrigerator fared no better, but she did have some cheese. Easy choice tonight. Quesadilla it was. While the cheese-and-bean tortilla fried, Nora filled a glass with water at the sink, and her eyes caught on the picture frame in the windowsill. A family portrait taken in a studio, where everyone looked stiff: her dad's shoulders set at an angle that had caused him to perch awkwardly on a stool; her mother with a terrible early-nineties bob; and Mario at thirteen, in heavy grunge flannel. She was only three, so her smile was natural and goofy, her dimples extra deep. The thing about the picture that gave her a pang was how none of them looked at the camera because their gazes were all trained on her, smiles soft, eyes lit up like she was their sole entertainment.

She turned from the picture to flip the quesadilla and had to blink against a stinging in her eyes. Nora had been an accident baby—a late-in-life gift, her brother used to tell her, that utterly surprised and delighted her parents. He'd been ten years old when she was born, an older brother and later, after the accident, a substitute parent until the weight of it all became too much for him to bear alone. When she was little, she'd understood he was sad. She missed Mom and Dad, too, but her aunt was soft and warm and hugged her a lot, and her uncle took her on long drives in his truck and told her stories about her parents.

They tried with Mario, too, but he pushed them away and wouldn't come out of his room. Sometimes it had made Nora angry with her brother. Why couldn't he try harder?

The burning of her quesadilla stung her nose, and she yanked the pan from the heat and slid the crispy cheesy circle onto a plate. Her phone buzzed and she grabbed it from her pocket, pulse racing. But when she saw the message, her heart took a nosedive.

You okay? Amanda, not Mario.

Not really.

Want to talk about it?

Nora's thumbs hung over the screen, and in her mind she typed paragraphs explaining why she was not okay, a novel about how lonely she felt, how sometimes she wanted to leave it all behind: her worry, the guilt she couldn't shed no matter how much she did for others or for Mario.

Not tonight.

You sure?

Amanda had been there for her, a shoulder to cry on, a friend to spend long hours searching homeless camps, an optimist when Nora thought all was lost. But Nora felt a tiredness sink behind her eyes. She didn't want to put more of her burden onto Amanda. It was wearing their friendship thin; she'd begun to feel it in the way she had with past boyfriends, other friends, even with her aunt and uncle. Amanda had lasted much longer than most, but she'd grown tired of hearing about Mario and had said as much. Told her one afternoon after Nora had again canceled plans last minute that she should focus on living her own life and let Mario go. When it came to her brother, people always wanted to tell her what she should do.

The wind feathered across the window, and Nora set her phone on the counter without responding. She let everyone down eventually.

She settled herself on the couch, turned on the television, and ate dinner while she flipped through stations until she found a documentary on the pyramids. Outside, the wind turned the branches of the aspen tree into drumsticks that beat a tuneless song against her windows. Thinking about her brother out there—alone, cold, hurting—tainted the quesadilla, but she finished her meal anyway.

It didn't take long to clean up after dinner. Her apartment was not elaborate, and her decorations were minimalistic, except for the walls of the hallway that led to her bedroom, which she'd covered in pictures. Nearly every square inch too. Mismatched frames hung from the ceiling to the floor with pictures of her parents when they were young, of Mario, including every year of his awkward school photos, collages of her twin cousins, mostly photos she'd downloaded from Facebook, including a recent one that showed them celebrating their twenty-first birthday together, all dressed up in cute matching tops and jeans. She walked past the pictures, looking at each one, touching a face here or there, soaking up the smiles, the traditions captured in old Christmas morning ones with Mom and Dad in robes, Nora as a chunky baby in a walker, and Mario in plaid pajamas playing with a *Star Wars* figurine.

She slid into bed, pulling the covers over her, skin prickled from the cold outside. She tossed and turned, and as on most nights, thoughts of her brother became a funnel inside her mind until all she thought about was him. Was he warm? Safe? Inside? Or exposed to this weather? When everything was bleak, when she was a little girl who cried at night because she missed the smell of her mom's hair, Mario would hear her and he'd hold her in his skinny teenage arms, rocking her gently, his voice murmuring against her hair. *It'll be okay, Peaches. You'll be okay.*

He'd been a sponge for her, soaking up her pain so that she could breathe again, even as he suffocated from it.

Her apartment walls creaked from the wind, and she snuggled deeper under the blankets, but the warmth felt wrong when she thought about her brother.

On the Thanksgiving when Nora was nine, Aunt Sophie had spent all day preparing the turkey and all the sides, despite having only just had the twins a month ago. She hummed and danced while she cooked, giving Nora a spoonful of mashed potatoes, a nibble of the ham with the sweet crunchy crust, and a lick of the apple pie bowl. Uncle Victor had laughed. *Is this your Thanksgiving pregame, Nora?* They were all in a good mood. Mario was coming. After he'd robbed their neighbor, her aunt and uncle had scraped together whatever money they could and paid for a thirty-day rehab program for teens. It had yoga and hiking and a family immersion component that encouraged families to attend therapy sessions and other healthy activities that replaced bad habits. But it was difficult for them to attend with the new babies and her uncle's job. They tried; Nora remembered they tried.

Mario had been late. Thirty minutes became an hour, the babies started to cry, the turkey was cold. It was dark outside when he finally stumbled through the front door. He'd sat down at the table and, without a word, started to eat, shoulders hunched, food on his face. Her uncle said something about respect. Mario kept eating, slugging water, reaching for Uncle Victor's bottle of beer. He yelled at Mario, and the chair fell back when Mario shot to his feet. He pushed their uncle up against the wall and held him there with his hand against his neck. Their aunt was crying, the babies were screaming, and Nora remembered how it felt like her ribs were squeezing her lungs until she couldn't breathe. But she got to her feet and ran at Mario and pushed him so hard she slipped and fell, hitting her head on the side of the table. Everything stopped then because Mario let her uncle go and fell to his knees, touching her forehead. His fingers came away red.

Oh, Nora, I'm so sorry, I'm so sorry.

She scrambled away from him and into her aunt's arms.

Mario looked from her to her aunt and back to Nora again, and he had to balance on his hands, swaying like he might fall to one side. *I'm sorry, Peaches. Oh God, I'm so sorry.*

But Nora was angry. It filled her chest and squashed her throat and made her scream at him with her hands curled into fists. *You're ruining everything, Mario! Why can't you be like before? Why do you have to be so mean to everyone! What's wrong with you?*

He'd looked at her, stunned. *I don't know, Nora,* he'd whispered. *Something's broken in me.*

Then go get it fixed and don't come back until you do.

She hadn't meant it, not the way he heard it. She'd figured that he'd go and do just that and then come back and be her brother again. It had felt like the right thing to say. Brave and strong.

But when he came back, he was dying on their front lawn, and Nora knew that she had made a terrible mistake and broken her brother all the way through.

The softness of the bed beneath her hips, the walls that kept the cold wind from rushing over her body, brought on a surge of guilt that plagued her sleep, so she grabbed her phone, opened the Travel Channel app, and picked a show on the world's most beautiful waterfalls. When her phone rang a few minutes later, she had begun to drift off to the narrator's voice. But she was instantly awake and answered quickly.

"Hello?"

"Hi, this is Ed. I'm, uh, I'm returning your phone call about Mario."

She sat straight up in bed, heart beating fast. "Yes, hi, Ed. Do you know where he is? He called from this number and he was—"

"I'm sorry, I don't." He exhaled a sob that left Nora cold. "He called me about my son, Adam. Then he packed his bags and left. I have no idea where he went."

She swallowed hard. "Adam was your son?"

"Yes. I have to go. I'm sorry, really I am. I understand what it's like for you, but I can barely handle my own stuff right now."

The line went dead and Nora stared at the screen, her eyes wide open. She watched one show after another, huddled under the comforter, until her alarm went off the next morning.

CHAPTER TWO

NORA

The door to the library opened, bringing with it a swish of air dusted with snow and a woman wearing a puffy maroon coat that fell to her knees. Where the coat ended, an enormous pair of winter boots began, engulfing her calves, the tips sticking out from her feet like clown shoes.

Nora rose from her chair behind the library desk, smiled, and tried to keep her eyes from drifting to the woman's boots. "Good afternoon, Marlene. Snow's coming down already, hmm?" The winter storm had been upgraded overnight and was now forecast to hit much of Colorado, with their foothills town expected to get some of the highest amounts. It wasn't unusual to get storms well into April, sometimes even May, but this late-March storm was shaping up to be a doozy.

Marlene pulled a thick winter hat—the kind with flaps that hung down to cover the ears—from her head, shook it out over the rubber mat by the front door. Her thinning white hair was the kind of color that once might have been blonde. "Feels like the storm of '03." She inhaled sharply into what sounded like a half-hearted laugh. "You know, I had to shovel for three days straight before I found my car." When Marlene struggled to pull her arms from the wet coat, Nora hurried from around her desk and helped her out of it. Marlene gave a tight nod and took the coat with a sniff. The woman had a fierce independent streak, and she hated to admit when she needed help, even now. So Nora simply stepped back.

The storm of '03 had dumped seven feet of snow on their mountain town. Nora was only twelve years old then, but she remembered it like it had been printed in the pages of a book, because it had been during a time when Mario was sober and visiting her regularly. After that horrible Thanksgiving and then his overdose, he'd disappeared for a while, but then, when she was ten, he'd come back. He'd stood before her aunt and uncle, his ball cap crushed between his hands, and apologized. Tears turned his eyes a caramelized brown. Nora still remembered how she'd felt like they were all standing in the center of a white light. Like everything had finally fallen into place. He'd moved to the city, he told her, had an apartment and roommates, a job, even a girlfriend with red hair and green eyes. Nora had seen a blurry picture of her on his phone. He'd seemed happy, but she remembered how later he'd started to change, acting distracted when he'd come to visit. Fidgety. And he'd end sentences halfway through, like he'd forgotten he was talking. Nora had thought it was funny, ignoring the alarm bells and the worried pinch of her aunt's mouth.

On the night of the storm, Mario was supposed to take her out to dinner like he did every Friday night. But he never showed, and Nora remembered sitting on the couch by the front window, watching the snow pile up on the brown grass, an anxious energy snaking through her body. He never called, and Nora spent that night curled into a ball on her bed while snow tickled the window, convinced that he'd driven off the side of a mountain. She'd sobbed into a pillow to keep from waking her twin cousins. He called three days later. Alive. He'd forgotten, he told her. At the time, she blamed the storm. But the next time it happened, there was no storm to blame. After the fourth missed visit, her uncle sat with her on the old slipcovered couch, her hand between his calloused palms. He was a kind but serious man, and the look in his eyes had an underlayer of steel. It made Nora want to pull her hand away. *Sweetheart, he's never going to change.* Nora's body had gone stiff like wood. *Alcohol ruined my father, and drugs are doing the same to Mario. You can't keep hoping he'll change, because it will only hurt you. Let Mario go. You were saved in that accident for some reason, and you need to live the life God gave you to find out why.*

Her aunt had come into the room, staring between her uncle and Nora. *Victor, no.*

Nora's eyes had heated with tears and anger, and she'd stood up, pushing against her uncle's hard bicep to get away from him. Her aunt had stepped toward her, face soft, arms open and waiting, and Nora knew that she could let herself be held, let herself be loved. She knew even then that if she wanted a family, they would love her through it all. But then she remembered spying through the crack in Mario's door and watching him cry without sound, so alone and sad, and Nora backed away from her aunt, turned from her uncle, and hurried from the room.

Sometimes it shocked her to think about the past, to realize how little had changed for Mario, while the rest of the world had moved on. She peered outside into the frenzy of another storm. The air was a whirling dervish of snow, pasted white across the tree trunks, freezing on the pavement. She pulled her sweater tighter across her chest, shivered. "You really think we'll get as much as we did from the storm of '03?"

Marlene nodded, hung up her coat. "It smells the same."

Nora scrunched her nose. "How?"

"Dirty. Like it won't give up until it's done."

With a laugh, Nora returned to her desk. She had a pile of new books that she needed to shelve, and there was one she wanted to set aside for Johanna, the elderly woman who came in every month for the Old Broad Book Club. Johanna was the founding member and a regular library volunteer and, Nora liked to point out, the one who came up with the name.

Still shedding her winter attire at the front door, Marlene pulled the oversize boots from her feet and set them on the rubber mat. Nora trained her gaze on the books, trying not to stare at Marlene's labored progress and ignoring the pang it gave her. She'd known Marlene for a few years now, and the two of them couldn't be more different. Nora had first met Marlene's husband, Charlie, who was an active volunteer and former board member at the library. They had a shared interest in travel, Charlie having worked his entire life with the aim to start his adventures in retirement, and Nora having put it off year after year. His friendship had rekindled her love for the idea, even if the reality of it was far out of her reach. Marlene was quieter than Charlie, and Nora had struggled to find common ground with the older woman.

Maybe Marlene might finally be interested in joining the book club. Johanna had invited her on more than one occasion, and Marlene had refused each time. But now . . . Nora jotted a note to herself to speak with Marlene because maybe she'd reconsider. She looked up from the books. Marlene's movements were stiff and slow from years of dealing with fibromyalgia. Nora knew this not because Marlene had shared it with her. No, that was quite impossible—Marlene hardly spared a smile for anyone but Charlie. She was of mountain stock, private to the core. Nora knew about her illness because Charlie had told her one day, not too long ago, when Marlene was seated at a computer wearing headphones and taking an online Spanish class. She and Charlie had a trip planned to Mexico for their tenth wedding anniversary, Charlie's idea, and Marlene was determined to learn Spanish first so she'd know if one of the locals was trying to cheat her.

"Umm, excuse me?" A soft voice.

Nora popped her head up from the books to find a teenage girl standing opposite her and shifting her weight back and forth. She wore a Denver Nuggets sweatshirt that was puffy and too big, in the way many kids seemed to prefer their sweatshirts. Nora thought it looked cozy and warm, perfect for a day like today. She smiled. "Can I help you?"

The girl shrugged and wiggled her phone in the air. "Yeah, um, what's the Wi-Fi password?"

Nora pointed to the placard near her desk with the password and studied the girl while she typed it into her phone. She had a crew of teenage regulars who came to the library. But this girl had been in only once before—last week, she was sure—with a younger girl Nora assumed was her sister, and she searched her memory, trying to come up with her name. The girl had already wandered away, head down and eyes trained on her phone, and in the way of kids who've grown up with smartphones attached to their palms, she easily navigated her way into the back room without bumping into anything. Nora smiled. She'd get her name later.

A familiar *tsk* sound came from Marlene, who sat on the bench, pulling a pair of loafers from a cloth bag. "You know it's why they don't read anymore." She tapped her temple. "No attention spans."

"But she's at the library." Nora gestured around the room. "Where books live."

Marlene slipped on her loafers and didn't respond. When she straightened, she cast a glance outside the expansive bay window, mouth pursed. "They've moved closer, you know. Like ants. There's one at the bottom of the stairs. Brought his own cardboard box and everything."

Nora tried to smile, hoping it would alleviate the edginess she felt at Marlene's words. Sometimes she wondered if the woman said things just to get a rise out of others. Charlie often described Marlene as a bee with no sting but a lot of buzz, and sometimes her buzz was deafening.

Nora softened. Charlie had a lot of buzz too.

A few years ago, Nora had set up a table in front of the library with baskets full of Thanksgiving meal supplies for families in the community who would be going without. After her uncle had lost his job, money was tight, and the stress of it was reflected in the deepening worry lines that tracked his forehead. They'd had to accept charity from others until they could get back on their feet, and while it was hard, it was comforting too. Nora had wanted to give back, and the library was a perfect vehicle, so she'd organized a food drive, storing the dried goods in the basement along with laundry baskets that would serve two purposes for families. The problem was, the board liked to have a policy or procedure for everything, and once again, she hadn't run the idea through the proper channels. Partly because the idea came to her rather late in the game and partly because she didn't want to hear no or wait for a decision.

But Charlie had championed her idea the entire time, steamrolling over protests that the library had rules and structure and policies that the new librarian should heed. *Are your policies more important than a family going without this Thanksgiving?* Nora smiled, thinking about the dropped gazes and fidgeting bodies of the board. Charlie had assured her that they weren't bad people, just older folks not used to change. Marlene had been on the board then, too, Nora recalled, and back then she'd been quiet and unsmiling, but she'd been the first to say yea when the board voted on the new Thanksgiving drive at the library. Nora still held it to this day, in addition to a holiday gift tree and a book drive.

Marlene had been on the board for only a few years, but Nora had heard that it was a rare appearance from a woman who everyone in town assumed to be a hermit. They said that Charlie had managed to bring her out of her shell.

Marlene pointed outside. "You need to discourage them. Is this a homeless shelter or a library, Nora?"

Nora suppressed a groan. Maybe Charlie could have left *some* of her shell on.

But Marlene was right, of course. The library wasn't a homeless shelter, and yet, for Nora, it had been like another home, her safe place where she could escape when things with Mario got worse. The building itself was special, over a hundred years old and rich in architectural details like the rolled columns out front, dark wood trim that gleamed, and arched ceilings that lent a modest grandness to the tidy space. Nora loved every unique aspect of the old library, often wishing she could have seen it in its heyday. It was small, only a few rooms plus a moldy basement that Nora was determined to convert into a teen hangout spot. One day, when she had the funding.

Mario had taken her the first time, held her hand when they walked past the lamppost that looked like something from a movie set and inside through the fancy arched door. *When I was your age, Mom used to take me to the library for story time*, he'd told her. *'Course, that library was ugly compared to this one. This one seems special, doesn't it?* Nora had stared up at him the entire time, and when they stepped inside, he smiled. A real smile. The kind that made his eyes get brighter and gave her a warm feeling in her chest. He'd squeezed her hand and she'd squeezed back, and for the first time since the accident, she felt close to happy. In the children's section, he'd pulled a huge picture book from the shelves, and she'd climbed onto the couch and snuggled beside him while he read to her, breathing in the mingling smells of paper and plastic, worn fabric chairs and old wood.

Later, the library became a place she'd escaped to when the volume at home rose with screaming babies and then whining toddlers that competed with the hushed but strained voices of her aunt and uncle drifting through paper-thin walls. And later still, it was where she went when Mario's visits grew sparse and his messages waned and she needed something to distract her from her own powerlessness.

The library had been the only place where Nora felt seen, where she wasn't the burden she knew she was at home, where she could forget about her growing fear that her brother was being eaten alive. The library had been like finding cool water in the midst of a desert, a refuge, and the books inside, her escape.

Nora dipped her chin ever so slightly to the older woman, who waited for an answer with her arms crossed. Marlene's eyes were squinted and hard, like her insides were stone, but Nora saw her shift her weight, noticed the wrinkle appear between her eyes—the telltale sign, as Charlie had once told Nora, that Marlene was in pain. Her honest answer was, yes, this library was a shelter for anyone seeking knowledge, information, or connection. Like Marlene, like Nora. A place she wanted to share with other lost souls, whether they had a zip code or not.

But she didn't say that, of course. Not only because Marlene was a patron but because Nora knew enough about people to understand that sometimes the best way to open someone's mind was by listening, not arguing. So she shrugged and smiled at Marlene. "It's a library, of course." But she didn't elaborate.

The corner of Marlene's mouth twitched; then she sighed and turned from Nora to the dark-haired security guard whose chair was across the small entryway, opposite Nora's desk. "Vlado," she called.

Despite the coziness of the room, Vlado's head stayed bent over a book spread open on his desk, too engrossed in reading to register Marlene's sharp tone. It wasn't unusual. Vlado was easily absorbed in reading, often jumping when Nora tapped him on the shoulder. But he was quick with a smile, and when he looked at Nora, she had to fight the urge to touch her hair or straighten her shirt. She didn't go to bars or, really, any social function other than her occasional movie nights with Amanda. So she wasn't around a lot of people her age, and something about Vlado altered the air, made her unsure of herself.

"Vlado," Marlene said again, loud enough that his name hit the marble floors with more force. Vlado's head shot up, his eyes unfocused in the way Nora knew well. Nora smiled to herself. He was reading the electrical systems manual she'd pulled for him last week after he mentioned taking apart an old weather radio he'd found at a garage sale. Surprise flickered in his eyes when he noticed his audience. He cleared his throat, closing the manual and pushing to his feet, an easy smile replacing his earlier confusion.

Vlado was the first security guard the library had ever had, and the cost of it put Nora's plans for the basement on hold. There had been an incident last summer when a man, in the middle of a mental breakdown, had barricaded himself inside the bathroom, refusing to leave. Nora hadn't been working that day, so Linda, the other librarian, had called 911. When the police arrived, the man grew violent and broke a faucet handle, tore the paper towel dispenser off the wall and smashed it into the mirror. It was an unsettling event, and the board had been unanimous about the need for a security guard. Nora had tried to argue for a softer approach, like working with mental health professionals to learn how to handle situations like that, but she was ignored and Vlado was hired soon after.

She didn't begrudge him the job; she just didn't love the concept of free books and information needing a security detail. But Vlado was an even-tempered man who chatted easily with patrons aged five to one hundred and was quick to help someone find a book or look up a fact, no matter how arcane. Once, she'd found him at a writing table in the corner, reading over a high-school boy's college essay. Vlado had smiled sheepishly. *He needed some editing help, and I can't concentrate at my desk.* She'd had to stifle a laugh and didn't question whether security was the best fit for a man whose attention was more often focused on a book than on the people coming in and out of the library.

Vlado smiled at Marlene. "Well, hello, Mrs. Johnston. How are you today?"

"I'd lock the doors if I were you," Marlene said. "They'll be in here looking for a free place to ride out this storm if you're not careful." She was talking about their town's increasing population of homeless people. "Before you know it, they'll set up camp in the basement, and you'll never be rid of them." She made a *tsk* sound, stuck her thumb at Nora. "Florence Nightingale here won't keep them out, so it's up to you, young man, to protect our library with whatever authority that little badge gives you."

Vlado just smiled and nodded, and Nora shot him a grateful look. Marlene shared her opinions freely and with vigor, not always thinking— or caring—about how her words might be construed. But now wasn't the time to disagree with her. When neither Nora nor Vlado responded, Marlene sighed, shrugged, and headed to the computers. Spanish lessons, Nora knew, and pressed a hand to her chest. The anniversary trip to Tulum would be Marlene's first trip outside the states, and Charlie had told Nora that Marlene was nervous and having second thoughts. Nora thought of all the exotic adventures she'd had planned and then delayed, believing they would happen someday, and hated the idea that Marlene might do the same. She swayed on her feet, fighting the urge to follow. She wanted to tell the woman that Charlie knew what he was doing when he booked their tickets and that she should go and feel the sand between her toes and see the Mayan ruins. Instead, Nora turned back to her desk. She and Marlene hadn't really said more than perfunctory hellos since December and Nora just didn't have the heart, or the guts, to bring it up.

She returned to her desk and brought her attention back to the work at hand. Outside, the snow fell in big, fat flakes that had quickly accumulated. These spring storms often included a layer of ice below the snow, making for treacherous driving conditions. She'd close the library early if she absolutely had to, but maybe she'd encourage Marlene to head home before things got worse.

A man in a sodden coat, his bald head unprotected against the elements, walked past the window, and she wrapped her arms across her chest, feeling cold for the person outside. On Nora's fifteenth birthday, her aunt had left the twins with a babysitter and taken Nora shopping. She'd splurged on a pair of name-brand boots. *To keep your feet warm when you walk to high school.* Nora had been touched—they usually shopped at the Goodwill—and a little excited to have something so new, cute, and warm. She'd thrown her arms around her aunt and hugged her. That same year, Mario ended up in the hospital with frostbite so bad he nearly lost the toes off his remaining foot. Her uncle refused to send him money, although from time to time, Nora saw her aunt slip a paid grocery store card into an envelope. They wouldn't let Nora visit Mario in the hospital then—said he wasn't himself and it wouldn't be good for her. The boots had felt like traitors, and Nora gave them to a girl in her science class.

The man paused outside the window, swayed back and forth, staring at something in the distance before moving on. Nora shot Vlado a look. The guard—who had returned to his manual, eagerly turning the page, his other hand taking notes in a small notebook—took no notice. She felt a pang, always wishing she had something to offer that was more than books. Blankets. Food. Hope. Something to assure people that their lives could be turned around. That it wasn't too late. She thought about the lonely tent by the factory and her brother finding the body of his friend. She squeezed her eyes shut. There was nothing she could do right now. No way to find him, but he would be okay. He'd survived so much; he could survive this too. She breathed in and opened her eyes.

Vlado stared at her from across the foyer, his face so kind she nearly gave in to the sad mess of emotions inside her. Instead, she straightened in her seat, cleared her throat, and directed her attention back to the stack of books on her desk. Sometimes it was unbearable, not knowing whether Mario was alive or dead, sober or not. So she kept busy because it felt better doing something instead of nothing.

She turned back to the books, affixed a note to one with *Johanna* written in neat print, and set it aside. Snow slid down the windows in soggy globs, and Nora noticed how the branches of the aspen trees bent low from the weight of the wet stuff.

Marlene was right about something: Nora wouldn't turn anyone away from the library. She sighed. Unless of course they chose not to follow the few simple rules, which included the rather obvious *no drugs or alcohol permitted* and *shirts and shoes at all times*, and after last month's debacle now also included *no sex in the bathroom*.

But she also understood Marlene's unease. Over the past few years, the number of homeless and drug addicts in Silver Ridge had seemed to triple, and she couldn't walk a block without seeing a body huddled in a doorway or camped around the town park. Some of the homelessness stemmed from the factory closing, leaving multiple people in the community without jobs, splitting families apart. All that trickled down to people moving and eventually other businesses closing as a result. Then came the drugs—prescription opioids, heroin, meth—which led to a rise in thefts and other small crimes. Silver Ridge was only about an hour's drive from the city, so Nora figured it was probably an attractive place to those seeking less crowded spaces, with room enough to set up camp, make a little money, without the constant presence of the police. And with the library being a public space, it drew all kinds.

Nora knew that bigger, more urban libraries had been dealing with these issues far longer and with dire consequences. She'd heard of addicts overdosing in library bathrooms or even among the stacks, in front of patrons or—God forbid—children. It's why she'd attended a training last month to learn how to use a nasal spray that would reverse an overdose in minutes. She'd done the training on her day off and purchased the spray with her own money.

Her fingers brushed the handle of a drawer on her desk, her jaw sawing back and forth, and her face hardened at the thought of ever needing to use it. Mario had been saved from overdosing more than once, yet it had never changed his life. Not even the threat of death seemed to be enough to make him want to change.

CHAPTER THREE

MARLENE

Marlene came to the library for the books, sure, but she liked to use the computers too. Do-gooder Nora had taught both her and Charlie how to use one a few years ago, and since they lived in a mountain canyon without the Wi-Fi, they used the ones at the library. She settled carefully into the plastic chair, pressing her lips together to keep an unintended moan inside, and with a squinted eye, looked around. If any of these busybodies from town gave her one of their head-tilting stares of pity, why, she would march right on over and tell them where they could shove it. Marlene's mother had always said she had a mouth on her. She did. One she'd gotten from her father, a longtime miner who, in his later years, couldn't breathe without oxygen and one day, when he was only fifty-five, stopped breathing altogether.

The library had emptied out since she'd gotten there, save for a girl who sat with her feet tucked under her in one of the big chairs in the corner, with her hoodie pulled over a baseball cap and cinched around her chin. Marlene gave a quiet *tsk* and turned back to the computer. Feet on the furniture. Hat inside. Kids these days hadn't been taught a thing.

Marlene shifted again in her chair, but every position felt like her muscles were being squeezed inside a giant fist. It was bad today. Part of the reason she'd decided to brave the s-curves from her cabin to come into town even with the storm moving in. Sometimes it felt better doing something, anything, instead of rereading a *Reader's Digest* from 1986 in front of a fire she had to keep loaded with wood every few hours and moaning with each new wave of pain. She hated to listen to herself. And lately, the cabin had begun to remind her of her mother. Marlene could still taste the menthol smoke from the cigarettes she'd burned morning, afternoon, and evening; hear the creak of the metal rocker out front, her phlegm-filled laugh when she was watching TV. Marlene had tried to keep the windows closed and aired out the curtains as often as she could, but still the smoke sneaked its way through the old cabin's cracks and crevices, and even now, twenty-five years since her death, Marlene would still catch a whiff of her mother's cigarette ghosts.

She moved the mouse to wake up the computer and then typed *Tulum* into the search bar, squinting to see the writing in the tiny search area. Up popped blurry pictures of turquoise water and sandy beaches. Marlene clicked the circle-arrow thing that Nora had told her to do if she couldn't get the thing to work. Still blurry. She clicked again, harder this time, and it hurt her fingers, which had, in the last few years, begun to curl from arthritis. Still blurry. "Damn computers," she muttered. "Waste of time." Her mother, Margorie, would have agreed. She had believed that anything beyond her shows was a waste of time.

A hand tapped her shoulder, and she cranked her head to look up. Nora. The woman had probably sussed out from the other room that Marlene was having trouble with the computers. Marlene's mouth turned down in the corners. Nora liked to help. She *loved* to help, especially Marlene. Especially now, and it was annoying. But that was Marlene's opinion, and she'd try to keep it to herself. Charlie often reminded her that not everybody loved to hear her opinions the way that he did. Her mother, however, had always been free with her thoughts. *It's best to keep your expectations low, Marlene, or you'll just be disappointed.* She'd look around the cabin, then back to Marlene, bitterness deep in the lines around her mouth. *This wasn't the life I was supposed to live.* More and more these days, her mother's voice had filtered back inside Marlene's thoughts. It'd been nice to think things would be different for her. But her mother had been right, of course.

Nora set Marlene's reading glasses beside the mouse, and she had to fight an urge to touch her face. *Of course* she wasn't wearing her glasses when they were right there in front of her.

"Found them on the bench and thought you might need them." Nora leaned down, peering at the screen. Her brown hair hung over one shoulder in heavy waves. "Wow, is that the place?"

Marlene slid her glasses on and turned back to the screen to find the picture clear and crisp, the water bluer than water had a right to be, the sand so white it looked soft—nothing like the Rocky Mountain sand, coarse and full of rocks.

"Yep." She waited, tapping her finger on the mouse but not clicking, and hoping Nora would take the hint. A second passed, then another. She tapped the mouse again.

"Okay, then, I'll leave you to it," Nora said. "But, Marlene, I'm concerned about the roads, and I'm thinking you might want to plan on heading back up before too long."

Marlene breathed in. Charlie said she could be short-tempered. That she didn't give most people the benefit of the doubt. As usual, he was right. He also said she was all soft and sweet on the inside, and it was just fine by him if she only wanted to share that part of her with him. Her hands trembled just the tiniest bit. Her mother had had a gentleness once. When she was younger and before years of miscarriages, a dying husband, and failed dreams had stretched her so thin that she was only an illusion of the self-directed woman who'd once worked a wartime assembly line building B-17s. Marlene used to think there couldn't be a mother and daughter more different. Now she wasn't so sure.

She looked up at Nora and pressed her lips together and did not say the first thing that came to mind, which didn't come from that soft part at all. "Nora, I have lived here my entire life, and I have driven these roads in all kinds of weather, including the time we outran a forest fire."

Nora's eyes widened. "Oh, I don't think Charlie ever told me about that."

Marlene kept her eyes on the screen while she spoke, but instead of Mexico, she saw flames jumping up a tree. "It was a close one. The smoke was so thick we could hardly breathe, and Charlie coughed for days afterward because we stopped for a dog."

The poor pup had been so scared that he'd lain down in the middle of the road and curled into a ball, like he'd just given up. It was nearly ten years ago, but Marlene could still feel the way her heart had beaten against her ribs, still smell the acrid smoke that seemed to melt into her skin, and taste the dry stickiness in her mouth from the panic that made it hard to breathe. They'd been married only a few months by then, and she knew it couldn't last—her mother would have told her from the start, if she'd been alive. But Marlene was the happiest she'd been her entire life. So she'd assumed the fire would kill them both, and she was okay with that because at least she'd finally known what it meant to be truly happy. But they did not die of smoke inhalation even though Charlie stopped for that damn dog. He stopped at nearly every house in their canyon to make sure their neighbors had made it out. He was a hero that day. To Marlene, anyway.

Nora was nodding, like she wanted Marlene to say more, her pretty brown eyes all soft like brown sugar and kind and *knowing*, and suddenly Marlene thought about where she was—in public—and who she was talking to—nosy Nora—and clamped her mouth shut. Without another word, she turned back to the computer. She knew Nora had left when the smell of roses faded. That woman and her perfume, like she thought she could singlehandedly summon spring by smelling like it.

Marlene rubbed her hands up and down her thighs. It hurt so damn bad today. Much worse than normal—of course, Marlene's definition of *normal* was a day when she didn't give in. And damned if she was going to do that today. The computer screen glowed with fantasy pictures of turquoise water and deep-green foliage, and Marlene imagined the heat of the sun warming her skin. She clicked on a picture of a cabana with white curtains, blue water only inches from the wooden structure. Their trip was coming up on May 1. Charlie had surprised her with the idea; then again, it shouldn't have surprised her, because all he ever read at the library were travel books. No fiction for him, he said, learning about the world was adventure enough. *Click.* More pictures popped up. This one of a white-sand beach below a wall of rocks covered in a green vegetation that Marlene had never seen before. Nothing was ever that green in Colorado.

At first, Marlene had been worried about going to a foreign country—at least, that's what she'd told Charlie, who had laughed her off, like he often did when she was being unreasonable. It was the same laugh he'd given her all those years ago when he'd asked her out on a date and she'd said no because she'd been fifty-eight years old for Pete's sake. Too old to *date*. Her mother would have asked her what was the dang point? Maybe when she was younger, maybe if this handsome man had asked her out when she was blonde and pretty in a quiet kind of way. But not as she was. A smile softened the edges of her lips when she thought about how he'd just laughed and said, *Well, I don't happen to agree with your answer. Guess I'll just have to keep coming back until you say yes.*

So he came back four nights in a row and sat at the counter, reading the paper and drinking a strong cup of black coffee. Each night before he left, he asked her again, and each night she said no. But between her serving pie and plates of eggs or corned beef, Charlie peppered her with questions about this or that, telling her stories of his own, and with so much life lived between them, the conversation flowed in a way that

Marlene didn't know conversations could. She even told him about her mother, how when Marlene was a much younger woman, she'd wanted to be just like her. Because Margorie had once been strong and brave and ahead of her time.

His eyebrows had wiggled high. *And are you like her?* She'd refilled his coffee, not wanting to answer or meet his gaze. She thought about dropping out of college to care for her father and how she'd always meant to go back and then never did and how the years of working at the diner and caring for her mother had made her world too small to hold her dreams any longer. Her mother's words echoed in her head: *Keep your expectations low.* She'd set the carafe of coffee on the counter and looked him right in the eyes. *I am exactly like her.*

Charlie had smiled and dipped his chin and said something she didn't expect. *Then she must have been an extraordinary woman.*

Soon Marlene found herself looking forward to his evening visit, a lift in her step whenever he walked through the doors in his gray overcoat and dapper hat. Until one night. Charlie drank his coffee, read his paper, and stood. *It's been a pleasure, Marlene.* And he folded his coat over one arm, put a flat cap on his balding head, and turned to leave.

It was for the best. Even then, her body had begun to betray her, growing old too fast. Her muscles ached at night, and her daily dose of ibuprofen barely touched it. But as she watched him leave, her heart did an anxious dance, and she spoke before she had time to think. Before her mother's voice had time to speak. *You're giving up that easy?*

He'd turned and given her a lopsided grin. *Giving up on what?*

Her wrinkled cheeks had actually blushed, like a schoolgirl's. She felt ridiculous, a pathetic portrait of an old woman in the last half of her life, desperate to be loved. But he had stood there, tall, with broad shoulders and a thin torso—no paunch on her Charlie—and stared at her like she was the most interesting person in the room. It had warmed her clear through, and from somewhere inside her, she mustered up a little bit of moxie. *Aren't you going to ask me out?*

He'd returned to the counter, set his hat and coat on the barstool beside him, and took a seat, still grinning. *I thought you'd never ask.*

The library was too stout a structure to creak from the wind outside, but Marlene imagined the cold sweep across her skin. With the relentless winter they were having and this new storm set to dump another few feet, Marlene had begun to think that the warm Mexican weather might feel good. She hadn't told Charlie, but what she was really worried about wasn't the foreigners; it was whether her body could handle a trip where they were supposed to visit Mayan ruins, learn to snorkel, hike jungle trails to see an ancient pyramid. Getting through a day where she hardly did more than add wood to the fire and make dinner was almost impossible. How could she manage a trip like this?

Her face stiffened. She knew the answer, so she opened up another window and found her way to where she could enter her website address—she shook her head—no, her *email* address into the line. Nora had walked them through the internet, but it was still a concept that Marlene found hard to get her head around. She had managed without it for almost her entire life, and she didn't see the point. But Charlie did and he had eventually convinced her, at least a little bit. Charlie could convince her of a lot of things. She pressed her lips together. Except about things she just knew to be true. Like the government was too big, welfare had created a generation that couldn't fend for themselves, drug addicts were morally bankrupt and—

The teenage girl in the chair spoke, loud enough for Marlene to hear her from across the room.

"I'm just chillin' at the library, Grandma. Yeah, I know it's snowing. Yeah, I have what I need." The girl laughed. "I know. I love you too. Don't worry; I'll be fine. See you soon." Her voice carried through the empty room.

Marlene craned her neck to stare at the girl. Had she ever heard of being quiet in the library? It's like parents had totally given up and created a whole generation of self-centered kids who would, of course, grow up to be nothing more than overfed, overindulged adults with no respect for true hardship. "Shhhhh!" Marlene said, then again to make her point, with her finger to her lips. "Shhhhh!"

The girl's head shot up, dark-brown eyes narrowed into a question. "Are you shushing me?"

Marlene nearly fell from her chair. Kids were unbelievable. "You're talking on your phone."

"To my grandma."

"This is the library."

"Sorry." The girl shrugged, then ducked her head and returned her gaze to the screen of her phone.

Marlene clamped her mouth shut, told herself that a lecture would do nothing, and besides, she wasn't this girl's mother—or grandmother, for that matter—and it was none of her business.

Back to the computer, she typed in her email address with a sigh: CharlieLovesMarlene@mail.com. It hadn't been her choice, but when Nora had shown them how to set one up, Charlie had picked the name, hunting and pecking at the keyboard with his typical self-satisfied grin. It wasn't that Marlene didn't love Charlie. She loved him from a place so deep inside it scared her. But she wasn't the kind of woman given to physical displays of affection—or verbal, for that matter. And she'd never truly understood why Charlie had asked her out all those years ago at the diner. Back then, at least she'd been a little more gentle, but over the years the pain had stripped her of that gentleness, left her one big open nerve, and it showed, especially in her short patience with others. So how could he love her like this? Marlene felt the way her back curved from the pain, the wrinkles in her cheeks that pulled when she winced. What could he love about her now?

She typed a short and to-the-point message to the Gulliver Travel Agency. To Anne O'Shea: Please cancel our trip to Tulum. We will not be going. From, Mrs. Charlie Johnston

When she clicked "Send," Marlene felt a sharp pain in her chest that she ignored. Some things just had to be done, and some people had to make the tough decisions.

She stood, using the back of the chair to keep her balance; but the chair had wheels that moved across the thin carpet, and Marlene lost her grip and fell to her knees, letting out a pathetic gasp and a whimper. Someone touched her elbow, and she jerked her head up to see the loud teenager from before, trying to help her to her feet.

"I can do this myself," Marlene said, angry at her weakness, and pushed lightly against the girl's side, feeling something long—like a pencil but thicker—inside the pocket of her sweatshirt.

The girl moved quickly away. "No, thank you," she said.

Marlene narrowed her eyes. "Excuse me?"

The girl crossed her arms, but Marlene couldn't make out her face with the ball cap she wore. It had a brim so wide it cast a dark shadow across her already-dark skin. "You should have said, *no, thank you.* Jeez, I was just trying to help."

The nerve of this girl. Marlene eyed the backpack she had slung over one shoulder. It looked stuffed, the zipper pulling apart in the middle. Hmm, could she be hiding something in her bag? Marlene wasn't around many kids, and neither she nor Charlie had ever had any of their own, but she watched enough news shows to see what had become of the world. And none of it was good. She smoothed the hair on the side of her head where she got thin flyaways that made her look like a mad scientist; then she wiped at the fuzz on her jeans and thought about the object she had felt in the girl's pocket. It wasn't a pencil. Or a marker. It felt like metal or hard plastic. Could it have been one of those things the kids used now to smoke drugs? Probably. She'd heard all about it on the nightly news.

"You don't fool me," she said, and at the way the girl's eyes widened, Marlene knew she was right. Something was off about her. She was hiding something. "Vlado might not be watching you, but I am."

Without waiting for a reply, she turned and headed in the direction of the travel books. Outside, the snow was coming down hard, the air so thick with it she couldn't even see the grove of aspen trees that circled the library. She envisioned the road up to her house, how the curve by the old mill always turned icy first. Then she shook her head and pulled out a book on the Mayan ruins, settling into a more comfortable sofa that had a wide view of the stacks, including the chair where the girl had returned and now sat with her legs slung over the side, her face lit blue by the screen of her phone. Marlene knew the road to her cabin like the back of her hand and could probably drive it with her eyes closed. So she could stay a little bit longer just in case. Make sure the girl didn't cause Nora any trouble.

CHAPTER FOUR

LEWIS

Her hair was different. Pink instead of green. Last week it had been green; he was sure of it. Lewis squinted but the windows of the diner were crusting over with snow, making it hard to see anything clearly. Nah, it looked yellow. He shook his head, wiped the snow from his scalp. Someone had stolen his hat. It's why he avoided shelters. Somebody always stole something from him. A huge SUV drove past the diner—gray, with shiny chrome wheels and grille, and slipping and sliding with its backend fishtailing all over the goddamn place. He grunted a laugh, shivered. Damn, it was a cold snow—heavy and wet and soaking through everything down to his socks.

The diner was the kind he remembered going to when he was a kid. Round barstools nailed into the linoleum, booths with stiff leather seats, now cracked and covered in spots with duct tape. A long and curved counter with a smudged display case showing off day-old slices of pie. Worn and old, like him. Lewis pulled his coat tighter and wondered how, with all the fancy breakfast places, it had not been bulldozed by now. History, he guessed. Some people liked their history.

Today the diner was mostly empty except for a woman at the counter with her cup extended and his granddaughter, Persie, standing behind the counter, pouring coffee and smiling at the woman. Lewis felt his old heart push hard against his chest.

Just a few weeks ago, he'd been in Denver, huddled in his sleeping bag with his back against a cement planter, counting the minutes to keep his mind off a gnawing pain in his belly, when his wife had walked past. He hadn't seen her in over a decade, but he'd recognize her anywhere. There was something about the way she held herself—straight up and down, graceful and long-legged—that made her stand out in any crowd. Her hair was short now, and snow white, and below her wool coat, she wore pants that hugged her calves and shiny heels that gave her stride purpose. She'd always been a beautiful woman and so far out of his league Lewis was never sure why she'd married him in the first place. She'd been a paralegal, whip-smart, and knew how to hold her own around men. Later, when she was forty, she'd gone to law school. An amazing goddamn woman and Lewis had nearly ruined her life.

The scent of flowers had trailed her, the delicate kind that smelled like a tropical beach. A perfume she'd worn her entire life, and it was so familiar and jarring that it had torn a jagged hole across Lewis's chest, and all his sadness spilled out onto the sidewalk. He'd gotten to his feet and started pacing, kicking at a trash can, scooping old dirt from the flowerpot and throwing it in a brown arc at the side of a building. People had stared. He'd picked up his sleeping bag and taken off down the street, muttering to himself, no idea where he was going until he ended up at the bus station. It took him a few days with a paper cup and an old sign, but eventually he had enough change to buy a ticket and he came to Silver Ridge, weary, feeling like death flanked him the entire way but wanting to see Persie, even if it was through a window.

In his few weeks here, he favored this bench across from the diner, where he could watch her while she worked. See the young woman she had become, the genuine smile that eased across her face and made him feel warm and proud, even if he'd had nothing to do with it. The last time he'd seen her had been when she was five and she'd scowled at him, all four feet of her. He'd been nothing more than a stranger on her doorstep.

The cold and the snow collecting in his beard made his nose run freely; he wiped it with the back of his sleeve, and it dragged across his chapped skin. Sometimes it hurt to watch her, to see how much he had missed. Damn it, who was he kidding? It hurt all the time. Right then, as though the girl had heard his thoughts, she lifted her eyes and looked out the window and straight to the bench where Lewis sat huddled against the cold, and goddamn if she didn't look him right in the eyes.

He fumbled with the collar of his wool coat, pulled it up over his jaw, and hoped he'd just imagined it. A memory poked its ugly head above the surface of grime and filth floating in the swamp of broken promises inside him. Of Persie when she was two years old. All chubby cheeks and "duckles." It had been Lewis's favorite description of a child's knuckles when they were growing but still bunched up into their tiny bodies. Duckles. In his mind, clear as day, he saw the sweet little dimples on top of the knuckles. He'd kissed each one and breathed in her baby-soap smell. He'd been going into rehab again, back when he thought he could still beat it. He felt his eyes get wet and wiped a palm across his face. An old sappy man on a bench in a strange town. Was there anything more pathetic?

His ears had gone numb, and his fingers were blocks of ice, searching his pockets for a spot even slightly warmer than freezing, and when he touched the bag, his pulse slowed. Already he could feel it shooting through his body, easing the tremors in his hands, soothing the jitters that wormed in and out of his muscles, and obliterating the ache in his chest that bloomed like an infection whenever he thought about everything he'd messed up.

The snow flew straight into his eyes, but Lewis kept his gaze on Persie. In the fluorescent diner light, her hair could really be any color. He focused on it again, arguing silently with himself. Maybe it was orange? He liked orange. It had been his daughter's favorite color. When

Heather was ten years old, she'd convinced him to paint her room orange, even the ceiling. He'd done it when his wife, Phyllis, was at law school. But when Phyllis came home to find the room she'd painted a few days earlier in girlish shades of pink and gray turned a garish orange, she'd sat down on the carpet and cried. It wasn't the first time he'd made her cry. And it wasn't the last either.

For a while, when Heather was young and before the knee surgery, Lewis had been a good dad, even if he painted rooms without thinking. When Phyllis was studying and going to school, he made sure to be home in time to cook dinner, play Heather in a game of backgammon, and tuck her into bed. He even planned her eleventh birthday party and borrowed a neighbor's horse, walking the kids in a circle in their backyard. Heather had cried happy tears. *You're the best daddy.* He'd never forgotten that moment. He also never forgot the look on Phyllis's face when he found her at midnight in the backyard, shoveling horse manure and trying to piece together torn-up patches of grass, like a golfer. He'd slunk back in the house, grateful he'd at least remembered to throw away the half dozen small liquor bottles himself.

Phyllis had deserved better.

He was a screwup, and his wife and daughter had paid the price. The question that plagued him now, the thing that drove him to come to Silver Ridge, was to see if somehow Persie had avoided his legacy. He'd purposely left his granddaughter alone, made sure to disappear from Heather's life. Had it worked? He watched Persie ring something up on the cash register, a concentration wrinkle in her forehead. She looked happy and normal.

Lewis jerked his hand away from the bag in his pocket. This was the game he played. Was Persie enough? Could he pull the bag from his pocket and throw it into the trash? When the drugs fell into the litter, would he feel lighter, square his shoulders, button up his coat, and cross the road? Would he smooth the remaining hair above his ears and open the door, walk straight to the counter, and say, *Hi, Persie. I'm your pop*?

45

Was she enough?

The woman at the counter had finished her coffee and started the process of piling on her layers. A man poked his head out from the kitchen, pointed at the front windows with a soupspoon, saying something to Persie, who nodded and untied her apron. She disappeared into the back, reappearing a few minutes later covered head to toe in winter gear.

Lewis had begun to shiver so badly it made his vision blur. He tried to focus on Persie, but he couldn't see her hair under her hat anymore, and his thoughts kept drifting to the bag in his pocket. To the numbness. To the quiet. To the peace.

He didn't notice the figure crossing the street until it was too late and she stood opposite him. He tucked his chin, stared at her boots, and couldn't swallow because something was in the way. A paper cup with a plastic lid hovered in his line of sight.

"I thought you might like something warm. It's black with some sugar—hope that's okay." Her voice was low and smooth and beautiful.

His goddamn eyes burned like they were on fire, but he wasn't about to cry in front of her. He pulled his head deeper into his coat, kept his eyes on the pink mittens she wore, and didn't move his arms, didn't take the coffee.

She stood like that for a minute, then set the coffee beside him on the bench. "Well, stay warm, okay? I think the Methodist church is, like, a shelter or something. Maybe you could go there until this storm passes?"

He didn't make a sound, but the blood pounded in his head, and to him it sounded like a train. She must have heard it too. He wanted to look up, wanted to see her face up close. Did she look like her mom? Did she have Heather's light-blue eyes? Or Phyllis's nose? Was she like him? He'd been a good dad once, maybe a good husband for some of the time, but it had been a sideshow to his real love, to the feeling he got when he could forget the coward that lived inside him. And they had known it.

He made a fist, punched his thigh. He hoped she was nothing like him. Nothing at all. Which was why he would not raise his goddamn head, would not meet her eyes, would say nothing.

When she finally walked away, he thought he might deflate from the way she seemed to take all the air with her. His hands were shaking—whether from the cold or her, he didn't know or care. He chanced a look up and saw an old Bronco slide to a stop. Saw Heather at the wheel, and it gave him a painful stitch in his side. She looked the same and different. Older, but still her. Persie climbed in, closing the door with a bang. Everything was muddied from the snow pelting his face, but he thought he saw Persie's head dip, her shoulders shake like she was crying, thought he saw Heather look up at him once before pulling away. He hit his thighs again. Could have also imagined the whole thing.

The Bronco drove slowly, the wheels sliding, then gripping the snow-covered pavement. Heather had always been a good driver in the snow. That's how Lewis had taught her, taking her out driving whenever snow came to Denver. Without realizing it, his hand had slid deep into his pocket and was fingering the baggie, touching the powder through the plastic. He wanted to forget the pain, forget the way he hurt everyone he loved, forget the goddamn thirteen seconds that had changed his life forever.

The coffee had cooled quickly in the paper cup, so he drained it before tossing it into the trash bin by the bench. He tried to get to his feet, but sitting in the cold had settled heavy in his bones and he fell back, burdened by the weight of his own damn body. He pounded the bench with a fist until a jolt of pain rushed up to his elbow. With an angry grunt, he gritted his teeth and pushed again to his feet, tensing his leg muscles to keep him upright and using the back of the bench for leverage. When he was steady, he tucked the sleeping bag under one arm.

"Damn right," he said and began to walk at an old-man-shuffling pace that irritated the hell out of him. When he was young he'd been barrel chested and strong, handsome in a Burt Reynolds kind of way, and he would have scoffed at an old man like him. He would have said to himself, *That will never be me.*

He shuffled along, leaving tracks in the snow like he was dragging a body, until he got to his spot at the library, where his sodden cardboard shelter had melted into the ground. Lewis stared at it for a long minute, grunted, then walked to the side of the building. A huge pine tree towered above the ground, and he settled himself against the base of the trunk. The thickness of the pine needles might give him a little bit of shelter from the dogged snow. With his back to the tree, Lewis stretched out one leg, keeping the other one bent, his hands deep in his pockets, finger rubbing along the bag.

He wanted to quit. He *always* wanted to quit. But he was weak, and the call of nothingness was stronger than anything else he wanted. The bag slipped easily from his pocket, along with a small card. He paused, held it away from his sad old eyes so he could read, and snorted. A library card with his name on it. Last week he'd gone inside to use the bathroom and got stopped by the librarian who gave him the card. Said she'd seen him around and thought a good story might keep the nights from being so long. *My life is one sad fucking story*, he'd said. He didn't mean to raise his voice but he must have, because the security guard was by her side in a minute, telling him to settle down. To her credit, the librarian seemed unruffled, her brown eyes calm, kind even. He'd had to look away. But she'd insisted, and just to shut her up, he took one.

He set the card on his thigh and poured a line of heroin across his name, using his fingers—which were thick, the skin split into deep crevasses that bled easily—to make the line thinner. From the bag, he retrieved a rolled dollar bill, and before the next gust of wind, he put the paper inside his right nostril and inhaled hard.

He waited, shivering, for the drug to kick in, anticipating the wave of calm that would erase the jitters in his muscles, take away the pain. Finally the cold, the snow that had settled across his shoulders despite the tree, his frozen feet, and hands went away with a warmth that crashed over him; he let his head roll back, the edges of his mouth turned up at the familiar feeling. But then it went wrong, and the warmth became a vise clamping onto his chest, and the calmness morphed into a panic that made it impossible to breathe. And then his head hit the ground and he couldn't see and he couldn't breathe, and his last thought was of Persie and her pink hair.

CHAPTER FIVE

NORA

The storm was shaping up to be everything the forecasters had hoped. Nora paced behind her desk. The part-time librarian, Linda, had already called to say she wouldn't make it in to help with the Book and Movie middle school group Nora had organized for that night. She'd already canceled it anyway. Too bad, because they'd finished reading *The Outsiders* and were excited to watch the movie. She'd even rented a popcorn machine to surprise them. She loved being around kids; it reminded her of her twin cousins. They were nine when she went away to college, and while she'd adored them, they'd been content with each other in a way she suspected only twins could be, speaking in their own made-up language, giggling late into the night, comfortable with one another. Nora had envied their closeness. With Mario gone, she'd felt more adrift than ever, loving her aunt and uncle for all they did for her but also resenting them for giving up on her brother.

She gave a worried look outside. It had started snowing less than three hours ago, and already Vlado had shoveled the front walkway three times. Only Marlene and one other patron, the young girl whose name Nora still couldn't remember, were still in the library. She was going to give Marlene fifteen more minutes to prove she was a tough mountain woman before escorting her to her car, along with the girl, who Nora would make sure had a safe way home. It was nearly six anyway, and she supposed she could close up early, given the conditions. Besides, the electricity had started flickering. Once it went, there was no reason to stay.

Vlado opened the door, bringing in a gust of wind and snow that dusted the carpet. He stomped his boots on the rubber mat.

Nora shivered. "How is it out there?"

"A heavy wet snow," he said. "Some of the branches on that big pine tree are hanging so low they are touching the ground."

Vlado was typically a man of few words, seeming to prefer books to conversation. But when he spoke, Nora enjoyed listening to the light accent that brushed over each word and his deep voice that seemed to resonate from his chest. To Nora—who had never been able to travel outside the US the way she'd once dreamed—listening to Vlado speak was like a small window to places she'd never visited.

"I didn't think it was supposed to get bad until later tonight," she said.

Vlado wiped a hand across his eyebrows, releasing bits of ice that clung to the hairs. "It's very bad now. A bus has slid into the sidewalk by the courthouse, but it didn't look like anybody was hurt."

Nora rubbed her arms. Spring in the Rockies was unpredictable. Yesterday's sun, with nearly sixty-degree temps, was like a dream when she looked out the window into a world of swirling white. She thought of the man who had been camped at the base of the concrete stairs these past three weeks. The one she saw last night huddled by the lamppost. Lewis. He was new, not one of the regulars Nora had come to recognize. And also not from around here, she surmised, since the others had taken shelter somewhere to get out of the snow, and he'd still been here when she came in this morning. "Did you see the homeless man?"

Vlado shook his head. "His box is there, but it's wet and caved in. I think he's gone."

Nora breathed out. "Good. He must have gone to the shelter." She thought of the empty tent.

"You worry about them." Vlado's observation was a surprise.

Their conversations were normal coworker back-and-forth. Nothing too deep, never prolonged, no watercooler gossip, which was how Nora preferred to keep things. His eyes were a deep hazel, with dark lashes that would make any woman jealous, and there was a sincere interest reflected in the depth of his gaze. She fidgeted, ran a hand through her hair. Sometimes with Vlado, she couldn't help but notice things like this or imagine what his lips might feel like. It was a nice distraction to imagine having someone to come home to, someone to cook or watch movies with, someone to share a weekend. All the couple things that were Instagram-worthy: decorating a Christmas tree, selfies on a beach, a kiss on New Year's. But those dreams were an exotic by-product of a different life, because the reality was that nobody wanted to share hers. Not when it included Mario. And she'd learned to accept it.

"Is there a reason you worry so much?" he said.

She straightened the books on her desk. "I happen to believe that everyone deserves a second chance or a third—even a fourth chance, if that's what it takes to turn their life around." But she couldn't meet Vlado's eyes when she spoke. It wasn't that she was ashamed of what she believed, but she knew that not everyone shared her point of view, and she didn't feel like getting into a philosophical discussion where she had to defend her actions. It had happened with other friends and other men in her life, and it never ended well.

Like her college boyfriend. They had met her freshman year, and everything between them just clicked. Dating him had been easy and fun, and when he said he loved her, she laughed and said it back. But that was back when she was going to travel the world with Amanda. Before her brother had come back into her life, sober and ready for a fresh start. Before he lived with her in grad school. Before he relapsed and her life spiraled out of control once again.

"Oh, good grief, there she goes again."

Nora straightened her shoulders at Marlene's voice and sighed softly to herself.

"Vlado, Nora's what my mother called a bleeding heart. Do you have those in your country?"

Nora pressed a hand to her forehead, shook her head slowly back and forth. "Marlene," she said through clenched teeth.

Vlado smiled. "I'm an American, Mrs. Johnston, remember? I've even got a card to prove it." Vlado's tone was even and warmed with an unflappable sense of humor. Nora didn't know how he always stayed so calm.

Marlene tilted her head, seemed to want to disagree, then closed her mouth. "Well, it means that she's an enabler. And that's what she does with all her free time. Enable people who should be working and taking care of themselves, not depending on handouts." She moved into the foyer and sank heavily into a chair by Nora's desk, like her legs had pulled her down against her will. "Charlie worked hard every day of his life until he retired."

Neither Nora nor Vlado responded to Marlene, and Nora hoped that the woman would take the hint and let the matter drop. She marveled, as she often did, at what an odd pairing Charlie and Marlene were, but Charlie adored Marlene, and when he was around, she softened like butter left out on the counter, and it always made Nora happy to know that people could find each other like that.

Charlie had moved to Silver Ridge a decade ago to work for the local electrical company and to retire if he ever made the decision to do so. He'd never intended on retiring, he'd once told Nora. As a lifelong bachelor, work was the best equivalent to a social life he was likely to get, and he didn't see himself as a solitaire-playing old man content to tend a garden or watch *Matlock* reruns until he was six feet under.

Nora had no idea what *Matlock* was, but she understood the desire to be involved, to stay busy. She felt a kinship with Charlie, having failed at so many of her own relationships. With all her volunteer work outside the library and her thoughts consumed with finding Mario, she just didn't have the energy or desire to make anything work. *So why'd you decide to retire in Silver Ridge?* she'd asked.

They'd been standing by her desk in the lobby, Charlie with his coat slung over one arm, and he'd glanced into the stacks and to where Marlene sat at a computer with her back to them, earphones smashing down her hair and repeating to herself in a voice worthy of a librarian shush, *Hola, me llamo Marlene. Cómo estás?*

A smile spread across Charlie's face, lit up his eyes. *Because Marly lived here.*

So he had moved to Silver Ridge, dated and married Marlene, and shortly afterward, decided to retire so he could travel the world with his wife. Nora adored Charlie. And not just because he was her stalwart supporter on the board who probably saved her from being fired on a couple of occasions for subverting rules and procedure. She never thought she'd return to Silver Ridge—it held memories both good and bad—but when she'd seen the position listed, it just seemed right to return to the library where so many of her good memories still lived.

Besides serving on the board, Charlie was a regular patron of the library, but after he retired, he started coming in more and more, and she always loved their conversations. Some days, he'd surprise Nora with a cup of coffee and a Danish from the diner, and if it was a slow morning, they'd talk. Their conversations ranged from their shared desire to travel to a mutual lifelong love of libraries. Last year, Charlie had been instrumental in helping Nora secure a grant for one of her library programs from the electrical company where he'd worked. Afterward, in a moment of surprising candor, he'd said to her, *Use the money to hire more staff and start living. You're too young to be so old, Nora.* She'd laughed and pretended his words didn't sting. Charlie had just shaken his head but never brought it up again.

Marlene was rocking slightly in her chair, like movement might help with the pain Nora guessed must be shooting through her body. Charlie had said that Marlene had been having more good days than bad, but Nora suspected that had all changed to a landslide of bad. Her throat clenched shut at the effort it took the woman to try to act normal, and she softened toward her, despite her callous words about Nora and the homeless. Everyone had their own story, and Nora knew that Marlene's was full of pain.

But Marlene, being her typical self, was not finished buzzing, and Nora squeezed her hands together under the desk, willing herself to be patient.

"I saw on my news program how most of these homeless, with their signs and their dogs, are actually not even homeless, just mooching off the sympathy of enablers like Nora." She widened her eyes, dipped her chin as though waiting for Nora or Vlado to agree with her.

Nora lifted her eyebrows. "That's quite a generalization, don't you think, Marlene?"

Marlene shrugged but it seemed that the wind had left her sails, at least for the moment. "Well, it's on the news."

Nora didn't even know where to start when it came to Marlene, whose news program beliefs were chiseled into granite. Normally, Nora would say something more, challenge her in a respectful way. Lately, though, she just didn't have the heart to contradict her.

Again her brother came to mind. He was always there, just under the surface of her thoughts. The reason she gave to people like him. And why she had to protect the tiny flame of hope she carried from the frigid winds of real life—that if she gave enough to others, someone, somewhere, would do the same for Mario. Call it karma, fate, kismet. She didn't know, but she had to believe that her good deeds counted and that if she couldn't physically bring her brother home, she could at the very least try to twist fate to work in her favor. She'd shared this idea with friends in the past, but it never seemed to translate to people who didn't understand that addiction was a monster that destroyed everything in its path. So she'd learned to keep these thoughts to herself and silently hope that her good deeds would ripple across the universe.

She tucked a piece of hair behind her ear and glanced at Vlado, then back to Marlene, who had risen to poke her head into the other room, making a *tsk* sound of disapproval. Nora sighed. When she shared personal bits about herself, it made her vulnerable to judgment and unwanted opinions. Like somehow hearing about her tragic life gave people the right to tell her what she should and shouldn't do. She'd shared a bit with Charlie because he knew how to listen and not judge. She didn't think Marlene had that same gift. As far as she knew, Marlene knew nothing about Nora and her brother, and that's how she planned to keep it.

"And speaking of lying." Marlene shuffled closer to Nora, gave a look over her shoulder toward the stacks. "There's a teenage girl in there doing drugs."

Nora stood a little straighter. "Did you see her doing drugs?" This complaint was not the first of its kind from Marlene.

Marlene cleared her throat in a loud *a-hem*. "Nora," she said. "I don't need to see it to know, but the girl is acting suspicious. Some people are just going to do the wrong thing no matter how hard you try to change them. I know you think you can save everyone, but you just—" Marlene pressed a hand to her chest, and Nora noticed the bluish shadows under her eyes, the whiteness of her scalp beneath her thin hair, the blue veins running under the skin of her hand. "You just can't."

Nora rubbed the back of her neck. Charlie once told her that he hadn't come alive until he met Marlene. And despite Marlene's predilection for a glass half-empty, Nora believed him because she could see it in the way he looked at her. As though he loved her as much for her faults as he did for her good parts. Nora felt a pang. It must feel wonderful to be loved like that.

Marlene continued in a softer voice, "You shouldn't let these hooligans walk all over you." Her voice had lost its hard edge, and a gentleness flirted with her words. "You're just too nice a person. Well, that's what Charlie thinks anyway." She paused, sniffed. "I think you're just sheltered."

The approval of her husband was as close to a compliment as Marlene would ever give, and despite her other words, Nora was warmed by the sentiment. But before she could address Marlene's accusation about the girl, the brass light fixture above their heads—the one that was in the center of the domed entryway—flickered off, then on, then off for a long moment before it lit up and stayed that way. Nora cast a worried glance outside. A wind had kicked up and the snow flew sideways. It looked bad. "Marlene, you need to head home. It looks like the forecasters were off. I think the bad part moved in early."

Marlene clucked. "Like I told you, the storm of '03. Maybe worse. But I don't need the forecasters and their models to know. I've lived here my whole life. I can feel it."

With the wind and the thick blanket of snow coating the windows, the flickering lights, the worry building inside about Marlene driving home, Nora fought against a growing uncertainty. She felt responsible for not closing up earlier. For not *feeling* the storm, or whatever nonsense Marlene believed. For not going to Denver last night to look for Mario or, hell, even this morning. His broken voice from the message kept replaying in her head, burned her eyes. Was he okay? What if he needed her?

An anxious energy wound through her legs, and she picked up her coffee mug and headed to the coffee station behind Vlado's desk. Well, not a *station* so much as a coffee maker she'd picked up from Goodwill, a couple of chipped mugs, and room-temperature creamer. She took a sip, the liquid from that morning tepid and bitter.

Vlado swiveled his chair around, his eyebrows raised, smiling. He stretched his long legs out in front of him and crossed his ankles. In the cramped space, the toes of his shoes were only inches from Nora. She stirred her coffee with a plastic straw, feeling the distance between them was too small. He was handsome. The thought heated her cheeks. She gave an awkward smile and turned to her desk.

"Nora." Vlado's voice was smooth and low, and the way he said her name made her duck her head, busy herself with stirring her coffee.

"Mm-hmm?" she said.

"Do you like to go to Denver?"

She shrugged, surprised by the question. "Sometimes." It had been where she'd lived during college and where Amanda still lived—and Mario, too, when she knew where he was. It was where she had spent nights alone, driving slowly through darkened streets, looking for her brother's face in the men who gathered around tents, against buildings, sprawled across benches.

He pulled his legs in, leaned forward with his elbows balanced on his thighs, and his forehead wrinkled. "I was wondering if—"

"So what are you going to do about her?" Marlene interrupted, and for once, Nora was relieved to have to tend to the old woman's complaints.

Nora drew a blank. "About who?"

With a dramatic sigh, Marlene said, "The girl who's back there doing drugs."

Nora tensed and glanced at Vlado, who shook his head, still smiling, and his unruffled demeanor made her relax. She crossed the foyer and set the cup down on her desk. "Thanks for the reminder. I'll go see if she has a way home. And it's time for you to go too. I'm closing the library."

Something crossed Marlene's face. Fear? Nora guessed she could be more nervous about the drive home than she'd let on. But then why had she come down in the first place? "Vlado, would you mind brushing off Marlene's car?" She glanced at the woman, unsure how she'd take the next suggestion. "If you're okay with it, Marlene, why don't you give your car keys to Vlado. He can warm up your car for you too."

Marlene's face hardened and Nora's pulse sped up, hoping something about *foreigners* and *thieves* wasn't about to pop out of the woman's mouth.

As if reading her mind, or perhaps because he'd worked here long enough to know, Vlado said, "I have a very nice car of my own. A brand-new lease, actually." He held up one hand, raised three fingers in what Nora thought might be the Boy Scout pledge or the Vulcan sign for peace. "I promise not to steal your car," he said, and Nora had to pinch the skin under her forearm to keep from laughing.

"Well, now, I would never accuse you of that," Marlene said, her gaze on the floor, one hand rubbing the back of her head. "But maybe . . ."

Nora didn't stay to hear what she said next and instead headed to the stacks to see about the girl. She found her in the plush armchair by the window that framed the aspen trees, reading a book. "Hello," she said.

The girl's head shot up, her dark-brown eyes narrowed. "That other lady already gave me a hard time. I'm just reading a book, you know. Is that illegal to do in the library?"

Nora smiled. "Not at all."

"Did that old lady say something about me? She's rude, you know."

Nora folded her arms, protective of Marlene but understanding all too well this girl's reaction. "Marlene jumps to conclusions, but she means well." Nora stopped, dipped her chin. "Most of the time, at least."

The girl slung her feet to the ground, gave Nora a look. "She's just plain mean, if you ask me."

"Can I help you find something? Anything in particular you're looking for?"

The girl grabbed her backpack, pushed to her feet. "Jeez, I didn't know I needed a reason to be here. I thought everyone was welcome at the library. It's what your sign says, you know."

Her eyes were a liquid brown that gave nothing away, but a faint quivering in her chin did. Nora touched her chest, empathy rising easily. The girl had likely come here for some quiet space, maybe to escape something at home, or because she'd had a bad day at school, or simply because she wanted to find a good book to get lost in, and instead she'd had to face Marlene's unjustified suspicion.

Nora understood wanting to be left alone. She'd been different from most kids her age. An orphan with a drug user for a brother, Nora didn't have the same cares as other kids, and it showed painfully in the way she tried to interact with others. Uncomfortable silences, stilted conversations about friends or crushes or a new show. She didn't know what shows were popular because she spent her time reading about addiction and how some chemicals changed a person's brain. She had nightmares about Mario as a zombie that woke her screaming and left her crying. So for her, the library was her respite, away from the chaos of her aunt's house, where she felt like an interloper. Away from school, where she was a loner, not cool enough for most kids, too weird for others. And the library, where Mrs. Washington—who, on Fridays, wore a pink cardigan that floated around her like cotton candy—worked. Mrs. Washington remembered when Mario first brought her to the library, and she always had something nice to say. *He's been through a lot, hasn't he? But he did right by you, Nora.*

By high school, Nora saw Mario only every few months, if that. And when he did come, his hair was greasy, his clothes were dirty, and all he wanted was money. His visits ended in her aunt crying and her uncle shouting at Mario to leave and Nora running after him. *Please get better. Can you try? Please? I miss you.* And she'd hug him and sometimes had to hold her breath because he smelled like old socks. *I'm trying this time, Peaches. I promise. Seeing you always makes me want to get better.*

Mario's addiction created a rift—with her aunt and uncle on one side, Mario on the other, and Nora alone in the middle. So the library was the perfect escape; its quiet, her sanctuary; the books, her refuge; and Mrs. Washington, the one adult in her world who seemed to both understand and not judge.

Yet by the way this girl stared at her—suspicious, guarded—Nora knew she didn't see her as anything like Mrs. Washington. She smiled, extended her hand. "I'm Nora. We've met before, right? You were in here with your little sister, I think?"

The girl nodded and took her hand; hers was small and dry. "Jasmine. Yeah, my sister was the one who spilled a juice box on the carpet. She's only eight and she's really loud. We just moved here."

Nora squeezed her hand before releasing it. "You and your sister are very welcome here, Jasmine. The library is a perfect place for kids, especially the loud ones." She glanced behind her toward the foyer but didn't see Marlene. "And I'm sorry about Marlene. She can be a little, well, opinionated sometimes and maybe stuck in her ways a bit."

Jasmine slid her hands into her sweatshirt pocket, shrugged. "Yeah, so can my grandma, I guess. Maybe it's an *old* thing."

Nora laughed and the girl rocked on her toes, seemed to want to say something else, but before she could, a gust of wind punched the windows, made the glass creak, and Nora was reminded of why she'd come in here in the first place. "Listen, Jasmine, this storm is really bad. Do you have a way home?"

"I'm walking. My grandma doesn't live too far."

"How far?"

"The Meadows."

The Meadows was a small neighborhood down Elk Falls Road. Jasmine was right; it wasn't that far on a nice day—just over two miles—but the road was two-lane and curvy, barely safe on a day without snow. Dangerous on a day like—

Outside came a pop, then a crash, and a small pine branch fell to the ground. The lights flickered again.

Nora's breath caught in her throat, but it wasn't from the violence of the storm. Through the branches, she saw a dark lump sprawled in the snow by the trunk of the tree—a figure, half on his side, face and head bare, snow flecking his black coat heavily in white.

It was Lewis. She could tell by the coat because it was a heavy wool that, despite the pungent odor it emanated, she remembered thinking was good to have with the oncoming storm. But he wasn't at the shelter. He was in the middle of the storm, lying down like—

"Oh my God!" With her heart pounding, she hurried to her desk and flung open the drawer. Her hands fumbled with the small package, her mind racing with questions. How long had he been out there? Was she too late? She ran out the door and into the storm, forgetting her coat, still wearing her flats, and ignoring the worried calls from both Vlado and Marlene.

CHAPTER SIX

MARLENE

She didn't care about the weather or how much the snow would hinder her drive home. It's why she and Charlie always saved enough for the extra nice snow tires, the ones that felt like the rubber suction-cupped to the road, no matter how much snow there was between tire and pavement. She'd even taken the precaution of driving Charlie's Jeep today for its extra clearance, instead of her more agile Subaru.

Vlado was pulling on his boots by the front door, intending, she supposed, to go warm up her car for her like Nora had suggested. Marlene fidgeted, squeezing her hands together. She didn't want to go home. Not just yet and not when she knew the storm would dump enough to keep the unmaintained road up to her house impassable until their neighbor, Jonah, with the plow on his pickup truck, could clear it for them. A deal Charlie had struck years earlier after helping the young family pay their winter heating bills one long, dark winter when Jonah had lost his job. Jonah had insisted and Charlie agreed but only for the one winter. The young man just kept doing it anyway.

"Vlado!" Marlene said, his name sounding sharper than she had intended. Everything always sounded sharper than she intended, her voice strained, sometimes breaking in the middle of words like her vocal cords had just given up. Which was exactly what she felt like doing these days. Her mother used to say that life was a boxer with a mean left hook. Marlene tended to agree. "I mean, I don't need you to—"

Just then, Nora rushed from the stacks and to her desk, face pale, eyes wild, hurling open a drawer and fumbling around inside before tearing out the door and into the freezing white in nothing but her flats and thin cardigan sweater.

"Nora?" Marlene and Vlado said at the same time. He met Marlene's eyes, and she noticed the worry lines that deepened in his forehead.

Vlado quickly finished tying up his boots, pulled on a thick winter coat and gloves, and with a puff of snow, he was out the door after her.

She watched him leave and tried to look out the window behind Nora's desk, but she couldn't see past the snow crusting the windows. What had gotten into the woman? Nora had looked determined, but scared too. Marlene started for the door, stopped. She should go out and help. In her younger years, she would have. She'd been strong, both physically and mentally. Spent much of her life nursing her parents in their last years. They had weakened like summer flowers after the first frost, quietly and quickly. First her dad, when Marlene was only in her twenties, and then her mother, decades later. And in between, Marlene had wilted, too, from a young girl who had a secret dream to paint people and places to a dutiful daughter who didn't want to see her parents die alone. She didn't resent them; she'd chosen to come home. Sometimes she just wished she'd nursed her dreams too.

Her legs itched to charge out into the storm, but life also had a mean right hook, and as soon as her mother had died, the pains had begun. First as a flicker, flashbulbs of discomfort that surprised her but didn't bother her enough to question it. Then the aching tiredness that kept her in bed, sometimes for two days in a row, until piece by piece she was stripped of the person she'd once been, reduced to the hobbled woman she was now who couldn't manage to walk out in a snowstorm to help a friend.

Marlene moved back and forth on her feet, watching the door for when they returned, and nearly forgot about the teenager with the drugs in the stacks, until she heard a soft curse. Relieved to have something else to focus on, she hurried to the back room and stopped in her tracks, feeling both vindicated for her assumptions and also disappointed that she'd been right. What people didn't know about her was that it was tough to be let down so often by the world.

The girl knelt on the floor, her overstuffed backpack zipped open in front of her, her head down while she worked the book into the bag. It was a library book, Marlene could tell from the lettering on the spine, and one that the girl had not checked out yet.

"Damn!" The girl swore again softly when the teeth of the zipper burst open. She shot a glance up at the window behind her, then another toward the front door, and that's when she noticed Marlene standing there, watching everything. The girl shot to her feet, bag pressed against her chest, and her glare was a mixture of defensiveness and plain old guilt.

Marlene sighed and leaned heavily into the doorframe. "Stealing from the library? I'm sure your mother's taught you better than that."

The girl's face changed then, jaw tightened, dark-brown eyes hardened. "I'm not stealing and you can't talk to me like that." She carried her broken backpack with the book tucked inside and moved past Marlene and toward the front door. Marlene's body jerked forward before it remembered what it could and couldn't do, and a searing-hot pain shot down her leg from her sciatica. She grunted against the sensation and followed the girl into the lobby.

The thing was, Marlene could lose her temper, sure, like anyone her age who spent too much time consumed with absorbing any physical sign of how much her body betrayed her with its aches, its pains, its wanton lust to compress her body into nothing but nerve endings. But she was good at hiding it—or had been at one point in her life, when she could focus on hikes with Charlie, dinners out, visits to hot springs, trips to Mexico. Just not anymore. And in this moment, it wasn't only the girl that was making her eyes heat up, her skin itch. It was so much more than the girl. But the *more* was what Marlene wanted to crumple into a ball and hurl out the window.

"Wait! You can't just take that book," she called. "This is the library!"

But the girl kept walking, and Marlene's chest swelled with indignation and regret and a sadness that had hardened into anger, and before she knew it her hand was reaching out to stop her.

Just then the lights flickered, and through the window by Nora's desk, Marlene saw a thick tree limb fall from the big pine outside the library, landing with a heavy thud. Pine needles from the branch scratched, but didn't break, the window. Both Marlene and the girl froze, and through limbs and under the tree, Marlene could just make out an odd trio of Vlado, Nora, and a man in a ragtag coat kneeling in the snow.

CHAPTER SEVEN

Nora

The snow filled her flats, squishing around her toes so that she felt like her feet were encased in plastic bags of freezing water. She tried to run around the side of the building, but her legs sank into the deep powder. It nearly came to her knees, and the part of her brain that wasn't reciting the signs of an opioid overdose registered the amount of snow with shock.

She kept going, ticking the signs off in her head. *Not waking up or responding to my voice or touch. Is breathing slow, irregular, or has it stopped? Are the pupils very small? Lips blue?* She felt her body shake from the cold. In this weather, her own lips were probably blue by now; how would she know if his were blue because of an overdose or the freezing cold? Snow wiggled under the tail of her shirt, slipped down the back of her pants. She kept moving, ignoring her labored progress and continuing to grasp for any remnants from the class she took. *Slow heartbeat? Weak pulse?* A chill ran down her spine that had nothing to do with the wet cardigan clinging to her skin. What if the guy wasn't breathing? Was she supposed to administer rescue breathing first? A knot tightened in the pit of her stomach, and her brain was suddenly empty of everything she'd learned in that class. The branches of the pine tree hung down like blackout curtains, blocking her view of the man inside. One branch bowed beyond what Nora thought was possible for wood, its pine needles resting on snow that had already piled heavy across the green needles, gluing its weight to the ground.

Beyond the sodden branches, she could just make out his form, sprawled by the thick trunk, and her heart beat so fast it flattened her lungs. She was thrown back to the afternoon when she was nine and had taken the trash out like she did every Monday. It hadn't been snowing, but it was so cold that her breath fogged the air, and she was so focused on that she didn't notice Mario sprawled in the brown grass, the zombie from her nightmares. She'd screamed so loud the neighbor's dog started howling. *You saved his life,* the paramedic told her later.

She pushed through the stiff limbs and found herself sheltered underneath the tree, shoving thoughts of Mario out of the way to make room for the box in her hand and the man on the ground. The snow was shallower in the protected space, and she was by his side in seconds, her mind spinning with instructions. *Lay the person on their back. Remove device from the box and peel back the plastic.* It had all seemed so easy in class, simple in a *How to Stop an Opioid Overdose for Dummies* kind of way. But it didn't account for a once-in-a-decade snowstorm or fingers that had grown so cold she couldn't grip the small plastic corner of the package. She squeezed her eyes shut, shook her head. Calm down, Nora! She was getting ahead of herself. Check him first. He lay at an odd angle, slumped low against the trunk. Her brother's skin had been gray, his lips more black than blue, and she'd been sure he was dead. *They said I would have died if you hadn't found me,* he'd croaked later from his hospital bed. *I don't know what I'd do without you, Peaches.*

The man's lips were blue; his eyes were closed, so she couldn't see his pupils. She put two fingers to his wrist, but feeling his pulse beneath the frozen pads of her fingertips seemed an impossible task, so she laid her head against his chest, ignoring the moist stink that mixed with the wool fabric of his coat. His heart beat but it was slow—too slow, she thought—and his breathing sounded like a wave that never quite reached the shore.

"Nora?" She didn't turn. Vlado's voice was recognizable even in a moment like this, where Nora was so far out of her league she felt like a stranger to herself.

"I need help." Her voice was hoarse.

"Okay." He was on the other side of the man's prone form in seconds.

"I think this man has overdosed." Her teeth chattered while she spoke, making her words come out in fits and starts. "We need to lay him all the way onto his back."

Vlado did just that and Nora was grateful to not be alone anymore, even if it was with someone who knew less than she did about how to save someone from an overdose. The class had been helpful, but it had also been calm and relaxed, nothing like reality. In reality, it was the hard grass biting into her knees, the stink of a trash bag split open by her side, the screeching cries of her aunt, and the splashes of ambulance lights across her brother's zombie face.

She fumbled with the package, the tiny edge of plastic slipping from between her wet fingers until she cried out with frustration. "Damn it!"

Vlado took the box, opened it, pulled out the device, and without a word, handed it back to her.

She fit it into her hand, thumb on the plunger, two fingers on either side of the nozzle that wobbled in the air with a shaking that skittered through her muscles. She didn't want this man to die. Not when she could do something to save him. Why was he here, near death and alone? Did he have a wife who cried for him? A son? Did they scour the streets like she did, feel the futility of searching for one person in the widening hole inside their chests? She would not let him die, but she was terrified that she was too late.

She slid one hand under his neck to tilt his head up, inserted the nozzle into his left nostril until her fingers touched his nose; then she pushed the plunger.

"Help me get him on his side," she said.

She pulled on his shoulders while Vlado pushed against his back, and they quickly brought the man to his side, where she positioned his hands under his head. Nora watched his face, waiting for signs that the medicine had worked. It could happen quickly or it could take a few minutes—that part she remembered. Mario's body had flopped like a fish when they compressed his chest over and over again. He wasn't responding; he was already dead.

The man's skin looked gray. She felt an ache in her jaw that she ignored as she waited, forgetting how cold she was, forgetting—

"Oh!" She pushed to her knees, soaking her pants on the wet ground. "We need to call 911."

Vlado nodded, pulled his phone from his pocket, and punched in the numbers. "Yes, hello, this—"

Just then the man sat up, his eyes wide and red, skin pale but less gray than before, the blue tint disappearing from his lips. He slapped the phone from Vlado's hand. It landed in the snow. "No, no hospitals. I'm fine, goddamnit, I'm fine."

He pushed his body up until he wobbled on his knees, hands on the ground as if he might keel over. Nora's arms shot out but hovered in the air, not quite touching the man but ready to brace him in case he started to fall. Vlado picked up his phone, looking to Nora as though waiting for her decision.

"Lewis, right? I believe you overdosed. I think you n-n-eed t-t—" She'd begun to shake violently, the adrenaline from before seeping out, leaving behind muscles frozen by the wind, skin so numb it lay on her like a wet blanket.

Lewis looked up at her, then swiveled his head, seemed to take in his surroundings: Vlado, the phone, the snow, his library card, and a rolled-up dollar bill on the ground beside a plastic bag. Moving slowly and clumsily, he grabbed the bill and the bag and stuffed them into his pockets, then sat back on his heels and rubbed his face roughly with one hand.

Nora stared at his pocket, surprised and slightly sickened to see him protect what nearly killed him. She blinked. "Sir, you need to get checked out by paramedics to make sure you're okay. You could still overdose once this medication wears off. And w-w-we need to get you out of the c-c-cold." Shivers racked her body and she wrapped her arms around her, tried to create warmth. A coat appeared around her shoulders, warm and too big, and she inhaled apples and some kind of woodsy manlike scent. She shuddered into it, grateful for the respite from the frigid air, and noticed Vlado, coatless and standing above her with his phone to his ear.

"She gave him something in his nose. Yes. He's awake and he's sitting up and talking. Okay, okay."

The man struggled to push to his feet. "I said no hospital, damnit, no hospital."

"What are they saying?" Nora asked Vlado.

Vlado pulled the phone from his ear. "They can't get anyone to us for a while. Roads are closed, big accidents all over the place. They say to get him inside and to keep an eye on him."

Lewis had risen to his feet but leaned heavily against the tree. Nora noticed his hands—thick with calluses, skin torn and hardened at the fingertips—and her chest hurt to think of the pain that must cause him.

"I have c-c-offee, t-t-tea, and hot chocolate inside," she said past numb lips. She thought about the day last week when he came inside to use the bathroom. How he'd kept his eyes down, hardly ever meeting her gaze, like he didn't exist if she didn't see him, like he was invisible. "It's r-r-really c-cold out here, Lewis. I could use something warm. H-how about you?"

His gaze seemed to take in her soaking-wet pants and flimsy shoes, but he still didn't meet her eyes. A deep fatigue sliced wide lines down his cheeks, and behind that Nora thought she saw something give way.

From above them came a loud crack, followed by a *whooshing* sound, and a massive branch tumbled to the ground not far from where they had gathered under the tree. Nora could not believe her eyes.

Vlado grabbed her arm. "We need to get inside. It's dangerous out here."

She nodded, turned to Lewis. "Please, Lewis, come inside with us. Please?" She could hear a raw desperation in her voice. Desperate because she knew she couldn't leave him out here to freeze to death, but she had no idea how she could force him inside without someone getting hurt. Already she was thinking of her brother. How she hadn't seen him in years, heard from him only sporadically. Her hands curled into fists. She had to get Lewis inside. This time she tried to keep her tone light. "There's coffee. Wouldn't it be nice to have something warm right about now?"

Lewis turned from them, back rounded, and for a heart-pounding second, she thought he was going to leave, but then he stopped and seemed to change his mind. "Okay," he said.

Nora breathed out, relief a temporary warmth. "Okay, Lewis. Good, good, let's go, then, okay? I even promise not to give you a replacement library card."

Vlado snorted and Nora saw the man's shoulders go up and down once. A sigh? A laugh? It didn't matter. All she cared about was getting him inside.

Vlado led the way and they trudged slowly out from under the tree and into the deeper snow, with the wind pushing wet flakes into her eyes and mouth, making it hard to see anything but white until they reached the library, and Nora walked inside to find that all hell had broken loose.

"Nora!" Marlene stood by Nora's desk, her hand gripping Jasmine's arm. "I *told* you this girl was up to no good."

Nora wanted to get Lewis settled in, then sink into her chair, take off her sopping shoes, and drink a hot tea. She didn't want to deal with Marlene. But the girl looked both angry and scared, and for a moment Nora saw herself kneeling on the grass—cheeks mottled by tears, her mouth twisted—and watching Mario leave on a stretcher. She gritted her teeth and, not for the first time today, wished for Charlie. He'd know how to talk to Marlene.

Nora approached them, her eyes on the older woman. There was a lingering chill in her voice when she spoke. "Take your hand off of her, Marlene. Now."

Marlene looked at the girl and jerked back, releasing her and seeming almost surprised that she'd been holding on to her arm in the first place. "Oh, but she stole a book, Nora. It's stuffed into her backpack." Her body seemed to deflate, and she slumped forward, leaning heavily into Nora's desk. "I knew she was up to no good, with her drugs and her phone and her hat on in the *library*." She said it as though she considered the deeds equally wrong but with less fervor than before.

Nora sighed. A pounding had started behind her eyes.

The girl snorted and moved toward the door. "She's crazy. I'm outta here."

Just then the lights flickered on, then off before extinguishing, and at the same time, every cell phone in the room emitted a shrill alarm. Marlene jumped.

Vlado held up his phone. "It's a weather warning. The storm is bad, roads are worse. It recommends that everyone should stay in place."

Marlene had moved to the window and was peering outside. "I told you," she said, sounding older, weaker than the force of nature Nora had come to know. "Just like the storm of '03, only worse."

The wind and snow battered the windows, and without the lights, shadows grew like mold into the corners of the old library. A memory of the storm from so long ago spread with the changing light. It rippled in the air around her, dancing with the panic, the fear that had become a familiar partner, that her brother was out there, alone and hurting, and there was nothing she could do to help.

"Miss Nora?" The timid note in Jasmine's voice caused her to shake off the memory.

She smiled at the girl. "Yes?"

"My grandma wants to know if I can stay here until she can come get me?" Jasmine looked sideways at Marlene and her jaw tightened. "Not that I want to hang out anywhere near *her*, but my dad is out of town and I don't want my grandma out in this. Her eyesight is real bad."

Nora took stock of the people around her. Jasmine fidgeted with the string on her sweatshirt, pulling it down one side, then retracting it with the other. The girl didn't look much older than fifteen and was probably as uncomfortable as a teenager gets around so many unfamiliar adults, especially with one of them accusing her of stealing and another filling the small entryway with a rather pungent smell. Lewis had slid to the floor, his back against the doorframe, exhaustion sloughing off him. He shifted with a grunt, squinted up at Nora. "Thought you said there'd be coffee."

Vlado leaned against the wall by Lewis, arms crossed and watching Nora with a look on his face she didn't quite understand. His brown hair was wet and tousled, and when their eyes met, his smile was warm.

By the window, Marlene seemed lost to her thoughts, her head tilted up as she watched the snow fall. "I shoveled for three days straight before I found my car," she said. "Lost power for a week and had to melt snow for water."

The last storm had been only the beginning. What had followed was a painful series of recoveries and relapses, hope and homelessness that took small pieces of Nora's brother, then chunks, like a building crumbling over time. This storm was no different because Mario was somewhere alone and hurting and there was nothing Nora could do to help.

She glanced at Lewis, who worked his hands in and out of fists, as though the feeling was just now returning to them. The only difference with this storm was that she was here with people like Lewis and Marlene and Jasmine, and they needed somewhere safe. And that was something she could give them; that was something she could do.

"Miss Nora?" Jasmine looked out at her from under her ball cap.

Nora smiled, clapped her hands, and said, "Is there a better place to be stranded than a library?"

CHAPTER EIGHT

Lewis

Yes, there was a better goddamn place to be stranded than the library. That was his first thought when the librarian asked the question like she was Mary Poppins offering a spoonful of sugar. But Lewis's toes were frozen, his eyes dry and gritty in a way that made everything a little blurry, and he didn't feel like himself yet. Not by a long shot. Everything was still a little hazy, and he wasn't completely sure what had happened or how he'd gotten here. So he grunted at her question and pulled his coat tighter around his body.

His head ached and his chest felt like someone had been sitting on it and just gotten up. The old woman by the window gave him a look that he ignored. He knew the type: opinionated and never wrong.

Over by the door, a girl stood, holding an overstuffed backpack against her chest. With her head down and baseball hat on, he couldn't see much more than her chin. Then she shifted and looked up, and he recognized her as a girl who worked at the diner with Persie, and then he saw Persie's pink hair in the diner lights. The girl in the library looked nothing like Persie, but they were around the same age, and it was enough to fill Lewis's eyes with sad old-man tears. He pushed a fist into the space between his eyebrows and cursed himself. *Men don't cry.* His father certainly never did—not when he'd buried his wife when Lewis was only ten and not when they buried his older brother, who came home in a box much too short for his six-foot four-inch body. *Men serve their country and men do what must be done. But they don't cry.* It wasn't something his father ever said; it was just an example that Lewis was meant to follow. So he did, and kept whatever he might feel about the war in Vietnam to himself. But he didn't want to go. Too many had already died, and for what? With his birthday looming and the draft like an ax blade on his neck, Lewis had no place to question. It was his duty, it was his job, even if it meant coming home in a box. He'd stuffed the recruitment flyer for the Ohio National Guard into his sock drawer. He'd already signed up when he told his father. Back then, some saw it as a way to dodge the war. His father had. *Coward,* he'd called him and didn't stick around to say goodbye. Lewis may have avoided the jungles, but he'd ended up on a hill, with a gun, and proving his father right.

The girl caught him staring at her and quickly pulled her hat down to cover her face, turned to the side. He shifted on the hard floor and sucked in his bottom lip. He'd made her uncomfortable with his staring. Of course he had. He pulled himself deeper into his coat and closed his eyes, overcome by a tiredness that seeped from his heart.

At some point, he felt the heat of someone close, kneeling in front of him, but he didn't open his eyes. Outside, he could huddle in a cardboard box, or a sleeping bag, or cover himself with newspapers to ignore the curious, the repulsed, the pitying gazes of people with homes and lives they hadn't fucked up. In here, the walls closed in on him, the people crowded above him, and he felt small and exposed.

"Coffee?"

He opened one eye. It was Mary Poppins, smiling. The kind of gentle smile that says *nothing bad has ever happened to me and I feel sorry for you, so I'll do nice things so I can feel better about myself.* He hated it but he wanted the coffee more, so he took the paper cup. It smelled black and strong and exactly like what he needed to smooth the aching waves behind his eyes. He drank and the bitterness of the liquid momentarily obliterated the foul taste in his mouth. "Thanks," he said.

"Of course. Here, in case you're hungry." She handed him a granola bar, which she had already opened on one end. It was a nice gesture, especially with the state of his hands. The cracks ran deep, and even something as simple as opening a wrapper was painful. He felt something twist in his chest. Did she know that? But he pushed the question away and ate, staying huddled deep inside his coat. It didn't matter why the librarian had done it. It didn't matter one bit because as soon as the weather improved, he was leaving.

The tall security officer bent over, his dark hair and youthful face reminding Lewis of a buddy of his from the National Guard. The one who'd missed that day because he'd suffered a compound fracture during training and wasn't deployed with everyone else. He'd been lucky, Lewis told him later. *Real lucky.*

"You overdosed," the security guard said.

Lewis didn't respond. He ate the rest of the granola bar and drained the coffee before returning to the inside of his coat and closing his eyes. He'd wait out the storm and then leave as soon as they weren't looking. They couldn't keep him here against his will, and he didn't owe her anything.

He was going to die; he could feel it. A man couldn't live a life like his and expect anything less. This time, he wasn't afraid. He'd only come back to see his granddaughter with his own eyes one more time. In his few weeks here, he'd seen enough. Phyllis had been strong, Heather even stronger, and Persie was nothing like him.

The librarian should never have saved his worthless life in the first place.

CHAPTER NINE

NORA

After flickering and teasing them with light and heat, the power finally went out and didn't come back on. While still pale and shaky, Lewis was mostly just withdrawn, appearing to sleep on and off, but otherwise did not seem to be in danger of overdosing. Still, she kept a close eye on him. Jasmine had wandered back to the stacks to sit in the wide chair by the window. She tapped on her phone but hadn't spoken much, seeming to want to be as far from Marlene as possible. Nora couldn't blame her. Marlene sat in a chair in the lobby, a travel book about Mexico in her lap, but based on the way her eyes flicked around the room, not reading.

Vlado had gone out to his car, returning soaking wet, the snow falling off him in chunks, and holding a weather radio. "I think I got this working over the weekend," he said, smiling, and set it on Nora's desk.

She raised her eyebrows. "Impressive."

He flicked on a switch and spun the dials. Nora heard mostly static melting in and out of robotic voices listing the counties under a severe winter-storm warning. ". . . be prepared for areas of ice and blowing snow with whiteout conditions likely. A windchill warning is forecast for the following counties . . ."

Nora's eyes widened and she shivered from her wet pants that clung to her skin and the old library, once a stout structure but worn down with time and already allowing the cold to snake inside through unseen cracks. She lowered her voice and leaned in toward Vlado. "If the power stays off, it's going to be hard to stay warm in here."

He nodded.

The voice listing the counties within the warning zone dissolved into a blowing static before briefly clearing. ". . . shelter in place . . . high country . . . unsurvivable conditions . . ." Again the voice was lost in static, and Vlado winced and shut it off. "I need to replace the antenna."

She pointed toward the manual. "Didn't you just start reading that?"

Vlado shrugged. "I read fast."

"And learn fast too." The more they talked, the more Nora wanted to know about him. It was an odd feeling since Nora tended to shy away from making new friends, because new friends led to conversations meant to uncover tidbits about the other. She didn't mind talking about the library or books or volunteering, but anything past that always led to Mario, and that only made people uncomfortable.

He smiled and returned to the radio, hesitated, then turned back to Nora.

She looked up at him, eyebrows raised.

"You saved his life."

The way he said it—a statement, a fact, with a solidness in the set of his shoulders and a look in his eyes that didn't hide his esteem. Her face grew hot. She did better with professional relationships. "Yes, well, I took a class on how to help if it ever happened here, so I guess it worked."

"You learn fast too," he said, and his eyes crinkled.

She turned from him and to her desk, feeling seen in a way she hadn't felt in a very long time and had no intention of encouraging. It was just past seven, and with no signs that the storm had plans of abating anytime soon, she needed to start thinking about what they were going to do to stay warm and how they were going to pass the time together in what had rapidly become a very dark library.

With her own deep chill lingering in the tips of her fingers, her thoughts kept drifting to her brother. Had he come back to Silver Ridge because he needed her? She checked her phone. No more messages. She twisted the ends of her hair, stopped herself from calling Ed back. When she thought of the man, her skin prickled. It could so easily be her getting a phone call like that. She put her phone facedown on her desk. No matter how much she wanted to, calling Ed was not the right thing to do.

Mario had been in a good place when Nora went to college, and she'd believed that the storm clouds had finally passed. College had been an exciting prospect. There had been pride in her uncle's eyes when she graduated high school, but Nora thought there was relief, too, and she couldn't blame him. Nora had been a quiet teenager, trying to stay out of the way as much as possible. She knew how difficult Mario had made things for their family, and she didn't want to add to it. But she had always been a reminder of the boy they could never help.

She'd managed to get a scholarship to Metro Denver, and she already knew that a job in library sciences was the direction she wanted. Plus, Denver was where Mario lived, and for the first time since he'd left home, they would live near each other again. Sharing an apartment during her last two years of undergrad had been his idea, a way for both of them to save money, but for her it was a second chance. Their childhoods had been destroyed by the accident, and Nora wanted those years back. For a while, it had been exactly what she'd hoped it would be. Life had seeped back into Mario, given him a peacefulness she thought he'd lost. They'd stay up late on the weekends, watching movies, eating popcorn, laughing. That's what she remembered the most about that time. Laughing.

Mario had worked at a bike-repair shop, and one day he brought home a purple-and-orange mountain bike for her. She'd tried to argue—money was tight for both of them—but he wouldn't budge. *All you do is study and work.* He pushed the bike toward her, giving her a smile that turned his brown eyes golden. *If you don't get outside more, you might turn into a vampire librarian, and that'll be bad for business.*

Pink-and-white plastic streamers floated from the handlebars. She'd run her fingers through the tangles, delighted at the odd pairing of childhood decoration with adult function. *Did you add these?* She'd laughed when he nodded. *What am I, seven?* she'd teased and punched him in the arm.

But Mario shoved his hands into his pockets, the lightness from before blown out like a candle. *Mom and Dad never had the chance to get you a bike.* His eyes had dulled and he looked away, kicked at a rock on the ground. *I don't know what I'd do without you.*

The streamers tickled her thighs, and the bike had felt heavy in her hands. It was a sweet gesture that reminded her of the noose around her neck. The one that woke her in the middle of the night, choking from fear that he was one stumble away from falling back into old habits. Her smile had felt fragile, but he didn't seem to notice, and she set the bike against the porch railing and flung her arms around him, squeezing like she could keep him whole if she held on tight enough. *It's perfect. Thank you.*

He'd patted her back. *You deserve it, Peaches.*

It had felt like a beginning, like the worst was finally behind them. But that had been her mistake.

She pressed a hand to her chest, cold to the bone both from memory and temperature, and reached for her phone. At the very least, she could email him.

Mario, it's bad out there, dangerous wind chill
tonight. I hope you're inside and safe from this

terrible storm. I'm sorry about Adam, but you
are not him. Please let me know that you're safe.
Love, Nora

She hit "Send," and instead of relief, it caused her heart to flutter, imagining her email landing unopened in an abandoned in-box. It was a Hotmail account he'd had since she was little. In the first few years, he'd answer her—not every time, but enough to keep her hopes up. Now, he hardly responded, but she occasionally still sent him a message because then she could pretend that he heard her.

The light outside had deteriorated, turning everything into black and blue shadows. It would be pitch black in here soon, and the thought made her lurch to her feet. They needed some source of light, or the hours that lay ahead of them would be interminable.

Vlado caught her eye. "Need help?"

"Maybe. I think I have a lantern in the storage room."

He followed her. "Good idea. Our phones won't last all night."

The storage area was a small closet just past the bathroom but large enough to store a few boxes and plastic containers, easels, and old posters. In the confined space, Vlado had to stand so close to Nora she could feel the slight heat from his body, and it reminded her of how long it had been since she'd been in such close proximity to a man. He held up his phone so that the light from it spread in a funnel above her head. She did the same and together they had a fair amount of illumination.

Vlado pointed his light at a poster. "'Young Authors Night.' I don't remember that one."

Nora smiled. "I have a group of kids every year who write a book. We start in April and finish up by September. Then we have a night where they invite family and friends for their book launch and author-signing event. It's one of my favorites. This year I had a kid who wrote a comic style of book, and his illustrations were unbelievable." Since she'd first started working here, she amped up the youth programs to make sure kids in the area had a place they belonged. It had been what Mrs. Washington had done for her and the best way for her to pass it on. She put a hand on her hip, looked for the lantern she knew she'd purchased at one point. "It must be around here somewhere. It was—"

Vlado's light swept the room again, stopped. "'Reading under the Stars'?" His lightly accented words betrayed his amusement.

"That's it." She pulled the box off the top of a stack, set it on the floor, and pulled out a battery-powered lantern, the kind meant to look old. "Aha!" She turned it on and it quickly illuminated the entire closet, and in the light she realized how close she'd moved to Vlado. She stepped back but her foot hit a box. He looked down at her, his eyes reflecting the glow of the lantern.

"'Reading under the Stars,'" he said again. "That seems difficult."

She pushed a piece of hair from her face. It had been a small group, mostly older adults who'd brought their own chairs but not their own light, which they'd needed because one lantern was never going to cut it. She'd passed out premade s'mores and a map of the constellations, and they'd had a nice evening, but she'd hosted the event only once because, well, reading under the stars was hard to do when it was dark. "A much better idea in theory than in practice."

His laugh was a rich sound that tickled her ears, warmed her skin. "You are very dedicated to your patrons, Nora. It is a busy library for such a small town. But I think I know why."

She stared up at him, trying to decide if he was making a joke, because the answer was obvious to her. "Yes, because it's where all the books live."

He nodded. "Yes, the books, and you. You provide so many resources for the kids and adults. I see them come through the door. Most of them go straight to your desk to tell you about their day or ask you something or to get your advice. They trust you. I think you are the reason people here love this library."

"Oh, well, that's not . . ." She trailed off and tried to look distracted. It was a nice thing to say but also completely wrong. So she put the lid back on the bin and eyed the other boxes, trying to ignore the heat prickling up her cheeks, and she focused on finding something that might entertain or, more accurately, distract Jasmine, Marlene, and Lewis from the fact that they were all trapped for the foreseeable future.

A rubber band of tension stretched between her three patrons, who, other than speaking directly to her, had completely ignored each other. If they couldn't leave the library, Nora felt like it was her job to fill the time with a distraction. Besides, helping them would get her mind off Mario. At least for a little while.

"What are we looking for now?" Vlado eyed the boxes, glancing inside a few.

"Something to occupy our hands and minds. And since we know reading is a bit difficult in the dark—" She paused, smiled.

Vlado laughed and hoisted the lantern. "As you cleverly figured out."

"Correct. So I thought an activity that could be done with little light might be best." As she grew older, she'd learned to stay busy. Keeping herself occupied kept her from worrying about Mario, and being out of the house let her pretend that the accident hadn't forever altered her aunt's and uncle's lives. So she volunteered at the library with Mrs. Washington, got a job at a secondhand store in town, and hung out at the diner before school.

She studied the boxes. What could be done in a library with no electricity? She looked over the boxes and saw what she wanted. "Let's see how they like knitting."

CHAPTER TEN

NORA

She brought the bin into the stacks area, then set it on the floor along with the lantern. Jasmine lifted her head and looked over her phone.

"What are you doing?" she asked.

Nora smiled. "Setting up an activity." She pulled a few chairs into a circle around the box and added a couple of floor pillows too. "Lewis? Marlene? Would you like to join in?" Lewis grunted from the other room, and Nora took that as a no.

Jasmine moved closer, settling herself on one of the pillows, her backpack on the floor behind her. Nora had noticed how the girl kept a distance between herself and Marlene, casting furtive glances her way every so often. Although she was curious about the book Marlene had seen the girl take, Nora didn't see the point in making that an issue at the moment.

"What's in there?" Jasmine said.

Nora lifted the lid and began pulling out spools of yarn in all shades: lemon yellow, cotton-candy pink, navy blue, deep maroon. On top, she placed several long silver needles. Jasmine picked one up and held it in her hand.

"There's a woman who teaches a knitting class here once a week," Nora said. "I've sat in on a few classes or at least listened to it from my desk. I'm not very good at it, but funny enough, I find it very relaxing."

Jasmine touched the yarn, her skin a deep brown against the soft yellow. "My grandmother knits sometimes. She taught me how to do the cast-on stitches, but that's about all I know."

Nora picked up a set of needles, unspooled some yarn. "Your grandmother lives with you?"

Jasmine played with the yarn. "More like we live with her. My dad has to travel a lot for work. It's why we moved here."

"It's too dark to see anything." Marlene's voice came from across the room. She held the Mexico travel book in one hand, the other swinging around in front of her like a blind person feeling their way across the room. "One lantern isn't going to make much of a difference."

Nora responded with "Mm-hmm." Because sometimes the best response to Marlene was to say very little.

Marlene moved closer. "You're knitting?"

Jasmine hung her head and didn't look up, her fingers busy working on a line of cast-on stitches.

"Would you like to join us?" Nora said to Marlene, who had settled into one of the chairs and begun to rummage through the bin.

"My mother knitted pot holders, scarves, clothes for my dolls, even socks." Marlene frowned at a ball of tie-dyed yarn, chose a purple one instead, and picked up a pair of needles. "Until her arthritis made it too difficult for her."

Nora gripped a ball of yarn and tried to keep her expression neutral. Marlene didn't normally share personal information about herself. "Charlie mentioned that you cared for your mother for many years. That must have been hard."

The needles in Marlene's hands stopped moving, her gaze on the yarn. "Well, yes, it was. My mother was a difficult woman to begin with, so by the end, well, it was not a fairy tale. When she died I was forty-five, and I thought that was all there was to it."

There was a silence that followed, broken only by the clacking of needles. Jasmine had stopped after she cast on several loops and now drummed the needles on the floor, probably bored out of her skull.

"But then you met Charlie," Nora said.

"Oh yes, then Charlie came along and ruined everything." Marlene's voice carried the same curtness as always, but this time it had something else—a hint of lightness around the edges when she said his name.

Nora smiled to herself. "How about you, Jasmine? How did you end up in Silver Ridge?"

"My mom died," Jasmine said, and Marlene's knitting needles hit the floor.

Nora stopped, rested her hands in her lap, and turned to Jasmine, who had wound a yellow piece of yarn around her finger. "I'm so sorry." It was all she could think to say without knowing Jasmine better. She didn't want to pry or ask questions that might cause her pain, so she simply left it at that.

The girl shrugged. "Yeah. She had cancer and she died really fast." Her hat covered her eyes and most of her face, but her voice cracked softly, and Nora felt her grief. "It was a few years ago, so, you know, it didn't just happen or anything."

They sat in silence for a few moments, with the creak of the windows a reminder of the storm raging outside. "That must be so hard, honey." Nora wanted to tell the girl she understood, that she'd also lost her mother at a young age. But after years of keeping personal bits like that inside, Nora found it difficult to share. She glanced at Marlene, whose mouth was pinched in concentration. In some ways, maybe the two of them weren't that different, which was probably why she'd always been able to find empathy for the older woman.

Marlene cleared her throat and leaned over, seeming to check in the bin for more yarn. "Girls need their moms. I'm sorry she's gone." Her words were clipped, tone even, but it seemed to affect Jasmine nonetheless because the girl gave an almost-imperceptible nod, her eyes on her lap, fingers playing with the yarn. Marlene pointed one of her needles at Jasmine's discarded ones. "Have you learned the knit stitch yet?"

"Yeah, I just can't remember it."

"Here, watch." Marlene moved her needles and fingers slowly to show the girl how to make the stitch. Nora watched, too, and seeing Marlene's tight stitches, she realized how very sloppy her own were.

The knitting kept them busy, but the conversation waned until Jasmine sniffed, set her needles on the floor, and pulled her knees into her chest, arms wrapped around her shins, shivering. "It's really cold in here," she said.

Nora realized that with the wind battering the old building and the electricity off, the temperature inside the library had begun to drop. It had gotten even darker, and Marlene was right: the one lantern didn't quite cut it for light. But it would have to do. She stood and, using her phone as a flashlight, made her way to her desk.

She returned with two blankets and gave one to Jasmine, the other to Marlene.

Marlene looked up at her. "You keep blankets here?"

Early in the winter, she'd left work one cold evening to find a woman outside, coatless and walking in circles, talking to herself. Her lips had turned blue. Nora had kept a blanket or two beside her desk ever since. "I keep a few for anyone who might need them."

"You mean the homeless." It wasn't hard to guess what Marlene meant with her sigh. "Charlie told me how much you volunteer."

She said it like it was a negative, but Nora knew Charlie thought her efforts were worthwhile. He'd even shown up at a soup line once with a few of the library regulars after she told him that volunteer numbers were down. Nora concentrated on moving the needles in a rhythmic motion, creating a line of stitches. It kept her hands moving and her mouth from responding with something rude. "I enjoy it, Marlene. I like helping."

"But why so much?" Something about the way she said it made Nora think the question was perhaps less judgmental and more sincere curiosity. "The way Charlie describes you volunteering, it doesn't seem to leave you much time for anything else. You know, like a life."

Nora bristled and took a moment to breathe, thought about the manuscript. The one Mario had found all those years ago at the obscure little library they had visited in Washington State. It had been the summer before her last year of grad school. He'd made solid steps in his life, going to meetings on a regular basis, getting promoted to manager at the bike shop; he'd even taken up cooking. There had been so many times that Nora had wanted to call her aunt and tell her, but she'd held back. She'd been confident that the worst was behind them, but it felt fragile nonetheless, and broadcasting it to the family who'd once told her to let Mario go seemed like tempting fate.

Let's go on a road trip, Mario had suggested one warm June evening.

They sat on folding chairs on the cement square they called a patio, staring above a crooked wooden fence, past rows of apartments, to the summer sky that glowed in the early evening.

To where? Neither one of them had the luxury of taking a day off work, let alone going on a vacation.

He'd sat up in his chair, leaned over the plastic arm, his face bright. His hair had grown long, brown waves that fell in shiny strands around his ears, and he was dating Allison, a high school mountain biking coach who had a pretty smile and a little girl he hadn't met yet. He was happy. *Let's go see that library you always talk about in Washington.*

The library was tiny and tucked away in the basement of a museum, where it housed over three hundred unpublished works of fiction, poetry, philosophy, spirituality, and everything in between. Nora had heard about it and loved the idea of a place where all manuscripts were accepted. So they went and spent three days combing through the writing, enjoying the perspective of authors who wanted their stories and musings to be curated and shared with others.

It had been on the last day that Mario found the manuscript. *Look at this one, Nora! It must be about you.*

At the time, she hadn't thought much about it, except that it was filled with fascinating observations and intuitive questions about life and meaning and purpose. But it had been fun to pore over it with Mario, who was convinced that it was all about Nora. But other than sharing a birthday with the title, she didn't see how it related to her alone. *Everyone has a purpose*, she'd said, expecting him to smile and agree.

Instead, something in his eyes shifted, and Nora had felt like she was seeing Mario for the first time—vulnerable, like he'd been hiding inside his own skin. *You think? So what's mine, then?*

She'd wanted to reach out and hold his hand, get him to talk, anything to scrub away the sadness that stained him. *It's to be exactly like you are right now.*

His lips flattened. *Sober?*

She'd elbowed him, smiling. *No, my brother.* It had felt like the right thing to say; she had meant it as something positive and good because to her, this Mario—the guy that made her laugh, the guy making something of his life—was the man he was supposed to be. Not the addict.

But what if I can't be anything more than that?

She hadn't understood what he meant, and she'd fumbled for something to say that would bring back the lightness in his eyes.

But he'd smiled and the moment passed. *Aw, Peaches. Don't look so serious; you know I love being your brother.*

He'd moved on to another manuscript, but it was like an iron curtain had dropped, leaving Nora on the outside with a gnawing sensation that she'd said something wrong.

A few months later, Mario was gone.

Marlene waited for her answer, and Nora looked skyward, thought about the hours stretching before them until the storm let up and needing something to distract her from her thoughts. "Well, like I said, I enjoy giving back but also—" She shot a look at Marlene, who was focused on pulling apart the yarn. "I believe it's something I'm meant to do."

"Like a calling?" Jasmine said from the floor. "That's what my grandma would say."

Nora smiled at the girl. "I guess, sure, like that."

Jasmine was looking at her, waiting, the light from the lantern flickering in her eyes. "So what's your calling?"

Nora smiled. "When I was in grad school, I found this manuscript—"

The girl's eyebrows met. "What's a manuscript?"

"Oh, well, it's a book, but one that hasn't necessarily been published formally yet." She was comfortable here, talking about books and libraries. "Anyway, this library is like a home for unpublished manuscripts, and there was one there that seemed like it had been written about me."

Jasmine's eyes grew round, and Nora thought she heard Marlene snort.

"It sounds silly, I know, but it spoke to me, and later when some things changed"—she hesitated, not willing to talk about Mario or how he fell apart a few months after their road trip in a way that left her breathless, scrambling for answers and all alone—"it just helped me to see my situation at the time in a different light. I guess what I'm saying—" Here she focused solely on Jasmine. "Well, it's what books have the power to do, speak to the reader. And this one spoke to me."

She'd thought about the idea of purpose a lot after that trip and especially during Mario's slide back into addiction. And she was left with the belief that she'd messed up somehow, said the wrong thing, hadn't done enough to help him stay positive, missed some opportunity to tell him she believed in him. And she didn't want to make that mistake again.

"Like music?" Jasmine said. "I listen to music all the time."

Nora brightened. "Yes! And poetry or art or—"

"A perfectly cooked egg," Marlene said.

Nora saw Jasmine's mouth lift and then, as though remembering that she didn't like Marlene, turn into a frown. "An egg?"

Marlene untangled the yarn. "Charlie has eaten a single egg every morning of his life and in every manner possible. Poached, fried, over easy, scrambled. He says that it doesn't matter what it looks like, because to him an egg is the perfect way to start his day." Marlene had begun to unwind the ball of yarn, letting it fall in a messy heap on the floor by her feet.

Nora felt a pang, remembering something Charlie had said to her not long ago. Was it too personal to share with Marlene? The woman's head was down, eyes focused on the yarn in her lap so that all Nora could see was the edge of her chin. Nora breathed in and said, "Charlie once told me that he loved eggs because it reminded him of the first time he saw you at the diner."

Marlene lifted her head, her mouth pressed into a line. "Charlie has vision problems, and I was a woman well past her prime. But those eggs were damn good."

Nora gave a small smile and returned to her knitting. Her hands had been busy, but all she had produced was a line of stitches in pink and yellow. She had a number of these at home. They were her stitches to nowhere.

"So what made this manuscript so special to you?" Marlene said.

"Yeah," Jasmine chimed in. "That sounds way more interesting than eggs."

Nora glanced up from their circle, letting her eyes adjust to the darker blue beyond the light. At some point Vlado had joined them, taking up space on the long couch, phone hovering above a different manual open on his lap, the radio beside him. Lewis had moved farther into the library as well and sat on the floor with his back against the wall. Nora supposed it might be a tad warmer in here, with its thin carpet and rows of books as opposed to the tile and high ceilings of the foyer. Plus, it had the only light, apart from the phones.

"Well," Nora began, suddenly unsure with her larger audience, "the title is what caught Mar—I mean, it's what caught my attention. It was called *October 6, 1990.*"

Jasmine leaned her elbows onto her crossed legs. "What's so special about that?"

Nora smiled. "It's my birthday."

"Cool," Jasmine said.

"It seemed like nothing more than a fun coincidence at first."

The rest of the summer after their trip had been busy. Mario and Allison were getting more serious, and he'd begun to talk about moving out, having his own space. *You should leave Colorado, Nora*, he'd said. *Travel, explore, live somewhere else. Finally go see the Great Wall of China.*

So she'd begun to make plans for after she graduated to join Amanda on an Eastern European leg of her next work trip. The Great Wall would have to wait. When she'd booked her ticket, Nora giggled, feeling free and so much lighter, like she'd been balancing something heavy across her shoulders. But that's how Mario affected her. He was the moon and his gravitational pull shaped her world, so when he stumbled, she did too.

First, he and Allison broke up. Mario had said it was mutual, but he looked lost, like he'd been broadsided. *She said I wouldn't be a good dad.*

He had changed in small ways at first. A late morning here, a missed shift there. His eyes had grown tired, a scruffy beard replacing his normally clean-shaven face. He had stopped watching movies with her, ate dinner standing at the counter, if he ate at all. She'd tried to talk to him, but he shut her out and she grew nervous, remembering the times he'd slipped when she was younger, the way it added another line around her uncle's mouth. So she started to leave sticky notes on his mirror with inspirational quotes; left books out on addiction, counseling, and getting sober; and checked the trash daily for bottles or pills.

By fall, he'd taken to smoking cigarettes on their square of cement, his knee jiggling up and down, cigarette ashing on the carpet of yellow aspen leaves. She'd known he was different, but she couldn't bring herself to face the truth. He was using again. The next few months became a nightmare of him disappearing for weeks, showing up hammered or high and sleeping for days. They fought, she cried, he promised to change, he tried, until he failed, and he failed so many times. She canceled her ticket, told Amanda she couldn't go, stopped dreaming about traveling, and started focusing on what more she could do to help him.

She smiled at Jasmine. "It just seemed like the author had written exactly what I needed to hear."

The author, she'd learned, had submitted sixteen manuscripts to the library. A chemical engineer by day and a philosopher by night who wrote deeply thought-provoking pieces. There was passion in his writings, in the observations he shared, and in his incessant questioning of the simple interactions between people and strangers, his desire to shed light on an individual's unique experiences that had led them to any particular moment in time. In the manuscript, he spoke directly to a newborn baby born on October 6, 1990.

"The author's writing made every birth, every person, seem significant, and I guess I was looking for something like that," she said. Her life may have started as an accident, and been defined by another accident, but Nora was determined to make it purposeful. She thought of what Mario had said about the manuscript and her purpose, and it became crystal clear to her then that her purpose was to stick by his side, the way her aunt and uncle never could.

"Yeah," Jasmine said. "I get that. My mom said stuff like that about people being important and all and how she'd already lived her purpose by being my mom or something like that." She uncrossed her legs, set them out straight in front of her, and Nora thought she saw the girl's chin tremble. "But I need her. And my sister really needs her now. And my dad's a mess without her."

Nora picked at the yarn, moved by the girl's strength despite her loss. Nora had been so young when her own mother died that she came to her in watercolor memories, vague in specifics, soft in the details but washed with longing. "I'm sorry, Jasmine," she said again, wishing she could say more, knowing that sometimes *more* didn't make anything better.

"But what about your manuscript?" Jasmine said. "I still don't get it."

Nora hesitated, unsure how much she wanted to share, but this part was important to her. It fueled her optimism; it was the reason she refused to give up, even when nothing seemed to change, but she knew how it sounded out loud. Like a person desperate to find a reason for a crappy life.

Vlado's head had lifted from his manual, sparked with interest. Lewis had raised his head a fraction as well, seemed to be listening, even if his eyes were still closed.

The light outside had shifted to a velvet black, and inside, the lantern spread gold fingers across the furniture and onto their faces. In the otherworldly light, Nora felt insulated, safe. "Well, it challenged me to see that we are each the sum of our experiences and that every decision we make, every experience we have, leads us to this single moment in time." She pointed to the floor for emphasis. "If all of our moments are important, then I wanted to use mine to help others, because you never know how it will all add up."

"Huh?" Jasmine said. "I don't get it."

Nora smiled at the girl. "I think that my purpose is to give to others, to help in whatever way I can. And if it adds to their moments and experiences, if it shows someone who doesn't think they're worth it that someone thinks they are"—she worked her jaw, glanced at Lewis, but he'd pulled back into his coat—"then maybe it makes one of their moments just a little bit better." It was what she wanted for her brother, for him to be reminded that he was special, that he was loved, that he was important to someone. And if she couldn't do that for him now, then she'd do it for others and hope that someone out there would do it for him.

"But, Nora, that's the problem."

Marlene. Nora bit her lip, focused on the yarn.

"How does giving them things do anything to make their situation better? How does that change their lives?"

Nora's pulse sped up, and before she could answer, Lewis spoke from his position on the floor, his voice hoarse and a little weak.

"What makes you think you know what anybody needs?" He pushed his back up against the wall, sitting a bit taller than before, and pinned his gaze on Nora. "Maybe people like me are exactly where we want to be. Maybe you should mind your own goddamn business."

Nora was speechless, feeling attacked and unsure of herself. Vlado sat upright and spoke in a firm, slightly loud voice that Nora had never heard before.

"Lewis, watch your language."

"It's okay, Vlado, he didn't mean—"

Marlene threw a ball of yarn into the bin. "I think he knows exactly what he means."

A hand touched her arm. "I think it's really nice that you try to help people," Jasmine said.

"Thank you, Jasmine." She turned to Lewis and tried to calm her racing heart. "I guess I never thought about it that way, Lewis. I don't think I know what anyone needs; I just want to help."

He pushed to his feet in a labored movement, and Nora's throat grew tight at the effort it took. He shuffled closer to their circle until he was only a foot away from her. In the yellow light, his eyes were a light green, the white part glassy, tired lines pulling the corners down so that he looked perpetually sad. "I don't need you and your good deeds." He turned and left the room, returning to his position on the floor by the front door.

Nora saw Mario, the way he'd look at her like he was underwater, drowning, and she stood on dry land, breathing all the oxygen. Like she had no idea how hard life could be. The same way Lewis had looked at her. She pressed her fingernails into her thighs and wished she'd kept the nonsense about the manuscript to herself.

CHAPTER ELEVEN

MARLENE

That was the problem with Nora. She believed what she believed about purpose and significance, despite the obvious truth about life. Marlene took a break from knitting to knead her thighs, hoping she could push the pain away with her knuckles. Marlene knew the truth, had seen it in a hospital room filled with flowers that smelled like death and felt it when her heart broke into a million pieces.

The truth was that life was unfair and unkind and full of broken promises.

Do-gooder Nora lived a Disney-movie life where purpose was found in magical libraries with mysterious manuscripts and every day was a new beginning. She couldn't know true sacrifice. Not the way Marlene did. Charlie once told her that she should reach out to Nora, that the woman seemed in need of a friend. And she nearly had because Charlie brought out a different side of Marlene, the side that *reached out* to others and said yes to dinner invitations and stopped to notice when the wildflowers bloomed. Marlene never did make the effort. But Nora seemed like she was doing just fine. Marlene didn't blame her for having a cushy life. She wasn't the type of person to wish her pain on others, but she did have more perspective, she believed, than those whose lives had been scripted to near perfection. Like about Lewis. Nora saw a man dying, and she decided he wanted to live. But maybe the old addict wanted to die, and all Nora had done was prolong his suffering. Had Nora ever thought about what he wanted? No, she had not.

The library had grown cold, but Marlene was sweating in her effort to stifle a grimace because her legs were on fire, stabs of white-hot pain digging into her joints, making her muscles cry out. It hadn't been that long ago when she was cruising through her days with the occasional blip: an afternoon recuperating in the big wide chair in front of the fire or a morning spent in bed, just until the medicine kicked in. But that had all changed, and now the bad days had piled up on top of each other, separating her from her memories of the good days, until she couldn't see over them to remember what it had been like on the other side.

It was late and she should have been home by now. She was due for another pill, but she'd left those on the kitchen table beside the *Reader's Digest* with the photo of the best small town in America on the cover. Not Silver Ridge, incidentally, which was what she'd remarked to Charlie, who thought it was a crying shame that they'd left the best small town in America off the list. She'd said he was the only thing that made Silver Ridge good. He hadn't agreed, but that was Charlie. Single-minded and stubborn and unable to see the faults in the people and places he loved.

She thought of her kitchen then. If she were home, there would be a fire burning in the woodstove, heating the entire nine-hundred-square-foot cabin. She wouldn't be shivering right now if she'd stayed home. But then her thoughts drifted back to the table with her pills and the magazine and Charlie's . . . oh, the needles clinked together from the shaking in her hands. She steadied them—she would not show her weakness here. No way.

She chanced a look at Jasmine, eyed her backpack, grateful to have something else to occupy her thoughts. She narrowed her eyes. The book was still in there. When Nora had dragged Lewis inside, Marlene had decided to let the book stealing drop. For the moment, at least. So much had happened at once, what with the old addict, who looked like the storm had tried to murder him, and the power going out, and the damn cell phones giving that earsplitting alarm. And Marlene's own rush of anger that had her gripping the girl's arm, surprising even herself. Besides, they were stuck here, so it wasn't like the girl could do anything anyhow.

And when Jasmine had mentioned that her mother had passed, Marlene felt the girl's grief, had lived it herself. She didn't wish that kind of loss on anyone.

She'd not been close to her own mother, but she'd admired her. In her youth, Margorie had been the real Rosie the Riveter, Marlene's dad had boasted, and her mother's cheeks would turn a very pale pink.

Why'd you stop working? Marlene had asked, and Margorie's face hardened further.

The men came home and the women weren't needed anymore.

Marlene supposed her mother had dreams that didn't include becoming a housewife to a miner in Colorado, but she never spoke of them, and Marlene imagined that she'd had to bury them long ago. She never understood how much that hurt her mother until she did the same thing years later when she left art school to come home.

The girl had set her backpack behind her, resting her back against it like a chair. Marlene squinted in the dark. Stealing just wasn't right, especially when she could have had the book for free anyway. She shook her head to herself, focused on her knitting. Nora was right about one thing: knitting was relaxing.

The girl stood, stretched her hands over her head with a loud sigh, and Marlene stared at the backpack. Someone should teach this girl that stealing was wrong, and Marlene doubted that Nora would be the one to do it. She'd likely take the book and not say a word to the girl. Or worse, when the storm was over, let her leave with it. And what kind of a lesson would that be? Surely this girl's mother wouldn't want that? Marlene *harrumphed* quietly, undecided. Or maybe she should just let it go. That's what Charlie would tell her if he'd come with her today. She sucked in her top lip, thinking.

"Problem, Marlene?" Nora's voice was kind—her voice was always kind—but Marlene sensed a frustration sifting through it that for some reason made her almost want to smile. Nora was unflappable, seeming to always be in control of herself. Next to her, Marlene felt like a quivering mound of pain and anger that had become as difficult to control as Jell-O.

She shook her head, going for a purl stitch this time. "I think the homeless guy has a point."

Nora's needles dinged. "And what is that?"

"Maybe it was his time to die. Maybe he wanted to die, Nora, and you got in the way."

"Oh, Marlene," Nora said quietly, and reached out like she was going to touch her.

Marlene jerked her arm away, and a burning sensation grew in her stomach, inched up like the heartburn that crept into her throat every night. An image spread in her mind, one that gutted her until she felt like a filleted fish. She was never one of those two-faced kind of women. The ones who could paste a smile on their faces even when they were miserable inside. The perfect housewives, the doting mothers, the ones who pretended their lives were nothing less than perfect. No, not Marlene. Never Marlene. She was of hardy stock. The kind that worked and didn't complain. The kind that knew hardship and didn't sugarcoat. The kind of woman who was perfectly content to live a life of solitude, until Charlie had come along and shaken her world right up.

She heard Nora make a sound, and the burning in her gut spread down her arms and legs and into her toes and fingers until she couldn't contain it any longer, and she stood up, hands clenched into fists, looking for something, anything, any*one*, to let out this terrible feeling inside, this injustice that no one here seemed to understand. And there it was, the backpack and the girl. Marlene thought of her mother's fingertips, hardened from her extra work as a seamstress, her father's spine, permanently curved from years mining in cramped tunnels. Kids today didn't respect the work of the people who came before them. They didn't know what hard work and hard labor meant. They were soft, weak, and didn't care about what was right and wrong. Like stealing a library book.

Her thoughts, fueled by her pounding heart and an anger that never faded, felt like a valve releasing inside, and before she knew what she was doing, Marlene stood, letting the yarn and needles tumble to the floor at her feet, and walked straight to the backpack, hefted it up, and unzipped it. Its overstuffed contents tumbled to the floor, including the library book.

Jasmine yelped and Nora said something, but Marlene didn't hear above the roar in her ears. She picked up the book and held it out to Nora. "I told you. She was stealing." Marlene had only a moment to see the title—something about birds and bees—and a wave of uncertainty weakened her arms. The roaring faded, left her standing in the quiet and cold of the small library, with the snow a white shroud covering everything outside. Her anger retreated like a wave, and she was thankful that the dark hid the burning in her cheeks. Nora quietly took the book but didn't look at it or at the girl, just kept her gaze steady on Marlene, and only in the twist of her mouth did Marlene sense Nora's own anger.

"I'm sorry about Charlie, Marlene. I'm truly and deeply sorry." She stood, setting the book aside, and faced Marlene squarely.

Marlene felt numb, her heart so heavy she thought maybe it would just break through her ribs. "Don't you dare," she said between clenched teeth.

But Nora did not stop. Instead, she touched Marlene's arm, and it felt like she'd plunged a knife into her bone, because Marlene couldn't pretend when Nora looked at her like that. She kept going and her words made Marlene shrink. "I miss him around here, Marlene. I miss our talks, I miss his corny jokes, I miss the way he laughed. I can only imagine how difficult these last few months have been for you."

Suddenly all Marlene wanted was to leave the damn library, drift out into the storm, and let the powdered ice bury her.

"I know you're hurt. I know you're grieving." Nora's face turned hard. "But you can't talk to Jasmine like that. You can't just be angry with everyone, and you can't treat people like they don't matter."

"But she stole a book." Marlene could only whisper because a creeping sense of shame had tightened around her throat. It wasn't about the girl, not really. But here she was, a seventy-year-old woman being schooled by Nora, a woman so young she could be her own granddaughter.

Nora softened again, tilted her head to the side. "Charlie wouldn't want this for you—"

Marlene took a step backward—she didn't want to hear Nora say anything more about Charlie—and had only stepped on a soft lump of yarn, but it was enough to make her stumble, enough to make pain race up her thighs, enough to ignite the anger she wore around her like a coat.

"How could you know what Charlie wants? You, Nora, with all your do-gooder work and guessing what people need? Pushing it on them whether they want it or not?" Her voice trembled and she hated it. "You have no life because you volunteer every minute of it thinking you alone can make things better. You have to know pain to understand it, Nora."

She left the room and returned to the foyer, where she took a seat on the bench by the door and ignored the man on the floor, and the ache in her chest that made it hard to breathe and the image of Charlie sitting next to her, giving her the look he always did when he was disappointed.

CHAPTER TWELVE

NORA

Nora's hands fell to her sides and she sat down, her heart hurting for Marlene yet still echoing her anger with the woman as well. She understood her grief, and Nora missed Charlie, too, but she couldn't let the woman take it out on the girl.

Nora and Marlene had lived in the same town for much of Nora's life, but Nora had never really known Marlene. Saw her at the diner, maybe, when she was a teenager and Marlene worked there; they'd never spoken, not that Nora could remember. But when she took the position at the library in Silver Ridge, Charlie, who at that time served on the board, had welcomed her with a bouquet of sunflowers; a bookmark with a picture of the library on the front; and a coffee mug with the words I'M A LIBRARIAN above a picture of Rosie the Riveter showing her biceps, and below the image: IT'S NOT FOR THE WEAK.

She wished she still had that mug. And she wished that Charlie had not died so suddenly. And that Marlene wasn't alone. It had been terrible to lose Charlie and to see Marlene without him, half a person, her eyes like windows to an empty house. Nora had tried to reach out, visiting their cabin in the woods, bringing meals that she'd had to leave outside the door because Marlene refused to answer.

"I'm sorry," came Jasmine's soft voice from the floor.

Startled from her thoughts, Nora looked down. The girl was stuffing the scattered contents into her backpack.

"I was going to bring it back, I just—"

From the foyer came raised voices: Marlene and Lewis. Nora sighed. Her night stuck at the library was quickly dissolving into what felt like a babysitting job. "It's okay," she said. "You can tell me about it later. I'm sure you have a good reason."

She grabbed the lantern and hurried to the foyer. Vlado was already there, standing in front of them and holding up his phone so that the beam of light was like an interrogating spotlight.

Marlene sat on the bench, arms crossed tight across her chest. "More drugs in the library. I told you, Nora, you're too nice, and that's why everybody walks all over you."

Nora set the lantern on the floor and ignored her. Marlene had only just started to come around since Charlie's death; losing him had hardened her, stripped the woman of the softness Charlie had unearthed.

Vlado cleared his throat and his jaw moved, casting shadows across his cheek. "Nora has done so much for you, Marlene. Be kind."

Marlene opened her mouth, seemed surprised by Vlado's tone, and closed it, shifting on the bench so that her face turned away from them.

Lewis held something in his fist, and Nora didn't have to see it to know what it was. He fumbled with the bag, his fingers—thickened with cracks—struggling to open it. He cursed softly.

"Lewis!" Nora knelt beside him, put her hand out, pulse racing. Would they have to tackle him? Rip it from his hands? Or worse? He would die if he did more drugs. She would not let him die. "Please!" The word came out like a screech, and she put a palm to her chest, tried to sound calmer. "Please, Lewis, why? This isn't the place or the time, and you nearly died—" Ribbons of anxiety brushed against her chest. "Please, Lewis, give it to me." She thought of Jasmine, turned to find the girl standing just behind her. Nora spoke between her teeth, anger fighting with her jitters. "She shouldn't have to see this. She's just a kid. Think of her, Lewis."

"Lewis," Vlado said, and his voice was polite but hard. "Hand me the drugs. You nearly died from that stuff."

Lewis gripped the bag harder, and for just a moment he wasn't an old man—he was Mario. And Nora was a college student and a child staring at the teeth marks of addiction.

She'd come home from a study group one night to find him curled into a fetal position on the ground outside the door. She hadn't wanted to see how bad things had become for him. Even if Amanda had prodded her, asking why Mario was late with rent again, where he went during the day if he wasn't working, why he was sleeping so much. It scared Nora to put a name on it because that meant it had never really gone away.

So she'd laughed, hoping he was being funny. *Lose your keys again, Mario?*

But he hadn't stirred and the closer she got, the air changed, burdened with a smell that made her eyes water and shot her back to the time she found him on the lawn when she was a little girl.

Mario? She'd knelt down and gagged, overcome by the stink of vomit.

That night became a rolling frame of repeated scenes through the years that followed: 911, emergency rooms, jail, failed recoveries, sleepless nights, frantic calls to ex-girlfriends. And then later, when he'd stopped trying to pretend and he was gone, slipping through her fingers like the powder he consumed. She could have given up. Nobody would have blamed her. But by then she couldn't separate his recovery from what she wanted any longer. The idea of travel lost its allure, overshadowed by her need to be in Colorado, near enough to help him when he let her. She could be the steady one.

"Lewis," she said, feeling the push and pull of time wavering around her. She could be here, she could be outside the front door of her old apartment or a little girl standing in the grass. A repeating cycle. "Can you give that to me, please?"

But Lewis didn't seem to hear her, caught up, she could guess, by the voice inside the bag that he held in his hand, gripping it like it held the air he needed to breathe. He huddled against the wall with his arms wrapped around his shins, his feet moving, tapping the ground like he was counting. The lantern glow combined with the phone light that Vlado directed at Lewis exposed the dirt smudged into the creases of his hands and his face forked with lines dug out by hard living and exposure to the relentless Colorado sun.

"Lewis," she said, more firmly this time.

It seemed to work, because his eyes shifted upward, unfocused, but looking past her. "Persephone's a good girl, isn't she? Hard worker, right? I'm so proud of her. I haven't told her that. But I am." It hardly seemed like he had enough air to push out the words, and his sentence ended in a hoarse whisper.

"Um," said Jasmine from behind her.

Nora turned. Jasmine had taken her hat off, and her black hair cascaded in tightly woven braids around her face. Small gold clasps in her braids sparkled when they caught the glow from the lantern. Her gaze shifted to Nora, then back to Lewis, and Nora was surprised by what she saw: Jasmine, smiling at Lewis, dimples deepening in her cheeks. Most teenagers would find it difficult to speak to a homeless person, or anyone who looked and smelled so different. Hell, most adults found it hard to make eye contact with people who made them uncomfortable because they were different or offensive in some way, or simply because it made people feel guilty to be reminded of all that they had and all that others did not.

Jasmine's brown eyes warmed. "You mean Persie? Oh, yeah, she trained me on my first day at the diner, and she's, like, the nicest." She tilted her head. "I didn't know her full name was Persephone. That's cool."

Lewis blinked, his mouth softened. "She's my granddaughter."

Jasmine moved closer, her smile wider. "Did you know she's, like, supposed to be the one who gives the speech to her class at graduation?" Jasmine snapped her fingers, thinking, looked at Nora.

"Valedictorian?" Nora said.

"Yep, that's it. She's really smart."

Lewis grunted. "No kidding."

Nora knew the girl, Persie, from when she came to the library. Hair that changed color frequently and a '90s-throwback style of clothes. Lewis's granddaughter? Could that be why he'd shown up in Silver Ridge? She felt a pang at the thought.

Jasmine sat down on the floor, elbows on her knees. The girl had a knack for making the floor look as comfortable as a chair, but the way she sat across from Lewis—relaxed, engaging—gave her the gift of making those around her comfortable as well. Nora admired her, wished she'd been so self-assured at that age. It was a rare trait in someone so young. Marlene sat on the far end of the bench, arms folded across her chest, listening—Nora could tell—but pretending not to. Vlado crouched on the floor next to them, his eyes shifting between Lewis's fist and Nora's face. Her nerves frayed. How would they get the drugs away from him?

"Persie's mother was good at school too," Lewis said to Jasmine, and Nora noticed that the bag was hanging from his fist now, almost like talking about his family loosened the grip of his need, if only for the moment. He was shivering, his legs, arms, torso shaking from drugs or the cold. Any warmth from the old boiler had dissipated quickly, and Nora thought she saw Lewis's breath fogging into the lantern glow.

Nora sat on the floor between Jasmine and Lewis, sitting as close as she could to the man and looking for any opportunity to grab the bag. For the moment, his focus had shifted away from the powder and to the girl, a desperate slant to his eyes, unblinking and fixed on her face.

"Her name is weird, but I like it," Jasmine said, and her dimples created deeper shadows in her cheeks when she spoke. "My sister's name is Olive and she hates it, but I think different names are cool."

"It's from Greek mythology, is that right, Lewis?" Vlado said, and his eyebrows arched high. "The goddess of spring growth. Persephone and her mother, Demeter, were worshipped in the Eleusinian Mysteries."

Lewis flicked his gaze at Vlado, his face wary. "I don't know about all that, except for the part about spring. Persie was born in April."

Vlado's eyes lit up as he talked, and Nora once again wondered at his choice to work as a security guard. The man seemed like he'd be more comfortable in a classroom—a teacher, perhaps—than as any kind of law enforcement. Vlado tapped his chin, and Nora couldn't help but notice that his fingers were long, like those of an artist. He caught her staring and she looked away.

"I believe their story reflected the idea of transformation," Vlado continued, and both Jasmine and Marlene looked interested. "The people who worshipped them believed their lives had an eternal purpose and that they weren't just living to die."

"Cool," Jasmine said and pulled the blanket tight around her, shivered. "My grandma believes something like that too." She frowned. "Except for the part about worshippin' goddesses. She does *not* believe in anything like that, trust me. It's Jesus or nobody else for Grandma." Jasmine laughed. "My mom was a Buddhist and that drove Grandma crazy."

Lewis had inched up from his hunched position, his back pressed against the wall, one leg stretched out in front of him, the other bent. He slid the bag inside his pocket, and Nora could just make out the tip of it sticking out. Her heart jumped into her throat, and she sat back, wrapped her arms around her legs. She couldn't get it from him now. She caught Vlado's eye. They'd have to look for another opportunity. He nodded, seemed to understand her thinking.

Lewis didn't notice. He looked at Jasmine and his mouth lost some of its hardness. "I heard what you said before about your mother. I'm sorry you lost her." His voice was weathered. "She was a Buddhist, huh?"

Jasmine nodded. "Yeah, she used to say that God made so many different people, so why wouldn't he have made lots of paths to understanding, too, you know?"

"Your mom sounds like a very smart woman," Nora said, impressed even more with Jasmine and a little bit more heartbroken that her mother wasn't around to see the young woman she was.

Jasmine fiddled with the edge of the blanket, twisting the corner of it into a sharp point. "My friend Brianna hates her mom. She can't wait to leave home. I told her she wouldn't feel like that if her mom was gone. She said I only think that way because mine's dead. She thinks I only remember the good stuff."

Marlene shifted on the bench and gasped, the wrinkle forming between her eyes. Nora had to fight the urge to ask if she was okay. "Well, that's just wrong," Marlene said. "My mother died twenty-five years ago, and I recall the good stuff as well as the bad stuff." She grunted. "Your mom sounds like she must have been an exceptional woman."

Nora blinked rapidly. It was touching and surprising to hear Marlene's kind overture. It was exactly what Charlie would have done. Jasmine nodded.

"Charlie thought something similar to your mom," Marlene said. "'Course, he was always a bit of a free thinker." Everyone was looking at her now, and it seemed to make Marlene unsure of herself, because she looked down. "I'm, well, I'm angry and not speaking to God or goddesses or Buddha or anything of the like."

"Me too," Jasmine mumbled so softly that Nora might have been the only one to hear her.

The room fell silent. Outside the storm raged, and through the snow-caked windows, the wind slammed against the glass. Nora shivered, grateful to be inside yet unable to stop herself from thinking about Mario.

"My phone's dying," Jasmine said, and Nora saw her concern knitted into her forehead and attributed it to a teenage girl's connection to all things social. She slid her hand into her sweatshirt pocket and held something that she didn't pull out all the way. She looked at it, then slid it back in, and from her other pocket, she pulled out a granola bar and munched on it in silence, tapping a message into her phone. Probably to her grandmother.

"My phone has plenty of juice, Jasmine, if you need to use it later."

"Yeah, okay."

She withdrew into herself and Nora wondered at the swiftness of it, the way she'd concealed whatever was in her pocket. Marlene seemed sure of what it was, and for the first time, Nora felt a twinge of doubt. The girl had shown up here when the weather had already turned bad and hadn't seemed too eager to leave. What could she have to hide?

CHAPTER THIRTEEN

LEWIS

He knew the girl Jasmine. Had watched her working alongside Persie, the two of them laughing, carefree, animated as only the young can be. While he sat on the bench across from the diner, feeling the weight of the bag in his pocket, the stinging breeze of his own history, the hourglass remnants of his future. He'd come to Silver Ridge hoping for what? Redemption? Forgiveness? The idea was a loaded gun sinking into his stomach, and he had to lean forward to eject its cold metal barrel. He'd missed too many opportunities to change his present, and he didn't deserve any of those things. He just needed to know that the stain of his mistakes didn't touch anyone but him. Phyllis and Heather had tried to help him, more times than he deserved. Alcohol had always been his go-to, the liquid a soothing tonic to the dream that woke him up with the stink of gunfire and his own sweating panic. But it was the pills that made his weakness spill out like oil.

At least Phyllis had been a better parent and had protected Heather from him, telling him to move out when Heather was in high school, putting their daughter first, even over their marriage. The last time—the last straw, as he thought of it now—had been back when Persie was a baby. When Heather and Phyllis had extended an olive branch: a counselor there at the house and a stint at a rehab place if he'd agree to go right then and there. He'd been holding Persie, looking down at her, and she'd reached up with a tight fist, knocked his chin with it. She'd smelled like clean laundry and bananas. His arm muscles had trembled in a goddamn reminder of what his body craved, but for a minute, maybe less, he saw himself through Persie's eyes. A man who could be more, if he tried.

So he had. And he'd failed. And now here he was, at the end of his days, his body wrung out like a limp dishrag, waiting for the storm to pass so he could leave and get back to the business of dying.

He'd leave now if he thought he could get away when they weren't looking, but his head ached and the color had only just now returned to the young librarian's cheeks, and if he was being honest, the cold was bitter and even sheltered inside he felt its power. If he tried to leave, he wasn't sure he could submit himself to the elements—not just yet, anyway. Besides, the librarian would come after him again, and damn it, he wasn't about to have her death on his hands.

Everyone had gotten quiet after the old woman had spoken, but they hadn't moved, instead were still grouped around him like they were Boy Scouts circled around a goddamn campfire. He pulled his collar around his chin, leaned his head back, and tried to fall asleep but couldn't stop thinking about what he'd heard them talking about. The old woman and her husband. Jasmine and her mom. The librarian and her lonely army of one. He knew enough to guess that something else drove her, something other than just wanting to be a good person. They all had their sad fucking stories, didn't they? But Lewis couldn't remember the last time he'd had a conversation with the same kind of people who usually scurried past him like roaches with their eyes down, jaws tense, hoping not to be seen by the crazy, stinking homeless man.

The security guard knelt on the floor in front of him and held out a big book. Lewis looked down at it, but the words blurred from the tremors running through his body. His clothes were heavy from how much snow had melted into the fabric earlier, and his pants felt like an octopus had suction-cupped to his legs.

"Um, here; take this, okay. Please?" Jasmine stood above him, holding out a blanket, and the security guard looked up at her, smiling. Lewis scrunched his nose. Hadn't the blanket been around her shoulders earlier? He couldn't remember, and in the dim glow, it looked orange. His thoughts scattered. Like Persie's hair. It changed colors so often he had forgotten what her natural color was. But he liked the changing colors, thought it showed her personality. Thought it proved that she was tough, and he didn't care what color she painted her hair as long as she was tough enough to take on whatever cards life dealt—tougher than him.

The girl tossed the blanket on his lap and moved back to the other side of the circle but not too far away. They'd all moved closer together, closer than Lewis was used to. Most people gave him a wide berth. But the cold prowled around them, fangs out. Lewis pulled the blanket up around his shoulders, down over his legs, and the small warmth was shocking, comforting. He coughed and silently cursed the burn in his eyes.

"Persephone and her mother, Demeter," the guard said, waggling the book he held and smiling like he'd just pulled a gold nugget out of a mountain. Lewis looked at it again: a large cover with illustrated pictures of women in flowing gowns and long thick hair.

Lewis understood that showing him this book was some kind of peace offering from the man in uniform. Something to say, *hey, I'll only throw your ass out if you put something up your nose or in your vein 'cause I'm a reasonable man.* Lewis was wary of his kindness. Being homeless automatically put him on the opposite side of any kind of law, and the drugs sealed the deal. The irony of it all was that once he'd worn a uniform. Had tried to keep the peace.

His mouth was dry and all he could think about was water. He grunted and straightened up against the wall, reached for the water bottle from the librarian. When the cool water slid down his throat, his hands shook, making the water in the bottle slosh back and forth.

"This is Persephone," the man was saying. "See, she is symbolic of the changing of the seasons, life and death and back to life again. It's poetic, no?"

He glanced at the open page, saw more illustrations of Persephone—some with her hair an ebony black, others a dark blonde, and even a few with deep-red curls. He made a sound that fell between a snort and a laugh, and it seemed to surprise everyone because they all looked in his direction. "Her hair color changes just like Persie and her hair."

The man looked pleased with Lewis. "Yes! And there are more similarities," he said and seemed to want Lewis to agree. Lewis had no idea what he was getting at. "You are like the seasons."

Lewis shook his head. "Like the seasons?"

Before he could answer, the librarian jumped in, her eyes bright with interest. "Vlado, do you study mythology when you're not fixing radios?"

There was something in her voice when she spoke to him. Admiration, he thought, and retreated back into his coat, happy not to be a part of the man's focus, content to disappear from all their prying eyes. He tried to tune them out, told himself that he wasn't interested, but he listened anyway. His life was an old black-and-white film, and this group was the first bit of color he'd seen in a long time.

"Yeah," said Jasmine. "It's cool you know that stuff. We've studied some of it in school, but you seem to know tons."

"Vlado's been going to college for years now." The old woman beside him spoke, gestured at Jasmine. "Nearly as long as you've been alive, young lady. Charlie told me all about it." She had light-gray hair and a mouth that settled into a pinched look whenever she wasn't talking. She reminded him of a woman or two he'd met, the kind that saw the worst in most things.

The librarian looked up at the guard. "I had no idea! What are you studying?"

But the old woman spoke up before the guard could answer. "Vlado's going for the big three letters, and it's taking him a long time." She seemed pleased to know this information when nobody else did, like a greedy raccoon in the trash.

The guard still knelt on the floor in front of Lewis, the big book balanced in his hands, and Lewis wondered if the tile floors hurt his knee bones. He had kind eyes that didn't give much away, and Lewis couldn't figure out if he was pissed or polite or just plain irritated. But he saw the muscles in his jaw twitch and Lewis settled on irritated. He'd be irritated too.

"You're going for a PhD?" The librarian's eyebrows rose. "In what? Wow, um, I mean that's great, but, uh, when do you study? You're almost always here." Her brown hair glinted red in the dim light, and her nose turned up at the end. It reminded Lewis of Heather. She had a nose like that, and when she was little, he'd kiss it when he tucked her in at night.

His eyes stung. "Damn it." And he wiped his sleeve across his face.

The guard gave him a look before answering. "In English. And I study at night, meet with my mentor on the computer, during weekends, and whenever else we can. I'm not studying Greek mythology; it's just always been an interest of mine. I find it a nice distraction, and Charlie liked to talk about it." He looked at the old woman. "He was a good man."

The woman made a sound in her throat.

The guard turned his attention back to Lewis, holding out the book. "Myths gave meaning to the world for people back then. Perhaps Persephone is your chance to come back to life again. To"—he gave Lewis a pointed look—"change your life for the better." The guard kept holding the book out like Lewis was going to take it and read it and find some sort of goddamn *purpose* in it.

"Oh, Vlado, I don't think it's appropriate to suggest that to Lewis right now, I—" The librarian spoke quietly but firmly, and if anything, the pity in her voice only served to make his fingers dig into his palms.

"Lewis is right here, lady." He could feel his lips wobble from a heat that boiled deep in his belly. How dare the guard or this librarian assume anything about him? They were so high and mighty, looking down at him like he was something pitiful and sad, like he was beneath them. He was not. This was his life, his choice, and damnit, he could do with it what he pleased. Leaving Phyllis and Heather and little Persie had been the right thing for him to do, the honorable thing to let them move on without him.

His nostrils flared thinking about what he put them through. His rebounds, his failures that had become a stockpile he returned to, no matter how many times he said he'd get better.

There had been a time when he thought things might actually change. A buddy who was a recovering addict had gotten him a job in Omaha. Lewis decided to take it, figured a change of scenery would do him good and being around someone sober might make him shake this thing once and for all. He hadn't seen Heather since just after the last rehab stint when Persie was a baby. This time, he'd shown up at her door one afternoon, jittery from too much coffee and pills and beers. Persie answered the door, five years old and with a stubborn wrinkle in her upper lip when she took him in.

You're not Sara. Then she'd run from the door and Heather had appeared, and when she saw him, her eyes dimmed and Lewis saw himself then. Jeans with dirt ground into the faded denim, a wrinkled and stained shirt with a smell that spun around him in the August heat. He rubbed his face, felt the thick stubble on his chin, the hard lines down his cheeks.

Dad? What are you doing here?

His back bowed and he found himself staring at the ground, wanting to unsee what had been reflected in her eyes: pain, suspicion, and a deep tiredness. He'd turned and left without saying a word, left them alone for good.

The librarian and the security guard and the old woman stared at him, and Lewis felt a simmering in his gut. What he did with his own damn time was nobody's business but his own.

He focused on the librarian. She kept her eyes even with his, hands folded in her lap, her face smooth and young and not marked with bitterness or loss. She had everything. How could she understand someone like him?

He leaned toward her. "I heard you talking about your manuscript and your purpose and how you think it's your job to save everybody." He ignored the ache that gripped his head, the stiffness in his legs, the thirst that raked his throat no matter how much water he drank. "It's not your job, lady; it's none of your—" He glanced at Jasmine, who stared at him—her chin in her hands, mouth turned down in a frown—and he felt a shift, his conscience poking at his insides. "None of your GD business."

The librarian's eyes had gone wide. "I'm sorry, Lewis. I just wanted to help. I didn't mean to assume—"

But he didn't want to hear her placate him, make him feel like a child. He wasn't a child. He was a grown man who'd made a mess of his life, but he owned up to it and he didn't ask anybody for anything, except to be left in peace and to use the bathroom once in a while. "Why do you need to save everybody else to have purpose?" He pointed a finger at her, and in the dark library, his voice was loud—too loud, maybe—because it bounced off the ceiling, showered back down on them.

The librarian flinched and the guard closed the book, leaned toward her as though he thought he could protect her in some way.

The lantern dimmed like the battery was dying, and the guard swore under his breath, but still the librarian was silent. Then she inhaled a breath that Lewis thought sounded desperate—sad, if breathing could sound like that—and his spine softened into the wall because he hadn't meant to hurt her, but sometimes he just went too far.

Her hands were in her lap, fingers threading in and out of each other when she spoke. "My parents died when I was six. We drove into a snow squall, and our car went off the edge, fifty-five feet into the canyon."

The room was silent and Lewis was afraid to breathe, afraid to make any noise that might draw her attention back to him. His eyes were wet and his chest had grown tight.

"Oh no," Jasmine said.

"My brother was driving."

The guard moaned and the old woman shifted in her seat, and Lewis saw how her face slackened in a look of surprise. Seemed nobody knew much about the librarian.

"What happened?" the guard said.

The librarian kept pulling at her fingers. "We were coming home. They'd let my brother drive. He was only sixteen but it had been a nice night and the roads were dry, but then they hit a snow squall on the pass and he just—"

Jasmine made a noise and Lewis saw the old woman rub her palms up and down her thighs. The librarian wiped a hand across her face, but she wasn't crying. Something thick rolled into a ball in his throat, and he had to look away from her or he thought he might choke.

"He hit a slippery spot and overcorrected." She spoke with little emotion. "They said my parents died on impact. My brother's leg was crushed, and he nearly died before they got him to the hospital. He lost the leg." Shadows played across her face, the light from the lantern moving across her nose and cheeks, making it seem like he looked at her through a kaleidoscope. "I walked away with a few scratches. I was only six but I can still remember feeling like I was flying."

Nobody spoke, and under the domed ceiling with the dimming lantern, the dark became an animal, circling them, pawing at their backs, hungry. Lewis pulled back into his coat, and the darkness licked him with shame.

Somehow the security guard still balanced on his knees, but his face couldn't hide his compassion for the woman.

"What happened to your brother?" This came from the old woman.

"Guilt is a terrible burden to bear," the librarian said.

Lewis wrinkled his forehead. What was her name? Nancy? Noreen? It came to him in a flash of memory from when she gave him the library card. Nora.

"It's like a cancer, quietly killing you from the inside out, and he found his own way of handling it."

The security guard cleared his throat. "Drugs?" he said, and Lewis knew, just how a man knows, that the guard wanted to reach out and hold her hand, put an arm around her, anything to give her comfort. That's what Lewis would want to do. But he didn't dare and neither did the guard.

Nora nodded, looked at Lewis. "And homeless, but lately he's been doing better, I think."

"You think?" the old woman said.

For a moment, the librarian looked lost and tired, and it was familiar to Lewis. His heart ached. Heather had looked at him this way, so had Phyllis, each time he'd crushed their hopes when he got high.

"He just lost a friend and, well, it's a tough loss, and he's been through so much." She pulled her phone from her pocket, checked the screen, then breathed in, and a smile settled on her lips when she looked directly at the old woman. "So I know a thing or two about pain." She said it all without a hint of *I told you so* in it, and Lewis noticed how the old woman sagged. "The thing is, if I can't help my brother right now, at least I can help others like him, and it lets me do *something* so I don't feel so powerless all the time." When she said this, she held her hands out in front of her, palms open, like she was asking them to believe her, and Lewis felt the emptiness of the action. Was this how he'd made

Phyllis and Heather feel? Powerless? He moved his body, tried to find a more comfortable spot, but regret was a nail poking into his skin no matter which way he turned.

Nora straightened up. "It wasn't his fault; it was an accident. My uncle told me once that I'd survived for a purpose, and I think he's right. It was to help Mario. He needs me." She shrugged. "Otherwise all of it would have been for nothing, right?"

Lewis pulled deep into his coat. Her optimism sounded thin and well worn, a ragged dress on such a young woman, and it hardened something in his throat. The darkness circled closer with the dimming of the lantern. Nobody said a word. Lewis rubbed at his soggy eyes and wished he could tell the librarian that she was right. But he had lived too long and knew too much, and so he said nothing.

CHAPTER FOURTEEN

MARLENE

There was a lot going on, what with the homeless guy trying to shove the drugs up his nose *in the library*, Vlado and his book smarts, Nora telling everyone about losing her parents and her brother, and Jasmine fidgeting with something in her pocket that only served to convince Marlene that she should find out what the girl was hiding.

She thought of Nora losing her parents like that and her brother being like Lewis, and she had to blink hard. Had Charlie known? The two of them had been close, getting into conversations whenever they came to the library that Marlene had to tune out during her Spanish lessons. If he knew, why hadn't he told her? But she knew the answer. Because it wasn't any of her business. Charlie respected privacy and he would have felt that it wasn't his story to share.

She closed her eyes, bent her head, and liked the way it shut out the rest of them. She felt the heat of someone beside her, the hint of woodsmoke in the air, and she allowed her body to lean into it.

You are too hard on them, Marly.

It had been his pet name for her. As a rule, she hated pet names, thinking them vain and self-serving, but she'd always liked this one and he knew it. She sighed, exhaustion weighing on her like the trays of food she'd lugged around as a waitress for so many years.

I know.

You don't have to do this alone.

That was the problem. Marlene had once had dreams—tepid ones, she knew, because all it took was her father's death and then her mother's caregiving as an excuse to let her dreams evaporate. She'd loved to draw and paint, and when she was briefly at art school, she'd fantasized about seeing her work in a gallery one day. If Marlene had been more independent, more passionate, more brave, more *anything*, then she would have stayed in school. Even if art had seemed self-indulgent, or frivolous, she would have stayed in college; she would have done something other than age into the woman she'd been when Charlie found her, hardened by regret. He had made the world brighter, full of possibility, and bit by bit she remembered the girl who'd wanted to paint, and the color seeped into her life one day at a time.

But I am alone, she told the empty spot beside her. *You left me.*

He wasn't there. She knew that. Marlene did not believe in loved ones speaking from the grave, and if he tried she wouldn't listen anyway because he was the one who up and died on her. She felt the rumble of his chest from his laughter. He would laugh at her for thinking that. Once, he said that being married to her was like being married to a favorite TV show and he always enjoyed the programming. She had retorted that being married to him was like being married to an audience of one. That made him laugh, too, and his laughter was contagious. Their life together had been brief, but it had been a good one— too good, she should have known, to last until the very end.

She missed him. In a way that made it impossible to see past the next day. In a way that made the pain that raked her body feel like fingernails on a chalkboard. It was the worst at night because the dark made the manner of his death play in her mind on repeat. *See, everyone is miserable. Everyone loses something,* she told imaginary Charlie. *I can't do this life without you.*

I know.

And I don't think I should have to. Silence. Because she knew what he would say to that, and she'd ignore him anyway.

Early in their relationship, Charlie had discovered one of her paintings in a closet of the cabin. They'd been dating only a few months, and it was the first time he'd been to her home. She was stirring a pot of chili, slightly annoyed by his snoopiness, equally charmed by his enthusiasm for the old place.

What is this? He held it out in front of him, the wrinkles around his mouth deepened with his grin.

Why, that's a painting, Charlie, she'd said, deadpan, and Charlie had laughed, nearly always delighted by her sense of humor. Sometimes she'd wondered what rock he'd lived under for most of his life, because there was nothing uniquely funny about Marlene.

Did you paint this, Marly? She'd nodded, turning her back to him to stir the chili, hiding her cheeks, which she was sure had turned pink. *You're an artist! Why is this in a closet? Oh, there's more!*

And right then and there, Charlie had pulled all her old paintings out of the closet, commenting on each one, how he loved this color or that perspective. He leaned every single canvas up against the log walls in the living room and kitchen, transforming the small space into an art gallery. The very last one he'd pulled out—the one she'd hidden way in the back, embarrassed she'd even pulled out her old brushes to paint it—he held between his hands with a look she couldn't quite figure out. *Is this me?* She'd nodded, stirring the chili. It wasn't a portrait—although those were her favorite—more of an impression of a man at a diner, newspaper folded on the counter, black coffee beside a plate of pie. Beside him, she'd painted herself, a first for her, sitting beside him at the counter in her waitress black, eyes on him, hand touching his arm, a soft smile on her face. *Well, now, is this how you feel about me?* She'd nodded and stirred the chili. After they got married, Charlie hung all the paintings up, saving that one for a place by his side of the bed. *So I can remember the beautiful way you see us.*

Marlene had to shake her head to get Charlie to go away. She thought of Nora, and it pained her to think of her losing her parents and then her brother like that. When Nora came to Silver Ridge, Charlie had been thrilled about the new librarian. He'd been part of the interviewing committee, and he came home excited, said she was smart and innovative and community focused, and would take their little library into this century and, oh, by the way, she had actually grown up in Silver Ridge. Nora Martinez. Had Marlene known her?

Marlene had given him a look, one she did quite often because she privately questioned if the man actually knew her at all. Apart from her job in town, she'd been the definition of an introvert, a loner, a mountain recluse. She worked long hours to pay the bills, which left little time for commuting to college, so eventually she let thoughts of returning fizzle. Between work and caring for her mother, there wasn't room in her life for female friendships, and the idea that she could meet someone or fall in *love* felt more and more out of her reach. Her mother's decline was gradual, turning her into a recluse who never left the cabin and relied utterly on her daughter until the day she died.

But then Charlie came along, and her days filled with hikes and people, dinners with neighbors and strolls around town, and everything she'd come to believe wasn't for someone like her. The surprising thing was that she liked it, but mostly because it involved being with Charlie. She loved spending any amount of time with him.

The ironic thing, however, was that when Charlie introduced her to Nora on her first day, after he'd given her that god-awful coffee mug, Marlene had recognized her with a sad kind of shock. Nora used to come to the diner—quite often, actually—when she was a teenager. She'd sit in a booth by the bathrooms, tucked away with her back to the restaurant and facing the wall. Always alone and always with her nose stuck in a book, sipping coffee, sometimes ordering breakfast, most often not. Marlene waited on her once or twice, but it wasn't her normal section. She remembered thinking how pathetic the girl had seemed. Acting older than Marlene, too young to be so sad.

The lantern sputtered and went out, and the night jumped on top of them, hungry and aloof. The cold had already crept inside, worming its way through the old building's cracks and crevices. Marlene felt a little bad for how quickly the building had shown its age. Like catching an old man without his dentures.

She sniffed, sat away from the empty space that was not Charlie. No dentures on him. He never even had a single cavity his entire life. She pulled the blanket tight, wishing she could seal the edges to keep all the air out, wondering if she should offer it to Nora or Vlado.

"Nora?" Jasmine said, and her young voice wobbled. "It's really dark."

"Did you know that when this library was first built, they would still use candles and oil lamps for light? So a little blip like now is just a walk down memory lane for this old building. Like coming home." Nora's calm voice cut through the room, silky smooth and warm.

Marlene knew it was for the girl, to ease her fear. Marlene thought Nora did a passable job of calming the rest of them too. With the blizzard outside and the thick clouds keeping any light from reflecting on the snow, it was a dense kind of dark. The glow of a phone, then another shone blue, lighting up first Nora's, then Vlado's face.

Marlene cleared her throat and Vlado shined a light on her, briefly blinding her. "There may be batteries or another lantern or flashlight in my car. Charlie always made sure to put emergency supplies in our cars in case, well, in case of situations like now, I suppose."

In the dark, she thought of the white beaches and blue water of Tulum. Felt the sand between her toes, on her legs, down her shorts, and all manner of places where sand shouldn't go but would anyway. Felt the sun warm on her skin, the sweat that would inevitably slide down her back and underneath her bra. The sky stretching above her, cloudless and expansive. It would have been a nice trip, even with the sand. It would have—

"Can I have your keys?"

It was Vlado, standing above her, holding his phone, which looked like a flashlight now between them so she could see his face. He was a handsome young man, with one of those long, straight noses that could either look too big or just right, depending on the face. Vlado was fortunate that his face accommodated it so well. But he was practically a stranger to her, and he'd already asked for her keys once today. There had been a show about something called catfishing, and it had to do with handsome young men like Vlado here luring susceptible and vulnerable women like her out of money and their dignity.

Now that's funny. You, vulnerable? You're the strongest woman I know.

She tightened her jaw and opted to ignore fake Charlie. She didn't actually believe Vlado meant her ill, but still, sometimes it was just the principle of the thing. Who goes around asking old ladies for their car keys, anyway? Charlie said her natural instinct was to assume the worst of people, a quality she'd picked up from her mother, who had reduced her own world to the size of the cabin and taken Marlene with her. Charlie thought it was her one flaw. She'd snorted at his blindness. She had so many flaws. But this was the only one he saw.

You should give people the benefit of the doubt, Marly. You never know what kind of day they've had.

That was Charlie, all right. He'd tried to convince her that most people wouldn't disappoint her the way she thought, and maybe they'd even surprise her.

Okay, Charlie, here goes. But when he steals it, it's your fault.

"He's not going to steal your car, Marlene." Nora's voice and Marlene sighed. The librarian could read her damn mind.

"And if I was, don't worry, I can't get anywhere tonight," Vlado said. "Not with this snow. But make sure you get your keys back tonight because tomorrow? Eh. Who knows?"

She heard Jasmine giggle, and even Lewis the drug addict made a sound that could have been a laugh.

Marlene *harrumphed* and elected not to say anything back. She wasn't worried about it anyway. Not really. It wasn't the handsome men who catfished, the show had explained. It was more often a woman pretending to be a man, which was somehow worse, Marlene had thought, for a woman to prey on the lonely lives of people like that. Unnatural. From her purse, she pulled her keys and held them out into the dark. Vlado took them gently and patted her hand in a gesture she guessed was meant to tell her he was joking.

Beside her Charlie laughed.

It took Vlado some time to layer up, and when he opened the door, wind rushed inside, bringing big fat snowflakes that stuck to the floor and their clothes and hair. So much snow it surprised even Marlene, who thought she had seen it all.

"What time is it?" Jasmine said, and Marlene heard a tremble running through her words.

It gave her a pang. This couldn't be easy for the young girl. To be stuck inside in the dark with strangers and one of them having accused her of stealing—which she had been, but still; maybe Marlene could have handled it differently. Her arms tingled and she ran her hands down her biceps. The pain would probably get worse when the morning pills swimming around her body began to die off. She tried to take her mind off it and thought about the book and the fact that a teenage girl without a mother was stealing a book about the birds and bees.

Charlie's words from before echoed in her head: *People might even surprise you.*

Fine, let's find out, then, Charlie. She leaned toward Jasmine, but in the dark she could only just make out the light color of her winter coat that she'd put on before the light went out. "So, Jasmine, help me to understand why you'd steal a book from the library. It's free anyway. Are you one of those adrenaline seekers? You know, cliff jumping, motorcycle riding, stealing?"

"Marlene," Nora said, a warning tone that Marlene ignored.

She thought of the title of the book. Had her mother passed before she'd been able to talk to the girl about the birds and bees? "Is it something, well, did your mom talk to you or—well, now . . ." Marlene was floundering. She'd never had kids and her parents were of the generation that never spoke of things that were best left to a marriage. But something about the dark made her bolder. "I'm sure Nora could find some books to help you learn, or don't the schools do that now, and maybe you could talk to your grandmother instead of stealing, or, well . . ." Marlene babbled out of words, unsure and slightly embarrassed herself.

"It wasn't for me," Jasmine said, and her voice sounded so small and young that suddenly Marlene imagined her not as a teenager with no regard for others but as a young girl, dealing with her grief and a life without her mom.

"It's okay, Jasmine," Nora said. "You don't have to explain yourself, not now and not to Marlene."

Normally, Marlene might take offense, but she was right and Marlene knew it. She shifted her weight, wanting to say or do something that helped, hearing Charlie's voice in her head and not being able to ignore it. "Was it for a friend?" She hated how she sounded, scratchy and weak, even more so as a disembodied voice in the dark.

The girl sat cross-legged on the floor, not far from where Marlene perched on the bench. Before the light had gone out, she'd been sitting with her elbows on her knees, chin in her hands.

"It was for my sister. She's in third grade this year and, um, well, my mom had this book that she read with me when I was little. I was hoping I'd find it here. But that wasn't it and I don't know, I was just—"

"Embarrassed?" Nora said.

"Yeah. I know it's stupid. But my mom was just amazing, and she was always there for me no matter how awful I was or—I guess I just wanted to do that for my sister because she doesn't remember her the way I do and . . ." She trailed off and the room went silent.

Marlene pressed a palm to her chest, the girl's grief a solid thing in the dark. Her own mother had lived much longer, but she'd been a hard woman who showed her affection by not showing anything at all.

"It's not the same book. I really wanted to find that one, and when I couldn't, I just—well, I took what was there, and I really was going to bring it back." There was a desperation in her voice, a plea for the adults in the room to believe her. And to Marlene's surprise, she did.

"What was the book called?" Nora asked.

"That's the thing. I don't know, except that I do remember the cover had a bunch of cartoon kids who looked embarrassed, and the inside, oh—" Jasmine giggled. "The first time we opened it, Mom and I laughed so hard. That's what I remember is how much we laughed."

"What was so funny?" Marlene said.

"The inside cover had a cartoon man and a woman standing naked in front of separate mirrors in really funny poses. I think Mom started laughing first, and then I did and, well, she made it fun and not uncomfortable, and she did that for everything and my sister's missing it and it's not fair!" Jasmine's breathing was ragged, and Marlene thought she saw her shoulders shaking. "I'm so sorry."

There was something about the absence of light that made Marlene taste the saltiness of the girl's tears, feel the enormity of her loss in an act of theft meant to fill the hole her mom had left behind. She thought of how she had grabbed the girl's arm before and later dumped out her backpack, and shame pricked her cheeks. Marlene pressed a cool palm to her face. She wanted to say something to make the girl feel better, but months of living in her own hole had allowed calluses to grow around her, and she didn't know how.

"There's nothing to be sorry for, Jasmine," Nora said.

"I want my mom."

"I know."

Marlene heard the rustle of a body moving, and she didn't have to see to know that Nora rubbed the girl's back. Nora, who had lost as much as anyone, yet she had space to console a girl without her mom. Marlene admired her for that, wished she had an ounce of her compassion.

You underestimate yourself, Marly. You always have.

I'm too old to change, Charlie, and you're dead.

The door opened and the storm tried to get inside once more, but Vlado shut it quickly. Marlene shivered, chilled to her bones and wondering if she'd ever feel warm again. Vlado stomped his feet on the carpet by the door and shook off his coat. "You had lots of supplies in your car," he said. "Charlie didn't want anything to happen to you."

Warm yellow light filled their little circle—a plastic lantern that Vlado set in the middle of them—and in the sudden illumination, Marlene could see Jasmine's wet face; Nora's hand placed gently on the girl's shoulder; and Lewis, not sleeping as she'd assumed but sitting straight up, his mouth twisted, eyes on the girl.

Vlado pulled flashlights from his bag along with a blanket and a pill bottle, which he handed to her. Her hands trembled when she took it. Pills for her fibromyalgia and a tiny note in Charlie's handwriting across the orange plastic. *For emergencies.*

She held the bottle to her chest, his absence a pit made deeper by his kindness, his thoughtfulness, his love that had him think to put some pills in the car for her *just in case.* In the soft light from his lantern, she felt her grief exposed just like Jasmine's, but for the moment, she didn't care.

CHAPTER FIFTEEN

NORA

Nora checked her phone. It was nearly nine o'clock, and over the last half hour, the storm had worsened. They weren't leaving anytime soon, and her toes were still frozen from going outside earlier. She wiggled them in her shoes, wondered how Lewis was doing.

"Are you warm enough, Lewis?" she asked.

"Better than being out there," he said, and Nora heard his voice tremble.

He had so many layers of wet clothes on his slight frame, from his heavy coat to his soaked trousers. She'd tried to coax him to take off his coat, but he'd been adamant in his refusal and she'd let it drop.

Jasmine called her grandmother, Evelyn, to tell her that her phone battery was low and gave her Nora's number. From the repeated times she'd said *I'm fine, Grandma*, Nora could tell that her grandmother was worried about her. She understood. An uneasy feeling had descended on her when the lantern light had gone out, compounded by her telling this ragtag group about her brother. Nora couldn't remember the last time she'd told anybody her story, except the time she'd come close to telling Charlie, but then he'd always been an easy person to talk to. Charlie loved the library because it had been built, he used to say, with quality of construction and purpose in mind but with an eye toward beauty and timelessness as well. The library was his favorite place in Silver Ridge, and after he retired, he'd come in for long afternoons, flipping through travel books and gazing out the window at the aspen trees or laughing with Marlene about one thing or another during one of their internet courses.

The floor was hard and radiated the cold up her spine, making her restless. Nora was always in movement because idleness didn't suit her. In the quiet lived the worry, the loneliness, the fear that on some level, she'd let her brother down.

"Let's move into the back," she said. "I think it might be a tad warmer."

Jasmine leaped to her feet and started for the stacks but was stopped by a beep from her pocket. Again, she put her hand inside, pulling it out just far enough so she could glance at it quickly without taking it all the way out. Her story about the book had made Nora's heart ache, but Jasmine's preoccupation with whatever was in her pocket gave Nora pause. Should she ask to see what it was? Nora gripped the lantern, unsure, deciding for the moment to let it be.

Lewis limped ahead of her, seeming to favor his right foot, almost dragging it as he moved. Nora bit the inside of her cheek. Could he have gotten frostbite? Sitting around in the cold library in his wet socks and shoes could only be making things worse.

They pulled the furniture closer together, the long couch, plus the two chairs and floor pillows. With the additional flashlights from Marlene's car, it was the brightest since the sun had set hours earlier. Lewis eased himself onto the floor with his back pressed into the side of a chair and his forehead wrinkled when he gingerly scooted his right leg out in front of him.

"Lewis, I'm worried about your foot. Maybe we should take a look at it? Get out of your wet socks?"

He leaned his head back and waved her away. "My feet are none of your business, lady."

"We'll see about that," Nora said out loud, and Marlene laughed.

"Well, now, there's a little bit of fire in you after all. I like it," she said.

Nora ignored her and decided to leave Lewis alone for the moment. But she was curious about him. He had a family who loved him, like her brother did.

"Here." Vlado passed out coffee in paper cups, and his hand lingered when he gave her the cup, briefly, but enough for Nora to feel for a split second that she wasn't alone. "I had a bit of coffee left in my thermos from this morning. It's still warm."

She took a sip, and the liquid heated her insides but didn't account for the burning in her cheeks.

In the glare of the lantern, Nora noticed Lewis staring at Marlene's hand, the one that gripped the bottle of pills. It had only been in a flash, but Nora had caught the look on Marlene's face when she read the writing on the bottle. Like a blanket had been pulled back, leaving her grief naked to everyone.

"What's in the bottle?" Lewis said.

Marlene gripped the bottle a little harder, gave Lewis a look that didn't hide what she was thinking. Nora leaned forward, preparing to handle whatever came next. Vlado did the same from his position on the couch.

Marlene sniffed. "I don't think that's any of your business."

Lewis smiled then, showing his teeth—a front one missing, the rest a dingy white. "We're not that goddamn different, are we?" He shivered under the blanket; Nora could tell from the way it shook, making the light undulate over the cotton.

Marlene's body stiffened in the chair. "I don't know what you're getting at, but we are very, very different."

"I started with those pills, too, you know."

"You have fibromyalgia?" Marlene's voice was hard as stone. Nora sucked in a breath. She'd never heard the woman verbally acknowledge it before.

Lewis's mouth spread flat, but there was a distance in his eyes, like he looked backward. "No, I had knee surgery and they gave me those pills afterward." He absently rubbed at his knee as though remembering the pain. "I should never have taken the damn things. They changed me."

Marlene straightened in her seat, smoothed her hair. "When I need a refill, I have to go to my doctor to prove I'm not addicted. They check my urine like I might be, and sometimes they treat me like I'm someone like you." She snorted. "And they're the ones who prescribed it in the first place."

Nora felt her face tighten. "Marlene, I don't think—"

But Lewis interrupted her. "I drank too much when Heather was little. I had the surgery when she was in middle school, and the pills made everything easier." He slouched against the side of the chair, legs out in front of him, so that the light hit only his profile now. He raised one side of his mouth in a half smile. "I'm sure you get it since you take them too."

"What did the drinking and pills make easier for you?" Marlene said.

Lewis raised one eyebrow, turned to glance at Marlene. "You don't have much of a filter, do you, lady?"

"My name is Marlene."

"You don't have a filter, do you, Marlene?"

"I'm honest."

Lewis sighed, leaned his head back. "Why I drank . . ." His head rolled briefly toward the group, and Nora thought he glanced at Jasmine before turning away again. "It's my own GD business."

Marlene nodded. "Fair enough."

Nora fidgeted in the silence that followed. Their knitting attempts from earlier sat discarded in the thick darkness outside the circle of light. She dug her nails into her palms. Mario was like Lewis. Wanting to be numb. Wanting to change his past but unable to. Could Lewis help her to better understand Mario's choices? She tried to bite her tongue, but the night was stretching long and the cold pierced her skin, sending an anxious jolt through her body. Hearing even a small bit about Lewis had made her more curious than ever, and without something to distract her, she couldn't stop the questions from spilling out. "Lewis?"

He grunted.

"I don't mean to be rude but, well, you have Persie and your daughter, and you came to Silver Ridge because of them, right?" There was a desperation in her voice. She clasped and unclasped her hands. "I'm sure they want to help you. I'm sure they love you and miss you. And Persie's the valedictorian this year? You could go to her graduation, listen to her speech."

Now that she had started, Nora didn't want to quit, even if she sensed that she was going too far. But if she could understand what motivated Lewis, maybe it would help her understand what Mario needed from her. Vlado was looking at her while she spoke, eyes soft in the dim glow, and he shook his head back and forth as though to stop her. She pushed up the sleeve of her sweater and ignored him. "I bet they would do anything to help you. I bet they would do anything to have you come home again." She was a little out of breath. "I bet they love you so much it hurts."

Jasmine gave a little moan. A hand touched her knee, and when Nora looked down to find it was Marlene's, the torrent of questions dried up, and suddenly Nora was staring into a mirror, and she remembered who she was—Nora the librarian, not Nora the social worker, or Nora the cop, or even Nora with the brother who'd abandoned her—and she hung her head. "I'm sorry. I shouldn't have said all that, Lewis."

Another hand, this one on her calf, and Jasmine's soft voice. "It's okay, Nora. It's so sad about your brother. I'd be angry too."

"Oh, I'm not angry." Nora inhaled, put a smile on her face even if it made her look ghoulish in the fractured light from the lantern. She wiped her eyes with her sleeve, surprised to find them damp. Like a moth to a flame, her thoughts drifted to the tent out by the factory and Nonnie from the shelter saying the man had a limp and was too young to be so bad off, and to the phone call and Mario, sounding more broken than ever. But he wouldn't have come back, would he?

She checked her phone again, noticed a text from Amanda.

This storm is vicious! My power is out so I'm binging Netflix till my phone dies. Let me know you're safe, k?

Nora sent a quick message. Stuck at the library but safe . . . worried about Mario.

A link popped up in the text thread to a podcast that Amanda sent yesterday. *Tales from the Flip.*

She exited her messages. Her phone battery was already low, and she couldn't spend the battery power listening to a podcast. She checked her voice mail once more, but it was empty.

Mario's message had been the first in more than a year, which wasn't unusual. But he had sounded different. Could the death of his friend have driven him to come and see her at last?

She straightened in her seat and caught Vlado's eyes. "Actually, it's possible that my brother is here in Silver Ridge. Like you, Lewis." She looked at Lewis, energized. Why hadn't she thought to ask him before now? "There's a man who set up camp out by the factory, and I've heard he's got a bad limp." She looked down at Jasmine. "Just like my brother." Jasmine nodded, but in the dark, Nora couldn't see her face. "I think it might be him."

"But then why hasn't he come to see you yet?" Marlene said, and Nora winced; hearing it out loud gave the idea substance. Why hadn't he? Her hands itched to call Ed, see if he'd heard anything from Mario, but she knew it wasn't the right thing to do. Ed's son was dead and he deserved to be left alone. She pushed the mail icon and her back slumped. Nothing new.

An uneasiness expanded and she chewed on a fingernail. The dark covered up everyone's reactions, turned their faces into shadow catchers, and with the storm pounding against the old building, Nora started talking. "Mario left me a voice mail message a few days ago, but I only heard it last night. I missed it somehow."

"What did he say?" Jasmine asked.

"His roommate overdosed and died, and Mario was having a hard time with it and needed to talk or hear my voice or something to keep him stable." Her heart pounded. "He was afraid he'd be like his roommate. Anyway, I called all the hospitals and rehab places I know of and his friends and ex-girlfriends, and I was planning on driving up to Denver after work too. But"—she pointed to the window—"then this storm happened, and right before that, I heard that the guy by the factory has a really bad limp." They had all leaned forward and the light flickered in their pupils; Nora was grateful for the dark. "I don't know for sure, but that could be Mario."

They were quiet and she let her gaze drop to her lap. She knew how it sounded, like she was desperate to believe anything.

"You've really put your life on hold for him, haven't you, Nora?" Marlene said.

Nora stiffened. She wanted to respond but she didn't know how.

"Lady," Lewis said. "It's none of your go"—he stopped, shifted his eyes to Jasmine—"GD business."

Marlene sniffed. "Fair enough; maybe it's not. But I did the same for my mother, you know, let her problems be my own." She leaned back, crossed her arms. "So I have some experience."

"He was a teenage driver who made one mistake. It wasn't his fault."

"And you feel responsible for what's happened since." Marlene's words were softer than the woman. "Why? You were only a child yourself."

Nora didn't know how to respond. She'd been told to let Mario go by her aunt and uncle, her friends, anyone she let get too close. Her uncle believed that she'd been saved for a purpose and she should live her own life to find out what that was. Aunt Sophie had said that Mario's path was his own. But nobody had ever put it quite the way Marlene had, and Nora couldn't argue with her. She was right: Nora did feel responsible. For telling him to leave that Thanksgiving, for having dreams he could never have, for wanting things that were just for her, and sometimes, secretly, for wishing he didn't need her at all.

"How do you know this man is your brother?" Vlado said quietly, and Nora was grateful to be interrupted from her thoughts.

"The more I think about it, the more likely it seems he'd come here. I went out there yesterday, but it looked like he'd left." She caught Lewis staring at her. "I think he went to the shelter ahead of the storm. That's so like Mario. He knows how destructive our snowstorms can be." Now that she'd shared her past with this motley crew, she couldn't keep from letting out everything she had been feeling, like it had been a caged animal. "I didn't have a chance to check the shelters this morning, but as soon as this storm lets up, that's the first thing I plan on doing." A look in Lewis's eyes, a glint that even in the dimness she felt. Pity? She bristled. Why would Lewis pity her? Because she still had hope and he'd lost all his? "So what I was trying to say earlier, Lewis, is that maybe this is your chance to make amends, if not for yourself, then for Persie. Because I love Mario and I will do whatever he needs to help him get better. I can help him; I know it." Her hands were fists in her lap. "And I bet Heather and Persie feel the same about you."

Lewis stared at her for a long moment, then looked away, tucking his chin into his collar, a turtle back into his shell. Nobody else spoke and Nora was left with her words hanging in the space around them, her initial burst of optimism wilting. She wanted to say more, to get Lewis to answer her, but she felt a shift in the room. Like all the attention was on her alone and not in a good way. More like she'd overstepped or said too much, and her cheeks flushed with embarrassment.

A deafening crack followed by the shattering of glass broke the silence. Nora jumped to her feet and felt the sting of snow on her face, the frigid slap of the wind, and when she lifted the lantern high, her stomach dropped. The branch of a pine tree had collapsed the edge of the ceiling, cutting through the building's exterior like it was soft cheese and exploding the window.

CHAPTER SIXTEEN

MARLENE

The wind howled inside, and what had once felt like a safe place to ride out the storm had turned into a wind tunnel that whipped snow through the room and tossed glass shards and pine needles across the floor. The library had become a C. S. Lewis novel that she'd read as a girl, and the stacks a wardrobe that opened to a fantasy world. Marlene felt a stinging slap across her temple, and the temperature plummeted so fast it took her breath away. A tall bookshelf wobbled violently before falling, spilling books onto the soaked floor.

Jasmine, who had been closest to the window, cried out and scrambled backward, hovering beside Marlene, and in the wobbling light, she saw pine needles sticking out of the girl's coat. Like they'd been arrows searching for a target. Lewis had pushed to his feet and hobbled over, standing just in front of Jasmine like he thought his old body could protect the young girl from another assault by the tree.

"Oh my God!" Nora yelled, and even then, it was hard to hear her above the wind. "We have to move the books!"

Vlado nodded and the two of them lurched forward, Vlado moving in first to try to push the large bookshelf back against the one behind it without toppling all of them, then handing Nora book after book.

But the process couldn't keep up with the snow and the wind pushing through the damaged building and tearing at sodden pages.

Charlie would be horrified to see his beloved library being attacked like this. Ignoring the ache in her head, and shivering into her coat, Marlene walked toward Nora with her hands out. "L-let m-me help!" she said, so cold her tongue had grown thick in her mouth.

At first Nora shook her head and continued running the books to the dry section, but then Lewis staggered behind Marlene, hands out. "C'mon, lady, you need our help!" His voice was so hoarse Marlene could barely make out his words.

Nora's shoulders dropped and she nodded with a tight smile, handing a small stack to Marlene, who gave those back to Lewis, and together they formed a sort of fire brigade with Jasmine at the rear in the driest spot, laying out the soggy books like pieces of laundry. Marlene's body screamed at her to stop, but for the first time since Charlie died, she felt like she was part of something and it felt good.

She had no idea how long it took, but by the time the last book had been salvaged, she couldn't feel the skin on her face and her fingertips were so numb that one of them was bleeding and she'd had no idea. Lewis looked even worse than before, his skin gray in the thin light from the lantern, eyes so red she couldn't see the whites.

Vlado had come back into the room with flattened cardboard boxes and was trying to cover the hole around the tree with Nora's help. The cardboard already sagged from the wet snow, but at least it gave the pretense of protecting them from the outside even with the tree limb dangling over the floor. With the window as secured as it was going to get, Nora picked up a lantern and held it high, seeming to get a count of everyone, which Marlene found funny. Like they were kindergartners on a field trip. "Let's move back into the foyer. It has to be warmer in there, and it's at least away from this window."

"What about the big window up front?" Jasmine said, stammering from the cold and sounding small and worried in the dark. "What if something crashes through that one too?"

Poor girl. She'd been quiet, probably scared out of her wits, but determined to help with the books. Marlene was sure that all she wanted was to go home.

Nora picked up a few chairs; Vlado and Lewis did the same. "We'll sit in the very middle of the foyer, away from that window and with our chairs really close together so we can stay warm. Okay?" Nora's hair was mussed, a few pine needles sticking into her thick waves and the skin under her eyes puffy and bruised in the shadows from the lantern. The woman looked exhausted.

"And I'll cover that window with cardboard, too, just in case, okay, Jasmine?" Vlado said.

Jasmine's dark eyes sparkled with the yellow light. "Thanks."

In the foyer, Marlene collapsed into a chair, and someone—Jasmine, she thought—put the blanket around her shoulders, and she pulled it tight, her toes like ice sticks, as she tried to take in everything that had happened. It smelled different inside now, a bitter mixture of wet bark and pine needles, and it made the walls of the library feel not so thick, the elements like a bear pawing to get in and flimsy cardboard their only protection. She shivered inside the blanket and the cold settled in a spot on her head that throbbed more than the rest of her.

"Are you okay, Marlene?" Vlado knelt in front of her, the skin on his forehead creased. He was a handsome man with kind eyes.

She shook her head, her thoughts muddled. Had she winced? Shown her weakness in a momentary groan? Hadn't she just helped save the books? She wasn't frail or useless, not yet anyway. She crossed her arms. "I'm fine, Vlado."

He touched her head with two fingers and brought them in front of her face. In the shadows, they were black, shiny with a coppery smell. Blood. She reached up. There were leaves in her hair.

"I think a branch hit you in the head, maybe some glass too."

A pounding in her skull, Marlene realized. One actually not related to her general aches and pains. There was some relief in having pain that had an obvious cause. "Oh, yes, that does hurt."

Nora came over, knelt in front of Marlene, and began to gently pluck out the leaves and bits of glass from her hair. "Oh, Marlene, are you okay?"

"I'm fine, Nora." She did feel a bit fuzzy, like someone had pushed a button and put her in slow motion.

"You're a tough old bird, aren't you?"

This from Lewis, who had resumed a spot between the chairs but on the floor, and for some reason, his words hit her in a way that felt like carbonated bubbles floating to the top of an ice-cold soda, and she laughed. It seemed to surprise Nora, who pulled back and looked at her as though she thought the injury might be worse. That only struck her as more absurd, which made her laugh harder, feeling younger, freer in that moment, even with the arctic wind pushing through the cardboard and the library dusted in snow.

Lewis made a sound in his throat. "The old bird's flown the nest."

She and Lewis laughed together at that, and for the first time in a long time, Marlene felt different. A door, a window, or maybe only a crack had opened up inside and let some of the bitterness and grief leak out.

CHAPTER SEVENTEEN

NORA

Nora used a damp paper towel to clean the wound on Marlene's head and apply some antibiotic cream she'd pulled from a medical kit in her desk. She was relieved to see it wasn't as bad as it had looked. The rest of them had formed a tight circle, everyone so close that Nora caught whiffs of an unpleasant odor she knew must be coming from Lewis. She noticed Jasmine trying to inconspicuously hide her nose in her sleeve; Marlene gave nothing away other than an almost-imperceptible scrunch of her nose. It made her sad and uncomfortable and wanting to do or say something to minimize it.

Vlado returned from the basement, carrying more flattened cardboard. He smiled when he met Nora's gaze, then said to Jasmine, "It's not plywood, but if the glass happens to break, it will at least keep it from shattering toward us."

"Thanks," Jasmine said in a small voice and Nora wanted to comfort her. With the wind howling against the building and whistling through the hole in the stacks, the girl must be scared. She patted her arm and Jasmine leaned into her.

"Plywood, huh?" Marlene said. "Charlie did that once for a wind-storm. Had gusts over a hundred miles an hour. Like a hurricane in the mountains."

Vlado stretched duct tape across the window frame, grunted. "I have a cousin in Pensacola. We were visiting him before Hurricane Ivan hit, and my dad and I helped him reinforce his windows before the storm blew in."

"You lived through a hurricane?" Jasmine's voice held a note of awe.

Vlado shrugged and smiled. Nora liked his smile—it was wide, familiar, and comfortable. That was the thing about Vlado. He always seemed at ease in his own skin, a feeling Nora had never quite per-fected. Not when she worried that people would judge Mario or her for supporting him the way she did. It made her keep to herself, even as a teenager, like she had some big secret to hide. She admired someone like Vlado, who seemed to be content just being himself.

"We left before it hit. My cousin was still very new to this country, and my dad went down there to help him acclimate."

"When did you come to this country, Vlado?" Marlene asked with her usual straightforwardness and Nora cringed.

"My parents and my grandmother and I immigrated to Colorado from Bosnia when I was twelve."

"Did you leave family behind?" Marlene said.

"Some, and others were already here."

"Why did you come here, then?"

Nora heard Lewis sigh. "Jeez, lady." And she quietly agreed but was also a little bit interested herself in this man she'd worked with for months and knew so little about.

Vlado seemed unfazed, and if anything, his smile grew wider. He finished taping the window and joined their circle, squeezing in between Lewis and Jasmine. The light from the lantern pooled in his cheekbones, highlighting his jaw. "We came for peace and freedom, Marlene. The American dream."

Marlene nodded. "I understand that. But freedom for what, exactly?"

"To love whomever we want. My father is a Croat and my mother is a Serb, and where we lived, that kind of marriage was dangerous."

"Wow," Jasmine whispered. "Your parents were brave, huh?"

Vlado nodded. "Yes, very."

"Are you close with your family?" she said.

"Yes, and like you, my grandmother lives with us too."

"Cool," she said. "I love living with my grandma. She tells me stories about my mom when she was a little girl and she makes the best jerk chicken on the planet."

"Nana makes the best gibanica on the planet."

Jasmine made a face. "That doesn't sound like food."

Nora smiled and found that the conversation had helped to calm her racing pulse, which was still elevated from when the tree had crashed into the library. At least they'd gotten most of the books laid out and drying. Only a few had been damaged beyond repair. But the accident had left the library frigid, and Nora saw it in the way her breath fogged the air in front of her face.

She cast a worried glance at Marlene, who, despite her mountain toughness, looked small and delicate, shivering inside her coat. And Lewis, who still wore his coat and pants that were probably soaked through from earlier. How long could these two survive in this kind of cold? Nora couldn't feel the edges of her feet or fingers. When would the cold become too much for any of them? She wiggled her toes, stretched out her fingers, imagined the blood flowing warm through her extremities.

"So, what is gibanica?" she asked, hoping to keep the conversation going, anything to keep them distracted for a bit longer.

Vlado chuckled. "It is a buttery, flaky, cheesy pastry that is absolutely perfect with a cup of black coffee."

"Mmm, that sounds good, except for the coffee." Jasmine leaned back in her seat and stuffed her hands into her coat pockets. "I'm really hungry."

Marlene nodded. Lewis grunted and Nora wondered again about the man's foot. His clothes still looked wet; he must be freezing in this cold.

Nora's own stomach rumbled, and she checked her phone. It was nearing ten and they hadn't had anything more than crackers and a few granola bars that they'd split among them. Jasmine had had a stash of treats in her bag, which she'd generously shared with everyone.

"You know what?" Nora said. "I think I have one or two small lunch sacks in my car."

"You keep lunches in your car?" Marlene said. "In case you get stuck in a snowstorm like this?"

"She gives them to people on the streets." Vlado's voice was warm. "I'll go get them. Where are your keys, Nora?"

Marlene made a clucking sound. "There he goes again. Asking for car keys."

From the lump that was Lewis came another laugh, and hearing something so light come from the tormented man was an unexpected shot of brightness in the cold night. "In my purse that's on my desk, outside pocket." The wind howled through the stacks, and Nora saw Marlene shudder and pull the zipper up higher on her coat.

"So, you work here nearly every day, and then in your off-hours you pass out sandwiches to the homeless, volunteer at the shelter, and look for your brother, too, I suppose?" Marlene's voice held notes of disbelief.

Nora straightened in her seat and tried to ignore the sensation that she was under Marlene's microscope. "Yep." She didn't elaborate, and for the next few minutes, Marlene let the matter drop.

Vlado returned, his cheeks ruddy from the cold, and ice and snow flicked onto the ground from his hair. He set the paper sacks into the cone of light.

"How is it looking out there?" Marlene said.

Vlado shook his head. "No sign of letting up. Our cars are nearly buried."

"Are we going to be stuck here all night?"

Jasmine's voice had a slight whine to it, and Nora could feel the worry coming off the girl, who had stood, hands in the pockets of her coat, shifting back and forth on her feet and looking for the first time agitated, uncomfortable. *She's a teenager*, Nora thought, *and probably starving and scared.* They were probably all a little hungry and scared.

"We might, but we're safe here, Jasmine, I promise. This old building has weathered even worse storms than this."

"I need to call my grandma." Jasmine slumped, pulled at a braid. "But my phone's dead."

"Do you want to use mine?" She held it out.

"Okay." The screen lit her face, and Nora noticed worry lines dragging across her smooth forehead. "It's me . . . yeah, it died. A tree crashed through the window! Yeah, but they patched it up and we got the books out of the snow. This is Nora the librarian's phone . . . okay, is Olive okay? . . . Yeah, tell her she's a brat . . . okay, I love you too."

They all sat very still while she talked, almost like they were afraid to ruin a moment. Warmth and love radiated from the one-sided conversation. Nora thought of her aunt, who'd tried to bring Nora into the family, to include her as much as possible, to make sure she knew she'd always have a home. But Nora didn't know how to have both the family she craved and be Mario's sister. So she'd chosen Mario. She was glad that Jasmine didn't have to choose between the people she loved.

Jasmine handed the phone back and gave Marlene a look that Nora couldn't decipher. "Oops, there I go talking on the phone again." Her voice was tentative, but with a lightness that made it seem humorous.

Marlene smiled, a rare sight that surprised Nora, and leaned forward. "And in the *library*."

"You're crazy."

They both laughed, and while Nora wasn't sure why, it made her smile and warmed the freezing air. She riffled through the sacks and divided the food so that everyone had something, splitting the sandwiches up as best she could. Not enough to fill bellies, but something, at least. "Sorry, it's not much."

Jasmine sat on the floor and peeked at the sandwich. Her fingers moved like she counted something. Nora's eyebrows rose. Was the girl counting calories? She felt a pang. Teenagers put such pressure on themselves.

Vlado crouched beside her chair. She inhaled woods and apples and damp clothes. "I know we don't know each other well, but if you need anyone to talk to, or, you know . . ." He cleared his throat. "I'm here for you, Nora."

It was such a sweet thing to say, and for a minute Nora couldn't speak, couldn't remember the last time someone offered something so earnestly. Then again, when was the last time she'd told anybody about Mario?

"Oh, Vlado, thank you. That's so kind, but I'm doing fine, really."

"Are you sure about that, Nora?" In the fractured light, Nora could see only half his face, but his eyes were dark and sad.

The skin on her face grew stiff, and she adjusted in her seat, crossing her leg and moving so that she faced away from him. "I'm quite sure, Vlado." This was why she kept to herself. Everyone had opinions and advice and suggestions on how she should live her life, when, in the end, it was nobody's business but her own.

Lewis stared at her and she stared back. He was probably the only person here who truly understood her. And he must have met the man out by the factory or at least heard about him. Knew something she didn't. Even a small bit of information, like the color of his hair. She breathed in. She had to ask. "Have you ever met the man who's staying out by the factory, Lewis?"

Beside her, Vlado rose to his feet and returned to his seat across the circle from her. She didn't look his way.

Lewis stopped chewing, his cheeks rounded from food, and held her gaze. Finally, he swallowed and it was so loud she could hear it from across the circle. "Once."

Her pulse sped up. Why hadn't she thought to ask him before? "What did he look like? Did he limp? Do you know what color hair he had?"

"Brown." Lewis took another bite and lowered his gaze.

She perked up, feeling a smile touch the edges of her lips. It was Mario: she was sure of it. And it made sense of this entire night: Lewis overdosing outside the library, the storm stranding them here, maybe even the tree crashing through the window that had seemed to bring them closer. Her uncle tried to tell her that she was saved from the wreck for a purpose. He thought it had to do with her, but after that Thanksgiving, she knew it had everything to do with Mario. "Was he missing a leg? Mario wears a prosthetic, but it's pretty old and may not fit the greatest anymore, so he might limp pretty bad."

Lewis shrugged. "I don't remember."

Nora shifted to the edge of her seat and ran a hand through her own hair, nervous and impatient. "But did he limp? Also, he's got a scar across his forehead, a pretty obvious one. It's from the accident. Did you see a scar?"

"No." He seemed reluctant to say more, but when he did, Nora felt her heart skip a beat. "I hope he's not your brother."

Nora wrinkled her forehead. "But why—"

"I need to go to the bathroom." Jasmine stood beside Nora, bouncing on her toes.

Nora did not want to be interrupted, but when she thought about the dark bathroom in the old library, she couldn't ignore the girl. "I'll go with you. It's probably a little scary in the d—"

"No thank you!" It was the loudest the girl had been, and it seemed to surprise everyone. She shoved her hands into her coat pockets, rounded her shoulders. "I mean, I'm fine on my own." She picked up a flashlight, and Nora watched the light bounce along the walls and floor as she walked. Then the squeak of the bathroom door opening and a thump when it closed, taking the light with it.

From somewhere to the left of them, by the window, came a wet plop, followed by another.

Nora looked behind her. "What is that?" A mushy sound like water hitting carpet came from just beyond the ring of light.

Vlado shone a flashlight over to the sound, up to the ceiling. "There's a leak," he said. "This snow is so heavy and wet it's probably more than this old roof can take."

"So the ceiling's caving in now?" Marlene looked up with a frown.

Nora bit her lip when she studied the ceiling. She had no idea what the condition of the roof was. Had it been checked recently? Was the heavy snow too much for it? She imagined a section of it caving in on top of them. The unknown made her feel like they were sitting ducks.

"It's just a leak, I'm sure." The ceiling looked fine, but light from the lantern didn't stretch high enough to see anything clearly. Another plop, and Nora thought it sounded like it fell closer to her desk. "I think there might be a bucket or two in the storage room." Nora started to move but was stopped by Vlado's hand on her arm.

"I'll get it." He left with the other flashlight and Nora sat down, chilled by the intrusion of the elements, and huddled around the lantern with Lewis and Marlene like it was a crackling fire, not a cold yellow light. Her heels tapped the floor. She felt momentarily useless, something that unsettled her, allowing room for doubts and worry to skitter across her skin.

"I know you don't believe me, Nora," Marlene said.

Her throat tightened and she would have preferred to ignore Marlene, focus on breathing deep and calming down. "About what?"

"Jasmine. She's a nice kid, but that girl is hiding something."

Nora didn't disagree, but she had no idea what to do and she was suddenly so tired. Her body weighted down like she balanced a tree trunk across her shoulders. Sometimes the heaviness of the world, the shattered lives of the people around her, the reality of her own life and her brother's addiction, became too much. She didn't want to believe that Jasmine was doing something she shouldn't. Nora needed to believe that not everyone fell down the rabbit hole when things got hard. She had to believe that even a child who'd lost her mother was strong enough to stand on her own. But Nora also knew the harsh realities of people in pain. And sometimes losing someone was too much to bear. Maybe it was the storm or the cold or the dark, but Nora weakened and she turned to Marlene and let it out.

"Why do you always have to think the worst of people, Marlene? Charlie never did." The words were out and she couldn't take them back. Her hand covered her mouth. Something about this night and the storm and the cold had brought everything she didn't want to feel right up to the surface. She wasn't herself. "I'm sorry," she said quickly, but the cruelty of her words hung in the air, ghosts of her regret.

The light played over Marlene's face, shadows getting caught in the lines across her forehead and down her cheeks. Her expression hadn't changed, lips still pressed together, yet a softness played around the edges of her eyes and it surprised Nora.

"You're right. Charlie was too generous with people." Her mouth bent upward, surprising Nora yet again because she was smiling. "I told him that all the time."

Nora fidgeted in her seat. "I'm sorry; I shouldn't have said—"

Marlene held up her hand. "Now, don't go and do that, Nora."

"Do what?"

"Get all weak and weepy and try to say you didn't mean it. You meant it and you're right. One thing I can't bear is someone who doesn't speak their mind."

Lewis moved closer to the light, nodded. "That's something we can agree on."

Marlene turned her head to look at him. "Nora here is right about you too."

"How's that?"

"You came to this town to see your granddaughter, I assume. Why? So you could put her through the awfulness of finding your dead body under the tree at the library?"

Lewis's head jerked back like she'd slapped him. The room was spinning and Nora needed it to stop. Needed some kind of order. "Marlene, that's not exactly what I meant." But wasn't it? Hadn't she had nightmares about finding her brother when it was too late? Images of his lifeless body burned into her brain? Didn't Persie deserve better? She pressed her arms into her stomach, trying to quiet an angry churning in her gut, because she knew this feeling wasn't about Lewis. It was about Mario. But she also knew that her anger was destructive and wouldn't get her anywhere. Or help her brother. She waited for the sensation to cool.

"No, damn it, no!" Lewis said. "Persie doesn't even know I'm here. I've stayed away. I just wanted to see her. Make sure she's okay," he whispered, as though the air had left his lungs. Light reflected against his wet eyes. He pulled his coat around him, slid farther into it. "I never wanted to hurt anyone."

"What happened to you?" Jasmine's voice was soft. Nora turned to find her seated on the floor beside her chair. She'd returned from the bathroom without Nora noticing. Lewis didn't answer but he stared at her, his face like stone. Jasmine said, "One time, when I was working with Persie, this old song came on the radio at the diner, and she said it was kinda about her granddad."

Nora felt her heart squeeze because Lewis's face was bare of his usual guardedness; instead, he looked open and vulnerable, with his eyes glued on the girl. "Persie talks about me?"

"Yeah, a lot. I think her mom tells her stories about you, when you—uh, well, when you were younger and maybe not, you know, like this." Jasmine bit her lip. "But this song came on and it made her kinda tear up." Her eyes rolled up, like she was trying to remember. "It was by someone called Cosby and Nashville, I think? Something about a college in Ohio?"

Marlene inhaled a sharp breath. "Kent State?"

He nodded.

"Yeah," Jasmine said. "She said you were there and something terrible happened and that it's kinda the reason she never saw you when she was growing up."

It'd happened in 1970, well before Nora was born, but she'd read about it, studied it a little bit in history. She knew that the students at Kent State had been protesting Nixon's expansion of the Vietnam War with the invasion of Cambodia. And that the National Guard was called in and four students were killed. "Were you a student then?"

He shook his head.

"Oh no," Marlene said. "Were you one of the national guardsmen?"

He nodded, still with his eyes on Jasmine, and Nora had to sift through the scant bits she remembered learning in school about the shootings at Kent State. The controversy that the National Guard had acted in fear, that nobody should have died. And Lewis was there? She pressed a hand to her chest, thought of Mario and his guilt, wondered what kind of scars Lewis carried inside.

He pulled his right leg up, and Nora noticed how he winced and tried to reposition, favoring his right foot. "What does Persie know about me?"

For the first time, Jasmine looked uncertain. "Just that her mom said it was hard on you. That guilt kinda destroyed you, or, like, made things really bad for you. She said you tried to forget it, but you just couldn't."

Vlado returned from the storage room, quietly putting a couple of buckets near the leaks before returning to his chair. For a moment, with the dark working its way in and around them, it felt like time had abandoned them, like they were drifting.

"Goddamn thirteen seconds," Lewis said.

"Were you one of the twenty-eight?" Marlene said.

Lewis nodded.

Nora stared at Lewis, trying to match up the shrunken man before her with a guard in uniform and a gun, firing on unarmed students protesting a violent war.

"I was scared."

It was all he said, but it was enough. Nora knew fear and how it could make you do things you didn't mean. She briefly reflected on her own choices. Her lonely apartment. Her solitary life. She'd given up so much because she wanted to be there for Mario when he needed her. Because she was terrified of letting him down again, like she had when she was just a girl.

Lewis made a sound that could have been a sob or groan, and he heaved himself onto his knees, pushed on a chair to stand, but when he did, his right leg seemed to buckle under the pressure and he fell hard.

Nora shot from her chair and knelt in front of him, where the stench of moist clothes and unwashed human permeated the air. She ignored it. "Lewis, what's wrong with your foot?"

"I'm fine, leave it alone."

"I think we need to take your shoes off and see." She touched the toe of his boot, and beneath her finger, the leather was squishy. "Your socks must be soaking. It's not good for your skin."

There had been another time Mario had overdosed after grad school, the one that Nora had been convinced would be his last. The doctor had told her that his feet were in bad shape—trench foot, he'd called it.

Isn't that what soldiers get? She'd been confused and he'd given her a kind look, full of pity.

We see it in homeless people too.

His feet had eventually healed, but Mario hadn't.

"C'mon, Lewis," Marlene said without a hint of gentleness. "Take off your shoes. Old-man feet are bad no matter who you are. My father had the thickest, yellowest toenails I've ever seen. Yours can't be any worse than that."

Nora wanted to pinch Marlene hard, but Lewis grunted a laugh. "Lady, you're too much."

And with effort, he slid his shoes off, then his socks, exposing his pale, wrinkled feet, which looked like they'd been soaking in water too long. On his right heel and toe were small white blisters, a few popped open and an angry red. Nora grabbed the antibiotic ointment from before and dabbed some on the blisters.

"You need to dry your feet out, Lewis," she said.

"But it's s-s-so cold," Jasmine said. "His feet will freeze, won't they?"

Lewis started to put his shoes back on. "She's right; it's warmer in my shoes."

"Your shoes and socks are causing the problem, Lewis."

"How do you know?" There was defensiveness in the glint of his eyes, and Nora imagined how he must feel with his damaged feet on display, glowing like little white fishes in the lantern light.

"My brother had something similar, although his was much worse."

Lewis didn't say anything, but he put his shoes down and left his feet bare.

Nora had an idea and hurried into the stacks, coming back with the box of knitting supplies.

"Oh, Nora," Marlene said. "I don't think more knitting will help the man's feet."

Nora ignored her and took out the yarn. There were discarded pieces in the bottom, ragged squares of past attempts, some big enough to wrap around his feet like socks. It seemed like a good idea. She took them out, held them up and wondered what she was going to do next. Vlado handed her duct tape.

Nora smiled. "Perfect."

Marlene snorted. "This seems like a really bad episode of a home improvement show."

She gently wrapped the knitted pieces around his foot, lightly securing it with duct tape so the air could still flow and allow his sodden skin to dry without giving him frostbite at the same time. She did the same with his other foot until he wore a pair of mismatched knitted duct tape socks. Marlene came over and laid the blanket that had been around her shoulders onto Lewis's legs. He immediately took it off and held it out, and it wobbled in the air from the shaking in his arm.

"Take it," Marlene said. "Now."

"You remind me of a drill sergeant I once had."

"Yes, well, I think I might have been an exceptional drill sergeant." Nora felt her eyes bug wide. Was Marlene joking? "Take it," she said again.

"No thank you, lady. You're as old and broken down as I am. Keep it."

Marlene laughed. "It's Marlene, and you're not wrong, but my clothes are dry, unlike yours, since I wasn't outside dying in the snow earlier. Take it. This is about as nice as I get."

A smile cut across his face, so broad it made a moonscape of pits and lines, but the look of delight that lifted his eyebrows was a first, and it lightened the mood almost immediately. She heard Jasmine sigh.

"That is a true statement, Mar*lene*," Lewis said and let the blanket fall to his lap.

Nora quickly tucked it around his legs and lightly draped it over his feet before he could shoo her away. The icy plop of water in the bucket, the sting of cold air on her cheeks, the tingling numbness in her fingers faded, and in the afterglow of the unexpected camaraderie, Nora felt warmed all the way through.

CHAPTER EIGHTEEN

MARLENE

Marlene's nostrils stuck together when she breathed in the cold air. The library was freezing now, so she huddled deeper inside her coat, still cold even with her hat and gloves. For the first time all night, Lewis looked a little less than frozen and a whole lot less almost-dead. She blinked hard, thinking about his feet, so white and wrinkled and vulnerable sticking out of the torn hem of his pants. She'd hated it for him and didn't want to say anything, but she also wanted the man to have some kind of comfort. He deserved at least that.

She watched Jasmine in a chair across from her, still pulling pine needles out of her coat, and Marlene grimaced thinking about her hand on Jasmine's arm, the way she had accused her in front of everyone about the drugs and the stealing. The girl had been in the wrong—nobody could convince Marlene otherwise—but she could have handled it better.

She was afraid she took after her mother more than she'd ever liked to admit. That she'd allowed the smallness of her world to make her small too. Charlie saw her as the person she'd once believed herself to be: an artist who observed and created painted worlds on canvas.

Marlene studied Jasmine, who was fussing with her phone. The girl was genuinely kind to everyone. Marlene wasn't around kids much, but she suspected that Jasmine was a rare one. It was too bad her mother wasn't alive to see it. Marlene blinked, wishing she hadn't been so awful to the girl.

Vlado leaned toward Nora's chair and touched her forearm. "You're bleeding, Nora."

Nora looked down, seemed surprised to find blood. "Oh," she said. "Must have nicked myself on glass."

Marlene shook her head, couldn't help but make a *tsk* sound. The woman gave too much. Just like Charlie, and look where it got him. "That's what I'm talking about, Nora. You only think about others. It's okay to be selfish once in a while. Notice your own cuts and bruises."

"Why are you so mean to her?" Jasmine said, and there was an edge to her voice that hadn't been there before now. The girl seemed preoccupied, knees drawn up into her chest, rocking in a nervous kind of way. It made Marlene think again about whatever she'd felt in the girl's pocket. What if Jasmine was struggling? Could Marlene blame her? Life was hard and losing loved ones was an avalanche of sad.

It's the tone of your voice, Marly. It keeps people out.

Marlene sighed. He was right. So she tried to speak more gently, even though the effort turned her voice scratchy like an old woman's. "I just tell the truth. Charlie admired you, Nora, but he worried about you too."

Vlado knelt beside Nora's chair now, rolled up her sleeve, and opened the medical kit. Nora watched Jasmine spinning her chair in circles, seemed not to notice when Vlado began to clean the gash on her forearm. "That's okay, Jasmine." She turned to Marlene. "He was worried about me?" There was a delicateness to her, a difference in the way she held herself. Marlene wasn't sure exactly how she had changed, just that it seemed like she'd lost substance in some way. She seemed smaller. And Marlene didn't like it. But she knew that Charlie's death must have been hard on Nora too.

"Of course he did. He also thought you were wasting your life and I agreed." Was she going too far? Marlene had no idea, had never been one to appropriately measure her effect on people. Before, she hadn't known about Nora's brother. Now that she did, though, did it make a difference? She cleared her throat. "He cared about you. It's why I called you to come to the hospital. To say goodbye. He would have wanted that."

Vlado had finished bandaging Nora's arm but sat back on his heels, listening, with his eyes on Nora's face.

"He would?" Nora's hands were limp in her lap.

Did Nora really have no idea how much Charlie had adored her? Marlene knew because he told her. And despite what most people thought about her, Marlene was happy when Charlie was happy. *If I'd had a daughter, I think she would have been like Nora*, he'd said more than once.

"What happened to Charlie?" Vlado said quietly, and the question sent an electric shock running through Marlene's muscles, awakening the pain that the pills had made dormant. She rubbed her fists up and down her thighs, lost in memory—the loud click of the monitor when it was turned off, the sudden quiet, and his breath that stuttered and stopped—each one a knife in her chest.

Only a few months ago now. That was what was so hard for Marlene to comprehend. Early December, he'd been alive, his body warm beside her in bed, his hand holding her own even in the library, his voice booming through the cabin, reading her another bad joke he'd found in *Reader's Digest*. "He fell off a ladder trying to hang Christmas lights for a neighbor of ours, and he never woke up." She'd sat beside him every day for weeks in a plastic hospital chair that made her cry out in pain from the way it dug into her bones, but she never complained and she never asked for another chair.

But the Charlie she knew, the Charlie she loved, was gone long before his heart had stopped beating. And when they asked her what she wanted to do, she made the decision alone, gripping his hand between her own, her eyes dry but her heart collapsing in on itself.

At some point, Nora had arrived at the hospital and stood quietly behind her, one hand on her shoulder. Marlene never turned around, never spoke to her, and after some time had passed, Nora squeezed her shoulder and left. It had been exactly what Marlene would have demanded from her, but when she was gone, Marlene had felt more alone than ever. She'd returned home that night to an empty cabin, cold and smelling of stale woodsmoke and burned coffee, and she'd ripped down every single one of her paintings and tossed them outside into the snow.

In the dark she couldn't make out who was crying, but she could guess because it sounded like the tears of someone too young to care who heard. Jasmine.

"I'm so sorry." Jasmine gulped. "That sucks. It's so awful. I get why you're mean. It's because you're so sad. I'm so sorry." A few more gulps and then she quieted. "I was mean to my sister after my mom died, and sometimes I'm really bitchy to my dad and I shouldn't be, but sometimes I just can't help it."

Marlene didn't know what to say, didn't know how to feel except touched. "Thank you, Jasmine." For the first time since Charlie had died, Marlene didn't feel so alone.

CHAPTER NINETEEN

LEWIS

He sat with his feet sticking out in front of him like one of the dolls Heather loved as a little girl. The ones with porcelain faces and shiny black shoes on their tiny doll feet that she lined up on the shelf above her bed. He was about as useless as those dolls too. When the tree had ripped the hole in the wall and they'd had to work together to move all those books to a safe place, he'd felt needed for the first time in years, and it had been good to use his body for something more than a dumpster for drugs. His feet still ached and tingled with the cold, but out of the wet socks and shoes that had felt like cement, he could move his toes, feel the bottom of his feet again. Had he said thank you? He couldn't remember. Nora was a good woman. It was a shame about her brother.

There was a constant breeze from the other room, and without moving around, the cold had settled into his flesh. He shivered and noticed that the others did, too, someone sniffling every few seconds, noses purple in the yellow light. Everyone had gone quiet—trapped in their own heads, he supposed—and for a second, Lewis didn't feel so different. They could be in the library or on a dark street, damaged people sharing a fire.

"It's like the blizzard of '78." His voice felt raw and small. Lewis wasn't used to being the first to say something. Their coats rustled when they turned his way, and he wished he hadn't brought their attention back to him.

"I don't remember that one," the old woman said.

"In Ohio, not here." Lewis was short, hoping they'd let it drop, but then the girl spoke and he couldn't ignore her.

"What happened?"

"It shut down the whole damn state. Three feet of snow with hundred-mile-per-hour winds that buried people in their cars and homes."

"Wow! What did you do?" Jasmine had leaned forward, elbows on knees, and Lewis was reminded of Heather and how she used to beg to hear the story of the great blizzard.

"The guard was activated and we spent days digging people out, delivering medications or taking folks to the hospital. Saved one guy who'd been buried by an avalanche from his own damn roof! Guy almost died." These were good memories, good times that made Lewis smile. "Persie's mom was born during that storm. I didn't see her until three days later, and damn if she didn't look just like her mother." Lewis felt his face relax, thinking about how proud he'd been of both his wife and his daughter and even a little bit of himself. But then the nightmares came back, stronger than ever, and thoughts of his baby girl, delicate and innocent, mingled with images of the young girl who'd been gunned down when she'd only been trying to get to class.

"Lewis?" It was the security guard. "Hey, man, you okay?"

It was all this talking about Kent State. It had brought everything back, and in the dark and cold, it marched through his head and he couldn't shut it off on his own. The last time he'd talked about that day had been in group therapy at the rehab place. He hated bringing it up. But the memory haunted him with the fear and chaos, the burned stench of discharged weapons, the screams.

He'd only been a damn kid. But they'd all been kids.

And it was the fear that kept coming back to chew on him. Fear had been a solid beast that day, wrapping its long tail around everyone, goading them, stoking the flames higher and higher. And when they had crested the hill, it exploded.

He could never come to terms with his own actions, could never scrub clean the stain they left behind.

Now he was an old man and it was only an excuse. An excuse for hurting everyone he loved. An excuse for being a piece-of-shit failure of a husband, a father, a grandfather, a man.

And he hated himself for it.

He had begun to shake from the cold. He'd been inside for hours now, out of the elements—a first in a long time—but the sudden drop in temperature when the tree crashed through the building was a cutting reminder of what waited for them outside. Another tremor had begun to run loops in and out of his muscles, but this was a feeling he knew well. This was a numbness he wanted.

In the dark, it was easy to think about the bag in his pocket and he slid his fingers inside, just wanting to touch it, to know it was there. Like the smooth river rocks he'd collected when he was a boy. The kind he'd hold in his palm and run his fingers across whenever he was thinking or anxious or needed something to do with his hands.

His fingers reached the end of his pocket, the rough skin catching on the cheap liner. Empty. It was empty. He tried the other pocket. Empty. His pants pocket. Empty. His breathing was fast and ragged.

"Which one of you bastards stole from me!" His voice cut through the dark, loud in his ears, and he liked the volume, felt it split open inside him, a release. He leaned into the light from the lantern, trying to see past the glare at their faces. His eyes ran over the old lady; the librarian; the security guard, who looked at him like he'd come from another goddamn planet.

He breathed in and out through his mouth, feeling the air flap against his lips. "It was my property. Mine! You can't steal from me!"

He was hot now, sweat dripping down his back through the thick coat, beading up across his forehead. He threw the blanket off and tried to get to his feet, but he slipped because of the knitted whatevers and because he was an old, broken man with a body that had given out. "You give me back my—"

"I took it."

It was the girl. And her voice in the night—sweet, lilting, but firm—and suddenly he saw Persie in the splintered light sitting cross-legged with her pink hair and big eyes that looked just like her mother's. Lewis's rage disappeared as quickly as a bolt of lightning, and his chest caved in. He leaned heavily on the chair, bent forward in case his legs gave out on him, because they might.

"You?" he said.

The girl pulled her backpack onto her lap, opened a front pocket, and took out his bag. The powder was white against her dark palm, and seeing it so close to someone so young, knowing what it could do, its destruction, its lies, its death, turned his legs into Jell-O, and he cried out, "Oh, no, girl, put it down!"

The librarian was on her feet, face so pale it glowed in the dark. She lurched at the girl. "Jasmine, no!"

The old woman didn't say a thing, but Lewis saw her mouth tighten. He fell back onto his seat and had to press an arm against his eyes.

The girl dropped the bag, and the librarian snatched it up, slid it into her own pocket. Jasmine wrapped her arms across her body. "I'm sorry," she said—defensive, Lewis could tell from the jut of her chin. "It fell out of his pocket, and I kept thinking about Persie and after what happened before with him I . . ."

Lewis pulled his head up just enough to look at her from over his arm. For years he'd felt ignored, unseen, just another drug addict, another homeless nut. But the way Jasmine stared at him, he smelled the musty stink of his coat, felt the dirt ground into his fingertips, tasted the spaces between his unbrushed teeth.

"Persie knows you're here," she said. "She saw you the very first day you were sitting out on that bench, and she recognized you from a picture her mom has. She cried her entire shift."

Silent tears leaked from his eyes. "No, I don't think so." His words were shaky. "I've never gone inside."

The old woman shifted in her seat and looked down at him huddled on the floor. "You're not invisible, Lewis."

Jasmine nodded. "Yeah. She knows it's you."

In the silence, the wind howled through the building, the snow battered the windows in wet thumps, and the library grew even colder. Lewis shivered, his heart beating too fast for someone his age, and he let his head fall into his hands.

Nora's chair squeaked when she moved. "I'm sure Jasmine's right, Lewis. I bet Persie would recognize you anywhere. The last time I saw Mario, he was walking out of a shelter, and I knew him right away." She laughed and it sounded distant, like she was somewhere else too. "And not just because of his limp. He's got these tight curls all over his head. When I was little, I used to be so jealous of his curls."

The way she spoke about her brother made his chest ache. He hoped the man at the factory wasn't him because she deserved better.

She pulled a hand through her hair. "Mine was always more frizzy than curly."

"Your hair is beautiful," said the security guard, who painfully and openly loved this woman. It brought Phyllis to mind. He'd loved her, too, but could never love himself enough to give her what she deserved. She'd remarried, he'd heard. And Lewis hoped she was happy.

"You've never seen him since?" the old woman—Marlene, he reminded himself—said.

"No."

Nora didn't speak and Lewis felt a desire to say something to erase what Marlene had suggested. "I'm still alive," he growled. "And if that isn't"—he felt Jasmine's eyes on him—"GD proof that you can make a mess of your life and keep on living, then I don't know what is."

Nobody said anything, but something touched Lewis's arm. A hand. Nora's hand. She squeezed once, and it took him a minute to catch his breath because it was the first time that he could remember being touched by a hand that wasn't a fist, or a shove, or a frisk of his pockets.

CHAPTER TWENTY

NORA

Nora had put the baggie into the pocket of her sweater, but even that was too close. She needed to get rid of it. A low buzz had started in her head and she struggled to keep her thoughts straight. Was Mario still alive? Doubt sprouted in her chest. She kept glancing at Jasmine. The girl had grown quiet, hunched down in the seat with her legs out in front, pushing the rolling chair back and forth with her heels. Unfortunately, Nora's doubts about the girl had begun to grow, a stubborn weed she couldn't remove. Why hadn't Jasmine handed the drugs over when she first found the bag? Why keep it in her backpack? There were no easy answers unless she asked, and Nora did not want to ask. Not yet. There had already been too much sadness shared tonight.

It was really late, toward the time when bed and home and warmth sounded better than trying to keep everyone's spirits up or to keep pretending that being snowed in at the library was anything more than dangerous when the power was out, the trees were trying to kill them, and they were all freezing. A breeze filtered in from the damaged side of the library, and it inched around her ankles, kept her feet in a constant state of near numbness. The *plop, plop* from the ceiling had not slowed. Would they be safer in the basement? It was dark up here with the storm and the windows covered in cardboard; the basement would be even darker, and that sounded much worse. She crossed her arms, her body shaking, worry knotted in her chest. After the tree, Nora had called 911 again to let them know she had elderly people and a girl stuck inside, but the roads were impassable, and the operator had said that the best idea was to stay put until the storm cleared.

She looked around: Lewis had curled back into himself, and Marlene sat with the Mexico travel book open on her lap, flipping through the pages by flashlight. Vlado had been the steady quiet man that she'd come to know, despite what must have been a turbulent childhood living amid such terrible violence. All she could recall about the Bosnian War was that it had been fueled by religious and ethnic tensions. It had to have been heartbreaking for his family to leave their home and start over in a foreign country, but Vlado exuded a contentment with himself and his life, even his past, that drew Nora like a moth to a flame. She'd never felt content, didn't even really know how it was possible to ever be at peace when her brother was so messed up.

Nora found it hard to keep her eyes open, but her thoughts were turbulent, running from Lewis to Mario to Charlie. She missed Marlene's husband more than she let on. He'd been kind and thoughtful and a good listener.

She'd almost told him about Mario once. On the day after she'd found her brother leaving the shelter. She'd been working at the library for only a year then, but Charlie came in nearly every day looking up one exotic place after another, making plans for his imminent retirement and all the places he and Marlene would explore together. Nora had been at her desk, thumbing through a review magazine but not reading, the cover images blurring one into another. Charlie set a plastic travel mug on her desk. Hints of orange and honey and a peppery spice filled her nose.

Marlene makes the best sweet-and-spicy tea, and I find it warms me right up. Everything okay, Nora?

Charlie had gray eyebrows that grew out like wings and an easy warmth that reflected in his eyes, and when he looked at her, she felt special and full of promise. She supposed that this was how her father would have made her feel. It must have been what broke her, his kindness and openness, the way he actually seemed to care even if her answer was, *No, I'm not okay, I don't think my brother will ever get better, and I don't know what to do without him.* She didn't say any of that, of course, but she did start to cry, big fat tears that ran down her cheeks and hit the desk and had her running outside and around the back of the library, where she hid under the big pine tree with the branches that spread out like a circus tent, mortified. He'd followed her, and the thing about Charlie was that he didn't say a word, didn't pester her with questions, didn't shame her for losing it. He simply stood beside her, one hand rhythmically patting her shaking back, and waited with her until her tears finally dried.

Then he handed her the travel mug, steam rising from the open mouth, the air tinged with orange and spice. *It'll warm you right up; you'll see.*

They never spoke of it again and he never asked, except in small gestures and little kindnesses that let her know he was there if she ever wanted to share. Charlie's death had been too sudden.

Her nose started to run, the tip of it cold, most likely red if there was enough light to see it by. She didn't have the kind of complexion that looked radiant in the dry and cold. When it was cold, she looked cold, always with tissues in her pocket to keep a runny nose at bay. She shivered into the fluffy down of her coat. The library felt trapped inside a snow globe, but the bag in her pocket burned, and she itched to get rid of it. Where?

Her gaze went to the dark hallway that led to the bathroom. She stood, taking one of the small headlamps from the plastic bin by Marlene. "I'll be right back," she said, but nobody replied, seeming trapped within their own snow globes.

The bathroom was the kind of dark that horror movies are made of, and as one of the first rooms to have seen any kind of renovation, it had been stripped of its original charm and now had a seventies hospital vibe, with cheap metal doors and industrial sinks that reflected the headlamp in multiple shiny points. She hurried to the first stall and pulled the bag from her pocket. Her hands shook when she opened the top. The powder couldn't hurt her, she knew that, unless she injected it or snorted it or whatever else could be done with it, but she hated the stuff. Hated it like it was a person—a kidnapper, a murderer, a sociopath who reveled in the destruction it left behind. But this was only powder. And all she could do was dump it into the toilet. So she did, watching the powder swirl into the water, the beam of her headlamp pulling shadows into the bowl. There was more of this stuff out there, most likely circulating around her brother's body. And she couldn't flush it all down the toilet.

She put soap and water into the plastic bag and washed it out completely before throwing it into the trash. When she left the bathroom, Vlado looked up at her, eyebrows raised.

She stopped by his chair and leaned down to whisper, "I got rid of it." She glanced at Lewis, but the man appeared to be sleeping.

"Good idea."

She balanced on the balls of her feet, about to return to her chair but not wanting to sit down, needing to move a bit, even just to stand. A voice chirped from Vlado's phone, but he pressed "Pause" and set it on his lap, looked at her expectantly.

"Oh, I'm sorry. Keep listening. I just needed to stand for a bit."

Vlado pushed to his feet and started to swing his arms around, stretching. "It has been a long day, hasn't it?"

She smiled. "A very long day." She pointed toward his phone. "Listening to music?"

"Oh, no, that is a podcast."

She brightened. "I love podcasts. Have you ever listened to *This American Life?*"

"It's one of my favorites," he said. "And *Hidden Brain.*"

"Oh, me too."

They stood there—awkwardly, it felt to Nora—swinging their arms like they were Olympic swimmers preparing for a meet.

"I'm really cold. My feet feel like blocks of ice," Jasmine said. "And I'm bored too. I mean, like, so bored my brain hurts, and all I can think about is how cold my feet are."

"Wiggle your toes, stand up, and move; it'll help." Nora thought of the podcast Amanda had suggested. It would be nice if she could respond, let her know she'd listened to it. It's what they used to do when Nora was a better friend—trade podcasts and book suggestions, then discuss them over coffee or wine. It might help everyone to take their minds off the bitter cold, and the storm that would not quit. "Vlado, do you have enough juice on your phone to listen to another podcast? Mine's getting a little low."

He picked up his phone. "Yes, plenty."

While Jasmine did a few jumping jacks and ran in place, Nora told him the podcast name and he opened it on his app. They chose an episode from the current season and he pushed "Play," turning the volume up as far as it would go. It was narrated by a woman, Sam, who had just moved into transitional housing near downtown Denver. Sam had been living on the streets for years, having escaped an abusive stepfather when she was young but eventually turning to prostitution, which led to drug use and years of barely surviving. She documented her first week staying at the house, where she had her own bed and a door and a bathroom. She talked a lot about the bathroom. This was her last chance, she kept saying. She shared a room with three other women. It narrated in a freewheeling journalistic fashion, with her recounting her struggles, interviewing one or two of the other women about theirs, sometimes just recording the sounds of them eating and laughing together in the communal kitchen, other times recording a disagreement about whose turn it was to clean the bathroom. It was engaging and heartbreaking and hopeful, and by the end of the episode, Nora was left wondering how Sam was doing now. Did she stick with the program? Had she transitioned into a more permanent one? Was she safe?

She didn't realize her jaw was sawing back and forth until it started to ache. Why had Amanda sent this to her? Was it to give her hope for Mario? Was it her way of being supportive? She caught Vlado staring at her across the small circle, his face so full of compassion and tenderness, like he saw straight into her heart. She blinked fast and looked away. Jasmine and Marlene had scooted forward, both of them staring at the phone as though it were a TV. Lewis stayed huddled in his coat.

There was a brief silence, and Nora thought the podcast was over, but then the host started to speak, wrapping up the show and giving an update on Sam.

But Nora couldn't hear what he was saying anymore. Her jaw started to twitch. She couldn't feel her face, her hands, her body. She knew why Amanda wanted her to hear this; she also knew why Amanda probably hadn't wanted to share it.

A strangled sound started in her chest, moved up through her throat and into a moan.

"Nora?" Vlado's voice came from a distance. "Are you okay?"

She shook her head. No, she was not okay, she was not okay at all because she would know that voice anywhere.

It was Mario.

CHAPTER TWENTY-ONE

NORA

"Nora? What's wrong?" Vlado pulled his chair close to hers, touched her shoulder.

Everyone stared at her, even Lewis. The podcast ended and her brother's voice faded, making the library colder and quieter than before. Like a tomb. She grabbed his phone, flipped back through the seasons to the very first episode from two years ago. Her fingers hovered over the "Play" button, but the title stopped her cold, vanquished any uncertainty she might have had.

To Peaches.

"It's him," she said, and her voice was a monotone, devoid of the opposing emotions vying for control inside her. In all this time, she'd envisioned emotional reunions, sobriety anniversaries celebrated together. But never, not once, had she ever thought it would be like this. A punch to the gut.

"Who?" Vlado said.

She held up the phone, pointed its screen out. Jasmine, Marlene, and Lewis scooted forward, squinted at the phone, except for Vlado, who kept his eyes on Nora.

"'Peaches'?" Marlene said.

In the blue light from the phone, Jasmine scrunched up her nose. "Who's that?"

Her shoulders rounded forward. "It's me."

"You?" Marlene said.

"He loved Super Mario Kart, and I wanted to be called Princess Peach since he always got to be Mario." She held up the phone and felt something sharp stab her in the chest. "This is my brother, Mario." She shrugged, her eyes burning. "With his own podcast. Doing really well, I guess." Without her help, without her.

"Oh, Nora." There was so much compassion in those two little words, and coming from Marlene, Nora saw herself for how she must look to all of them. A fool.

Suddenly she wanted to be away from everyone, part of her wanting to run out the door and scream into the wind, let the snow fill up her mouth and eyes and her ears. She got to her feet, gave Vlado back his phone, grabbed hers and a headlamp and, without a word to the others, headed to the bathroom. It was the only place she could be alone. And she needed to be alone.

~

She sat on the bathroom counter, her back to the mirror, legs criss-crossed beneath her so that her ankles dug into the hard surface. Her phone battery was low. She thought of Jasmine; she shouldn't use it, but she couldn't help herself. She needed to know. She had to understand why he was sober and had never called or reached out or thought about her at all. She didn't know how to feel, so she pushed "Play."

Hey, there. So, I'm Mario, and, um, well, this is my podcast, Tales from the Flip.

The audio was muffled but not enough to hide the flutter in his voice. He'd been nervous.

I'm an addict, but that's not what this podcast is about. He coughed, a hacking sound that came from deep in his lungs. *Sorry about that.* He gave a nervous laugh, and underneath it was the sound of clothes shuffling, uneven footsteps on pavement. *I had pneumonia and it's taken me a while to kick it. That's what I get for smoking most of my life.* Another laugh, this one deeper, more genuine. *Another thing I quit and another thing that this show is not about.*

Threading in and out of the audio were sounds of the city: a car honking; a puff of exhaust from a city bus; a shout, another one, and then a different man's voice came into range of the audio. *Mario, man, what the fuck? Where have you been? Tyler said you died, man.*

Mario laughed. *Do I look dead, shithead?* There was the sound of hands clapping and then Mario, his voice steadier, more serious. *I'm doing a podcast.*

Right now? No shit, man.

Yeah, right? It's a project of mine. Trying to stay clean, you know?

Mm-hmm. Cool, man. Peace. A light pounding that faded as the man walked away.

Mario laughed softly. *That's Regis. He's one of the good ones. Actually, that* is *what this podcast is about. People like Regis, like me, the ones you walk by and dismiss as lazy or criminal or addicts or thugs. The people you think are worthless. Too much? Too honest? Can't hack it? Then go find another fucking podcast 'cause this one's not for people like you.*

There was a long break punctuated only by the voices from a food vendor calling out an order as Mario walked by.

Still here? Cool. We're about to have some fun.

He was comfortable now, and she could picture him in a blend of the young boy she remembered with the man she saw last time outside the shelter—sunken, defeated, sad. She pushed the phone all the way to her ear, wanting to soak up the familiar timbre of his voice, breathe in the idea that he was sober. At last. And try to undo the grip of betrayal that clung to her heart.

The rest of the podcast followed Mario as he talked to different friends, people he knew or knew through others or total strangers. And he kept his promise that the podcast wasn't about addiction; it was a brilliant portrait of the people behind addiction and homelessness and bad luck. They shared laughs, told stories—some wild, others as mundane as watercooler gossip. And, like Sam, the stories made them real. Men and women facing hard times, hitting rock bottom. Families struggling to keep everyone together, even if that meant living out of a car. She flew through the episodes in that first season, hooked and briefly forgetting what she was waiting to hear: why Mario had transformed his life and never told her. Left her to sleepless nights of worry, endless days of searching.

At the end of the first season, Mario had grown into his role and developed an easygoing, natural way of bringing the listener along on his journey and into his conversations. It was intimate and real and so like the Mario she knew before everything changed for him. The older brother who had suffered guilt and grief from the accident, who blamed himself for taking their parents but who pushed that aside to read to her before bedtime and sing her songs, like their mother had. Who was her everything before he couldn't be any longer. She pressed a hand to her eyes, wished like she had a million times before that she'd been older, more capable of caring for him when he needed it most.

It wasn't until the end of season one that Mario said something that reached across the delayed waves of recorded podcasts and squeezed her heart.

I hope you've enjoyed this first season of Tales from the Flip. *This experience has been epic for me, and your emails and ratings and subscribing have blown me away. So, okay, I know I said this show was not about addiction, but it does happen to be a huge part of my story. And today I'm one year sober. Woo. Fuckin' yeah.*

There was silence and Nora thought the podcast was over, but his voice came back on, almost like he'd recorded it at a later time.

I miss you, Peaches.

The battery icon on her phone had turned red, bringing up the warning that her battery was low. Her thoughts flitted to the others. She should conserve her battery. What if Lewis's feet got worse, what if Marlene had a heart attack, what if—but she couldn't stop thinking about Mario.

Mario's been sober for years. WTF Amanda? she texted. How long have you known? She knew how it sounded, knew it was rude, but she felt betrayed and it heated her from the inside out.

No dots, nothing.

??? Amanda?

Nothing, and then the dots and Nora stared at the circles flashing across the screen until a message popped up.

Not long. I didn't know how to tell you. Your whole life is Mario. I didn't know what this would do to you. It's good though, right? He's sober, Nora. It's a good thing, right?

Instead of answering, she flipped through the episodes to the current year, the one she'd listened to with everyone was the last one of the season, and it had been aired back in November. What had happened since? Why hadn't he recorded more?

The screen went blank. She pushed buttons but realized with a sinking feeling that she'd let her phone die. What had she done? That left only Vlado's phone. And with Lewis's general health and Marlene's age, she should be putting them above everything else. Once again,

Mario had taken center stage, and now she couldn't stop thinking about him.

Without the light from her phone, the bathroom felt like it stretched around her, a black hole. She turned on the headlamp and pushed off the counter. A heaviness had settled across her back because it was familiar, this disappearing act. Since she was a little girl, her brother had done it too many times to count. She thought of his message and the fear in his voice. It echoed her memory of the Thanksgiving she told him to leave and the look in his eyes when he did. Like she'd betrayed him. Like she'd been the only one who'd survived the accident.

CHAPTER TWENTY-TWO

MARLENE

Nobody said anything when Nora ran off to the bathroom. Vlado just sat there, staring after her, his jaw twitching, and he didn't move when Lewis extended his finger and pushed "Play" on Vlado's phone.

"Just one episode," Vlado said. "We need to save the battery."

They chose one from the very first season. Her brother had talent, Marlene would give him that, for putting the listener right into the shoes of someone else. Marlene's attention was captured by their stories, and her mind created its own images to attach to the voices. The problem was that so many of the people he interviewed sounded so normal, and she knew that they most likely looked and smelled more like Lewis. A man who, only a few hours ago, she had reduced to an ant.

Oh, Marly. Such unkind thoughts. You sound like your mother.

They had inched their chairs forward, and the added warmth of the others, however slight, was a shocking difference to the blast of coldness that surrounded them. Marlene's hands were numb inside her gloves no matter how much she opened and closed her fingers. She needed to warm up, so she stood and tried to walk in place. Lewis watched from his spot on the floor. The man was in bad shape, and Marlene was growing worried about him.

"Join me, Lewis." His feet probably still hurt him. "Sit on a chair and move your arms and legs around. Get your blood flowing."

Jasmine and Vlado joined her, each of them doing their own version of stand-in-place exercise. After a few minutes, Lewis climbed into a chair and moved his limbs around. "Worse than any drill sergeant," he mumbled. Marlene smiled in the dark.

The podcast played.

One interview was of a family, a young father and mother who couldn't make their mortgage payments after long hospital stays and an extensive treatment plan for their daughter. The father lost his job in the middle of it all and held on by delivering pizzas in the evening and working at a fast-food restaurant during the day. They scraped by on what they could until the bank foreclosed on their house and they had nowhere else to go but their car. They kept mentioning that she was better now and how it had all been worth it to see her healed. The mother said they'd be back on their feet in no time. Marlene was touched by their resilience.

Then at the very end, after Mario whooped for his sobriety, he added *I miss you, Peaches*, like it was an afterthought, a cute sign-off meant to do what? Appease the sister who'd given up her life to find him, to help him? Marlene tapped her foot, annoyed with a man she'd never met and thinking about Nora listening to all this alone.

When it ended, Jasmine blew air out through her nose. They'd sat back down, and the two of them huddled close together now. Marlene inhaled a pleasant mix of cherry and vanilla, and when she noticed the girl shaking in her coat, she tentatively put an arm around her shoulders, and to her surprise, Jasmine leaned into her.

"P-poor Nora," Jasmine said.

Lewis grunted.

Jasmine pulled a granola bar from her backpack and chewed quietly, her eyes closing and opening. She held it out to Marlene. "You want some?"

"No thank you." Poor girl, Marlene thought. Hungry and tired and having a lock-in with a bunch of old people. Not a teenager's typical night out. She pushed to standing, her body screaming at her from the cold that locked her muscles in place. She took a few of the quilted scraps and made a pillow on the floor.

"You look like you can't keep your eyes open, Jasmine. Why don't you lie down for a bit?"

Lewis shifted in his chair, held out the blankets. "I'm warm now; give these to her."

Marlene hesitated—the man did not look warm—but there was a tautness to his shoulders, a firmness in his eyes that made her take the blankets. Sometimes dignity was more important than comfort.

Jasmine hesitated, her eyes shifting from Lewis to Marlene, but Lewis pointed to the floor. "Get some sleep."

The girl smiled and lay down. "Thanks, Lewis," she said softly, and Marlene covered her with the blankets. The girl's eyes were already closed before she laid her head on the yarn. "Marlene?" she whispered.

"Yes?"

"I'm so sad for Nora and Mario and Lewis and Persie, and for you about your Charlie and . . ." Her words trailed away and her breathing deepened.

The sentiment, coming from the girl who, hours earlier, Marlene had accused of using drugs and stealing books, caught her square in the chest.

"Me too, kiddo; me too," she whispered.

CHAPTER TWENTY-THREE

LEWIS

Without the blankets, the icy air worked its way past his coat and through the holes in the knitted socks Nora had made and sank its teeth into his skin. He shivered, trying to find any bit of warmth in his still-damp coat. He'd been freezing before, more times than he could count, but there was something different about this time. Something about the warmth that came from being around people that made the near-unbearable temperatures inside the library tolerable.

He glanced at Jasmine, who had pulled the blankets up to cover her face, and something burrowed under his heart. He was glad she was warm.

Lewis had seen some sad things in his life. His own life, for one, was a carnival of a shit show. He tried not to look backward or think too hard on all that because what was the point of something that couldn't be changed? Besides, it gave him nightmares when he did, a feeling in the tips of his cracked fingers that he'd let something go he could never get back.

But listening to Nora talk about her brother, hearing how desperate she sounded to have him back in her life, made Lewis shake with a longing to get high. Anything to maim this beast of a feeling that clawed at his stupid old heart, baring layers of shame and regret and the things that haunted him because he couldn't change the past. Couldn't take back the hurt and the lies that had led to him now: a sad sack of an old goddamn man.

He shoved his hands into his pockets. If he could just get high— even a little high would make it better, at least for the moment. But his pockets were empty, and he remembered the girl had found his drugs and the librarian had taken them, and he was too damn tired to get angry.

When Nora heard her brother on the radio show, it was like she'd lost her footing. She'd seemed different, not that Lewis knew her at all, but in the time he'd been around her, she was calm and pulled together with what seemed to him a superhuman kind of strength. But that unraveled in the course of a few minutes, and Lewis couldn't stop thinking about her. And thinking about her brought Heather and Persie to mind. Did they worry about him like Nora did about her brother? Did it make them unhappy? He'd imagined them going about their lives, relieved to be rid of him—better off, even. But the idea that they could be like Nora made him search his pockets again and wish more than anything that he had something to take it all away.

The old woman sat in a chair beside him, so close her elbow brushed his arm. Since the tree, they'd huddled together, looking for any bit of warmth, and none of them had looked at him funny or wrinkled their noses. The security guard slumped in his seat. He kept glancing toward the bathroom, jiggling his knee up and down like he might rush in there any minute to check on Nora.

"I'm sorry, if I, um . . ." Marlene's voice was gentle, and she hesitated like she was unsure of herself. It wasn't hard to guess that she was hardly ever gentle. "Lewis, I'm sorry for making assumptions about you."

He shrugged, happy to have any kind of conversation to distract him. "I don't know what you assumed about me, but don't beat yourself up. You're probably right."

Marlene's laugh was dry. "True. But after listening to that podcast, well, I think there's probably more to you than meets the eye."

He lifted one side of his mouth. "Like you?"

"Oh no, I'm a what-you-see-is-what-you-get kind of woman. Dry like toast. No surprises here."

They both laughed, and for the first time in a long time, Lewis felt halfway normal. "I'm not so sure I believe you about that. Seems that Charlie of yours knew a good apple when he met one."

Marlene's smile froze and Lewis crossed his arms, wondered if he'd gone too far, been too chummy. It had been so long since he'd had normal conversations; he was suddenly unsure if he even knew how anymore.

"That's a very nice thing to say, Lewis—apart from comparing me to an apple, of course."

His muscles relaxed. Back in the day he'd been easy on the eyes— and charming, too, always with a joke to make the ladies laugh. It's how he got Phyllis to go out on a date with him.

Marlene leaned toward him, and her eyes were shrewd. "But what got you here, Lewis? You seem to love your family, from a distance at least. Nora is partly right. You did come back here to see your grand-daughter. But if you're not going to even say hello to her, why did you come back at all?"

He wrapped his arms across his body. "It was a mistake," he said and turned from Marlene. He'd had enough with halfway normal.

"So you're forever in purgatory, huh?"

That seemed to perk the security guard right up, and he dragged his eyes from the bathroom door and sat straight in his chair. "Like Sisyphus and the boulder."

Marlene sighed and there was a slight fondness to it. One night stranded in a storm and the old woman was getting soft on everybody.

"Please educate us, Mr. PhD," Marlene said.

Vlado smiled and did just that. "Sisyphus was a trickster who tried to cheat death twice, and his punishment was to roll a boulder up a hill for all eternity. You are like that, Lewis, except the part about death—although you did cheat death once today, so . . ." He shrugged. "But you seem too honest to be a trickster."

Marlene pointed at Lewis. "Vlado here is right. You do sound like Sissypants—"

"Sisyphus," Vlado said.

Marlene waved him away. "Close enough. Your mistakes and your—uh, well, I'm just going to say it even if Nora disapproves—your *drug addiction* arc that boulder, and you just keep pushing it and pushing it up the hill. If you want to, you could let it go and get on with whatever life you've got left. I know it wouldn't be easy, but what have you got to lose?"

The last time anyone had been so honest with him had been back in rehab, but that was a long time ago. Right now he was weak and so cold there was a permanent shiver in his leg muscles. He was not at all on solid ground when it came to talking to these two. But all he had was the truth, and what did it hurt to be honest? "I've tried before." His voice was hoarse. "And I did it on my own once when Persie was five."

A breeze whirled in from the hole in the other room, moving around them in a freezing stream. Without Nora and Jasmine, their circle had collapsed into a triangle where they clustered together, the only sources of heat in each other. Lewis knew he smelled; he knew he was dirty, knew the fuzziness on his teeth made his breath bad.

"What happened?" Marlene said.

"I'd gone to Omaha, thinking a fresh start would help. Had a job, even." He gave Vlado a look. "Like you."

Vlado raised his eyebrows. "A security guard?"

"Not as official as all that but not much different. I was a bouncer at a strip club."

"Hah!" Marlene laughed. "Not much different at all. Vlado once had to stop a couple in the bathroom having sex. Charlie told me all about it."

Vlado shook his head.

"I take it that things didn't go well back then, given"—Marlene moved her hand in a circle in his direction—"all of this."

Lewis blew air out of his nose, amused. The woman didn't hold anything back. "No, it did not."

They were quiet for a bit, and Lewis pulled back into himself. He knew his problem back then. He'd quit the drugs but kept on drinking. He'd thought drinking wasn't his problem. That it had been the drugs that destroyed his life. He'd been wrong. It had been all of it.

Outside, the wind seemed to have died down for the first time since the crazy storm had started. The snow would end, and he'd be back out there. When Nora had dragged him into the library all those hours ago, all he'd wanted was to leave. But in the time that had passed, something had splintered inside him, and now he was scared. Scared because he knew that the only thing that waited for him was death. So he started talking, like his own voice could drown out the feeling that it was all about to end.

"One of the girls was around Heather's age. She'd had a dad like me, a loser and a drunk, and she'd ended up in that shithole, dancing for creeps. She had a ten-year-old son, and she showed me pictures of him nearly every shift. She loved that boy."

He rubbed a hand across his face, squeezed his eyes against a burning. "The night she died, I could smell the alcohol on her breath, and the way she was acting, well . . . I thought I knew a damn drunk." He hadn't thought about her in years. It was too painful. The way she had died, his own assumptions that left her boy without his mom. "I asked her to wait, told her I would drive her myself, but she got this look in her eyes and I knew she'd never let me take her home." He stared at his hands. "I don't blame her. Men were dangerous to her."

"What happened?" Marlene said softly.

"Her car went off the road, hit a pole."

"I'm so sorry, Lewis. But it doesn't sound like your fault—"

His head shot up and he stared at the old woman. "It was my own goddamn fault, lady. I was wrong."

"Wrong how?"

The door to the bathroom opened, hitting the wall with a thud, and Nora hurried toward them, the headlamp jiggling up and down in the middle of her forehead. "He's in Silver Ridge; I'm sure of it."

CHAPTER TWENTY-FOUR

MARLENE

"Here?" Vlado said. "How do you know?"

She sat in her chair and scooted it close to the lantern, like they all had.

"It just ends," Nora said, and her eyes searched each of their faces with a frantic intensity that Marlene had never seen in the woman.

Her chest grew tight. "What does?"

"The podcast. The newest season only has a few episodes. The last one was back in November." She nodded and jiggled one knee, seeming to want them to agree with her. "But I know what happened."

"What happened?" Marlene said.

"He relapsed."

Lewis cleared his throat. "He's been sober for what?"

"I'm not sure—two years, maybe three?" Nora said.

Marlene pressed her lips firm to keep an angry grunt inside. How could he do that to her? Not tell her. Let her assume the worst. Her eyes burned and for the first time in a long time, it wasn't for Charlie.

"But I don't know why he hasn't told me." She looked around. "Where's Jasmine?"

Vlado pointed to the lump on the ground. "Sleeping."

"Maybe he was scared," Lewis said abruptly.

Marlene tensed but Nora seemed unfazed, and it was painfully clear to her that Nora had heard and probably thought of every excuse in the book when it came to her brother. "Maybe, Lewis. But he needs me. We need each other. It's always been that way." Nora looked so lost and so young.

"Maybe you're too much—or, I mean, you expect too much." Lewis sounded hoarse. "Or maybe he didn't want to disappoint you."

Nora looked at Lewis like she'd never seen him before, like he came from a different planet.

"He's my brother. It's a pattern for him, and with his roommate dying . . . I think it was just too much for him to handle on his own. He needs a support network when he's sober to keep him strong." Her knee jiggled up and down. "But it doesn't make sense. Why hasn't he come here or called again?"

Vlado leaned in toward Nora, balancing his elbows onto his knees. "Nora—"

She turned away from him, started talking like he'd said nothing, "He's always so ashamed when he fails. I don't care, though, you know? I just want him better. Last time it happened, I lined up a rehab place for him straight from the hospital." She twisted the fabric of her pants. "But when I came back the next morning, he'd left."

Marlene's breath caught at the way Nora spoke: matter-of-factly, like it hadn't hurt her.

The young woman looked up, and her eyes were bright. "But you came back, didn't you, Lewis? You wanted to see your family, right? Because you know they want to help you."

Lewis shook his head. "You're wrong. They might want me back but only if I stay away from drugs. And I can't. I've tried." His voice weakened, grew hoarse, and his despair twisted around Marlene's heart. "I won't do that to them again."

Nora turned from him to Marlene, and she looked desperate now. "Well, I know Mario the way you knew Charlie, you know, Marlene? Like how you knew he didn't want to live like that? How you were strong enough to make the decision to let him go?"

Marlene stiffened. That was something she'd never spoken about, never acknowledged out loud to anyone about the choice she'd had to make. Only to the nurses when she'd had to tell them it was time, and even then she'd refused to look them in the eyes. Kept her own on Charlie for those last few excruciating minutes. Marlene had not cried once. Not when she called the ambulance that horrible day. Not when the doctors told her his brain had died. Not when he took his last breath. Not a single tear, because Marlene had no intention of doing this life without him, so why cry? She'd see him again or at least enjoy the blissful nothingness that came next. But now. She touched her cheek, shocked to feel the tears that slid inside the lines, pooled in the single tiny dimple on her face, the one Charlie loved to see deepen whenever he made her smile. Which was a lot. He'd made her smile more than she'd smiled her entire life.

When she wiped the sleeve of her coat across her face, she caught Lewis's eyes on her and Marlene froze, feeling like a small animal caught in crosshairs. Something hard lodged in her throat. More than once tonight, she was grateful for the dark that felt like a blanket she could wrap around her, and she did, shifting in her seat just enough so that she couldn't see him.

Marlene didn't want their sympathy or anything that might make her doubt herself or change her mind. Yesterday, with the storm coming and memories of Charlie in everything, deepening like ink into paper with each passing day, she knew she didn't want to face another day without him. Charlie would have disagreed with her. He had a way of finding meaning in the most delicate of threads, connecting one to another. He would tell her to hang on because there was purpose in her journey, meaning to her life that had nothing to do with him. She didn't agree, because she hadn't come alive until she'd met him, and that had been when her life was already half over. What was the point now, when she was nothing but a shriveled, lonely old shrew?

You're just so stubborn, Marly.

His voice from behind her, his hand on her shoulder. She reached her own hand up, touched empty space that left her cold. *I'm so lonely.*

You don't have to be.

She shifted in her chair, imagined his hand falling from her shoulder. The gun sat on her kitchen table. An old pistol that had been Charlie's. It waited for her—the answer to her pain, the end of her heartbreak. She'd nearly done it yesterday morning, with her window open and the cold breeze from the approaching storm bringing in bits of snow that made her hands shake. But imaginary Charlie wouldn't quit, his voice a companion in her head, his spirit a constant presence that nagged at her. *This isn't who you are.*

So she'd come to the library, hoping to shake the Charlie in her head, and now here she was, stuck in the dark and watching dependable Nora fall apart.

Nora had known all about Charlie, of course, but the librarian seemed to understand privacy, so for her to bring it up like that in front of everybody, Marlene knew that the woman was not okay.

Nora was still talking, completely unaware of the effect her words had had on Marlene. "Nobody knows Mario like I do, and I'm positive that he's relapsed." She looked at Vlado, held out her hand. "My battery died. Can I use your phone? I just need to listen to it again. Maybe there's a clue in there for me. And I need to call the shelters, ask around at the hospitals."

Vlado slid the phone into his pocket. "We only have my phone left, and it's really bad out there, and with the tree and Lewis and—" He cleared his throat. "I think we need to conserve the battery." His eyes met Marlene's, and they reflected her own sadness.

"But I think he's here, Vlado." Her voice cracked. "I just need to make sure he's safe. Please."

Lewis rose to his feet, unsteady but with a look on his face that Marlene had not seen before.

"Nora!" His voice was hoarse, the volume loud in their small circle, and Marlene glanced down to see if he'd woken Jasmine. The girl didn't move. "I have to tell you something."

"Okay."

"The man out by the factory," he said.

"Do you know him?" Nora stood so close to him that shadows flattened the lantern light around her. "You think he's Mario, don't you?"

Lewis looked down and his shoulders drooped like he was about to give up.

"Lewis! He's all I have left. Please."

When he looked up, Marlene noticed that his chin trembled. "I hope he's not your brother."

Marlene rubbed her arms.

"Why?"

"Because he died of an overdose."

Nora's jaw twitched and Marlene wanted to put her arms around the woman, do something to erase the desolation in her eyes. Nora hurried to the door, yanking on the handle with both hands. The door opened; ice splintered and fell from the frame, and snow spilled inside. Marlene stared at it in shock, trying to register the amount.

"Oh my God," Vlado said.

It came up to Nora's shoulders, a pile of wind-drifted powder. She started pawing at the snow, but it just kept spilling inside, avalanches that collected in small mountains around her boots.

Marlene stood. "Nora, you can't go out in that."

For the first time in hours, the air was clear; the storm had finally died down. From beyond the wall came the growl of heavy machinery, loud in the muffled stillness of the blizzard's aftermath. They were already trying to clear the roads. It would take hours, probably days, to rid the town of this much snow, but the sound of the machines meant the end of the storm.

Vlado hurried to her, putting his hands on her arms and gently guiding Nora inside and to a chair beside Marlene. He pulled at her gloves and cupped her hands with his own, blew warm breath over her skin like the man hoped it would take all the pain away. Marlene touched her arm.

"It might not be him," she said. Nora looked at her like she wanted desperately to believe her. Marlene wished it was true.

Everyone was quiet. There was a feeling in the air that things had shifted. The storm had subsided at last, and the hum of machinery had replaced the howl of the wind. Soon, there'd be a way out, and Marlene's hands tightened into fists at the thought. Vlado removed the cardboard from the big front window. It was still dark outside, but without the snow, the sky had depth again, with a hint of lightness weaving through it. Marlene was chilled to the bone from the cold, and her body ached from sitting but not as much as her heart, which hurt for Nora.

After such a long night, the idea of going home should have been a welcome relief, except that Marlene knew what waited for her. An empty, lonely cabin and a gun on the table.

There is more to life than me, Marly.

She wrapped her arms tight across her body. Charlie saw something in her that nobody else had noticed. And their ten years together had been the happiest she'd ever been. *You made life worth living, Charlie.*

You could paint again, Marly.

Marlene blew her nose into a tissue and ignored the voice that was her own imagination. It wasn't hard to guess what he might say to her. *My paintings are gone.*

Then paint more.

She turned from the voice, thought of the canvases she'd destroyed, the paints she threw in the trash, the brushes she'd snapped in half after he died. Charlie once said that her paintings were more a reflection of the real Marly than a portrait of someone else. That it showed her truest self, and that was the person he'd fallen in love with. But since his death, she couldn't paint and she was afraid she'd forgotten how.

They were all exhausted and freezing, and there was nothing much to do but wait for help. She studied Nora, huddled inside her big down coat, not talking, lost in her own thoughts, like Marlene, like Lewis and Vlado, who paced the space by his desk, picking up books they'd been reading and making a pile of them on Nora's desk. He seemed to not know what to do with himself, and Marlene shook her head. The poor man was lovestruck, and the object of his attention was so wound up in her own world that she would never see what was right in front of her.

Marlene made a quiet *tsk* to herself. It took one to know one, and Nora was as single focused as Marlene. But instead of caring for a mother, Nora had spent her life entrenched in her brother's addiction, and she couldn't see all that she'd given up. Her parents wouldn't have wanted that for their daughter. And she'd even guess that Mario didn't want this for his sister either. It was probably the reason he'd stayed away from her all these years. Marlene had to swallow hard because she couldn't stop seeing the little girl who needed her brother inside a grown woman who was all alone.

She put a hand on Nora's back; the contact seemed to startle her because her head shot up. "You're going to be okay, Nora."

Nora stared back at her, her eyes an opaque black. "Are you okay, Marlene?"

Marlene thought of Charlie, his easy smile, the way she'd felt in his arms. Like nothing bad could ever happen. "Well, Nora, no, I am not okay. So I guess we have that in common."

The growl of an engine and the sudden sweep of lights across the front window startled all of them. Nora shot to her feet, and Marlene and Vlado joined her at the window. Outside, there was a snowplow and another machine Marlene didn't recognize.

"That's not a snowplow," Nora said.

"No, it's a front-end loader." There was relief in Vlado's voice. "It will move a lot more snow. We should be able to get out of here in a few hours."

They watched the headlights of the plow wobble in the air, giving the front-end loader light to maneuver by. The snow rolled up and over the blade, but there was so much of it that it hardly seemed to make a dent.

"That's going to take some time," she said, and she felt the tension drain from her upper back. She wasn't ready to go home—not yet.

She settled back down into the chair, trying to get all the warmth she could from her coat. She'd almost worn Charlie's favorite winter coat—the one with the brown waterproof fabric that fell to his knees—but she'd already had on her own, and when she spied his boots, she settled on those instead. He'd been wearing them the day of the accident, and putting them on made her feel close to him, even if her feet swam inside.

Nora stayed at the window, staring out at the plows. Vlado took a flashlight and walked into the stacks. From where she sat, Marlene saw the light swing back and forth, making circles around the room until the beam caught on needles and a dark-brown branch sticking through the window. She heard Vlado whistle. A few minutes later, he returned, shining the flashlight at the front door, Nora's desk, his own desk, and down the hallway toward the bathroom.

"You look like a real security guard doing that," she said, and Vlado laughed.

"Yes, I am not cut out for this kind of work. I take it you noticed."

"Once or twice."

Nora turned from the window. "Why did you take this job, Vlado?"

Vlado swept the flashlight again, up toward the arched ceiling with the polished hand-carved trim, down to the beautifully tiled floor, the heavy wooden desks. "I needed a job and I've always loved these libraries. They were built all over the country in small towns like this through grants, each one a tiny, grand replica and built to withstand time. But now so many are gone or repurposed into something else. I guess there's just something special about this one, and I jumped at the chance to work here." He touched the small letters sewn onto a breast pocket. SECURITY. "Even if I make a poor replica of a security guard."

Marlene barked a laugh. "So you came for the library, and you've stayed for the thrill of the job? What about your degree? Don't you want to get that done so you can do—uh, well, do English PhD things?"

He turned the flashlight off, and the lantern caught the outline of his jaw. He smiled. "Teach, yes. I'd like to teach."

"Why is it taking you so long?"

"Marlene," Nora said softly but without her usual firmness Marlene had grown accustomed to.

"No, it's okay. She's right. I've dragged my feet a bit, but my parents have always worked very hard and I worry that the academic path is—"

"Self-indulgent? Frivolous? A waste of time?" It was easy for Marlene to finish his sentence because it was exactly what her mother had thought of her wanting to major in art.

"Marlene," Nora said again, but Vlado just smiled wider, nodding. "Exactly."

"Finish your degree, Vlado. I don't know your parents, but I can tell you that if you don't follow your dreams, they have a way of haunting you anyway."

A soft beeping sounded from the floor by Jasmine. Marlene leaned over where the girl lay huddled under the blanket. She had pulled her coat hood up and over her head, and the blanket covered nearly every part of her so that all Marlene could make out was the slim line of her forehead. "The beeping is coming from her," she said to Vlado. Jasmine shifted slightly, and it looked like her hand moved under the blanket. The beeping stopped.

Marlene hesitated, unsure what to do, but worry writhed in her gut and she didn't like it. Putting her hand on the floor first, Marlene knelt down and touched the girl's shoulder, jiggled her gently. "Jasmine?" The girl did not move and Marlene thought about the object in her pocket. Did she take something? Smoke something? Marlene bit her lip, angry with herself for not finding out what Jasmine had been hiding. What if she had done something stupid? After all, she'd lost her mother, moved to a town she didn't know, had a little sister she felt responsible for. She shook her shoulder, a little harder this time, and her pulse beat fast when the girl didn't stir. "Jas—"

Another beeping sounded, and the bundle of blankets moved. "Oh shit," Jasmine said and sat bolt upright, putting her hands on either side of her like she might fall over. With her hood up and her braids sticking out and her eyes squinting like she stared into a bright light, the girl looked confused and not at all herself. Her eyes finally landed on Marlene, but in them, Marlene did not see a beat of recognition. "Did you feel that?"

Nora joined Marlene. "Feel what?" she said, sounding as alarmed as Marlene felt. "Are you okay, Jasmine?"

Jasmine yanked her hood down. "I think we're sinking." She pushed up, tossing the blankets aside, and stood with her feet planted, arms held out on either side of her, balancing. "Yeah, we're definitely sinking, and we need to get the hell out of here now."

Marlene was not shocked by language, but coming from Jasmine, who up to this point had been nothing but polite and thoughtful, it sounded off, not like the girl at all. Marlene stood very still, unsure what to say or do.

"You're at the library, Jasmine." As usual, Vlado's voice was calm.

Jasmine turned to stare at him and did so for too long. Vlado shifted his weight. Then she started giggling, and the sound sent a chill down Marlene's spine because it didn't sound like the girl at all. Was she sleepwalking? "That's hilarious." She started pacing and moving her fingers in and out like she'd lost the feeling in them. "There it is again!" she yelled, and stopped moving, standing again like the floor wobbled under her and she couldn't keep her balance.

Lewis stood beside Marlene and stared at the girl. "What's going on?" he said.

Nora reached out to grasp Jasmine's shoulders. "Jasmine? Sweetheart? Are you okay?"

Jasmine wiggled out from under her hands, and Marlene noticed that the girl was shaking when she started to pace again. "'You okay?'" she mimicked Nora. "Okay, B-okay, S-okay, D-okay."

Nora looked wide eyed at Marlene. "What's wrong with her?"

Suddenly Marlene didn't want to be right, hated that she was, and wished for all the world that people would stop disappointing her. Especially this girl. Marlene wanted Jasmine to be the exception.

"I told you before, Nora, she had drugs on her. The girl is high on something."

CHAPTER TWENTY-FIVE

LEWIS

Something was wrong with the girl, and the old lady thought it was drugs. Lewis was afraid to find out the truth because he didn't want to think that Jasmine was like him. He wanted to slink out the door, wished he could take back telling the librarian about her brother. He kept sticking his hands inside his pockets, wishing he had something to help him forget, wishing he'd kept his distance instead of getting to know them.

He'd been ticking off the minutes, hiding inside his coat and waiting for the moment when he could escape the library. But now everything was going to hell in a handbasket because something was wrong with the girl, and from the way she acted, it wasn't hard to guess what. The thing that surprised him was his own reaction: his dry eyes had turned gritty with tears. He'd seen plenty of drugs in his years—overdoses, lives torn into pieces—and he'd had to shut it out because at the end of the day, the amount of suffering was too much, and to survive in the foxhole of it meant to stop seeing it.

Somehow seeing her like this was different, and he couldn't ignore it and he couldn't shut out the way it blasted open the sadness he'd buried like a corpse inside him. So he hovered behind them, shuffling from one foot to the other, feeling as useless as he'd ever felt and hating himself for it just a little bit more.

They stood around the girl, who stared back at them like they didn't understand her and couldn't see the world the way she did. Lewis understood. He'd felt that way, cocooned in the softness of a good high when the rest of the world looked miserable and dangerous. What was the girl on? Had she gotten into his stash before the librarian took it from her? Lewis moved toward Jasmine, and his back ached from the weight of his guilt.

Nora held her hands out toward the girl, left them hanging in the air, and she looked bewildered, like she'd chosen the wrong path and had just now realized how lost she was. "Oh, Jasmine, honey, did you, uh, get into what Lewis had?"

Jasmine fell back into a chair, and she rubbed at her head, squinted her eyes shut. "I just . . . it's so dark. I think I'm blind now."

She started laughing, and Nora turned, stared from Vlado to Marlene. "What do we do?" she said.

"What did you take, Jasmine?" Marlene said, and her voice was firm but nothing like the woman who, hours earlier, had torn through the girl's backpack to find the stolen book. "We just want to help you." Her words cracked and Lewis saw the old woman wipe a hand across her face.

Lewis stepped even closer. Jasmine worked her jaw like she was trying to chew a tough piece of steak. Something tickled his brain. A memory of the dancer from the strip club. Hallie. She'd come in every evening, fresh and energized, dancing as though the men's eyes and roaming hands didn't strip a thing from her. She'd had a purpose, Lewis knew. Her son. She'd told him once that stripping was just a job and the money was her son's ticket to a good life. That evening, though, she'd been different, bone tired, her normal exuberance faded to a weary smile. Her boy had gotten sick, she'd told Lewis, and she'd been up the last two nights with him, and her friend was watching him now. He was better but she hadn't had decent sleep in days. *Take the night off,* he'd said.

Sadness flickered in her eyes. *We both know that's not for people like us, right, Lewis?*

Shame warmed his cheeks. Yeah, he knew better.

But, hey, when you take your break later, would you mind grabbing me a burger from McDonald's? I missed dinner tonight, and I really need to eat.

He'd seen it when she rummaged in her purse for cash. A needle. And his heart sank. Hallie seemed like one of the good ones. He never got her that burger. An asshole had accosted one of the dancers onstage, and Lewis had to kick him out, punch him a couple of times in the parking lot. Then a fight had broken out between two of the girls, and he had to physically pull one off the other, which was tricky to do when they had so little clothing on. So by the time he saw Hallie later, it was when she was heading home. Keys dangled from her hand, and she passed him at the door, stepping out into the cool night in only her bra and a short pair of denim shorts. It wasn't her style. *Wait, Hallie, here.* He handed her the money from before. *Busy night; sorry about the food.*

She'd stared at the money, then gave him a vacant kind of smile that didn't touch her eyes. *Okay,* she said and kept walking, moving back and forth in the parking lot like she'd forgotten where she was headed. It set his alarm bells ringing, and he'd thought about the needle, hurried after her. *Can I drive you home?*

She laughed and it sent a puff of sweetened breath toward his face. The woman was drunk. *I'm not into old-ass men, Lewis. No thank you.*

He'd touched her arm. *But your son.*

She'd ripped her arm away. *Don't touch me! Don't you fucking touch me!* she'd screamed, and ran to her car. Lewis backed off, confused, annoyed, and angry. He wasn't about to get accused of something when he was only trying to help.

The memory faded but the air around Jasmine smelled just like Hallie. His pulse sped up and Lewis got down on his old knees and started rooting around on the ground until his hand touched her backpack.

"Lewis, what are you doing?" Marlene said.

Vlado was beside him. "Please stop, Lewis."

But he didn't. He pulled everything out, desperate, knowing in the excited beat of his heart that he was right and he needed to find it.

A flashlight shone in his face, but he ignored it and kept searching.

"He's looking for her drugs." It was Nora and she spoke in such a defeated way, like it was something she'd expected of him all along. He wanted to correct her, suddenly wanted her to see him differently, but he didn't have the time and he couldn't stop until he found it.

The backpack was empty and Lewis groaned, frustration scraping across his back. He was right; he knew he was right. He turned to the girl, noticed her sweatshirt with the front pouch, remembered Marlene saying something about the drugs in her pocket. He shuffled forward on his knees, ignoring the way the hard floor dug into his kneecaps, and reached out, heart pounding. It was in there. This was like Hallie; he just knew it. It had to be.

"What is he doing? Vlado!" Marlene's voice, shrill and loud.

Strong hands grabbed him at the elbows, pulled him to his feet, and dragged him backward, away from Jasmine, who had started to rock and rub at her head.

"No!" he yelled, struggling against Vlado, but he was weak and felt every bit the broken old man he was in the security guard's grip. "Check her pockets! Goddamn it, Marlene, check her pockets!"

Marlene stared at him but Lewis couldn't make out her expression in the pieces of light from the lantern.

"Please. It's just like Hallie, please!" For the first time in a long time, Lewis wanted to be heard, needed to be believed, because it wasn't about him. It was about this girl.

Marlene turned to the girl and put her hand into her sweatshirt pocket. Lewis saw the old woman's shoulders stiffen, and then she pulled a long slender object, like a marker, and a smaller rectangular electronic from Jasmine's sweatshirt. She held both into the light. "What is this?"

For a moment Lewis couldn't speak because the air had stuck like peanut butter inside his lungs. He wasn't 100 percent sure; it looked different from what Hallie had had in her purse, but it was close, medical looking in the same way. It rushed out of him. "I th-think she's diabetic. And-and I think she's in shock. We have to get her to a hospital or something. It's bad. She'll die if we don't get help."

There was a gasp from Nora, and Marlene covered her mouth with her hand.

"Oh my God," Vlado said from behind him, and he released his grip from Lewis's arms.

They all rushed toward the girl, sinking to the floor at her feet and talking at once.

"My phone is dead," Nora said. "And so is Jasmine's."

"Mine has some juice left." Vlado sounded breathy, unsure. "I'll call."

"What can we do?" Marlene whispered. "Does anyone know anything about diabetes?"

"No," Nora said, touching Jasmine's knee. "Jasmine, sweetheart, are you diabetic? We think you are in—what did you call it, Lewis?"

"Shock," he said. "That's all I know. But she needs a hospital."

Vlado started talking into the phone. "We have a young girl, and we think she has diabetes and we think she's in shock. We need help, please; we don't know what to do."

They sat around the girl, shoulder to shoulder, and Jasmine rocked, moaning once in a while but otherwise not talking.

"Yes, okay, sugar, a Coke, or orange juice?" Vlado took the phone away from his face. "Do we have that?"

Lewis fumbled around in the dark. "She had a granola bar in her bag."

Nora popped to her feet. "How about a Gatorade? I might have some left from earlier."

"Yes, they said both," Vlado said. "But she might have a hard time swallowing the granola."

Marlene took the package from Lewis, broke off a piece, and put it in Jasmine's hand. "Hey there, honey, can you eat this?" Jasmine stared at her hand, spun the granola bar in circles in the air. Marlene tried to push it toward her mouth, but Jasmine clamped her mouth shut and the bar left crumbs on her lips.

He started to pace, trying to remember the voice he'd used for Heather when she was a girl and he needed to reprimand her. "Jasmine!" Firm and fatherly, but it had been so long since anyone had needed him to be in charge that it came out dry and unkind. "You need to eat that now!"

She crossed her arms, smiled at him, and shook her head.

"Yes," Vlado said into the phone. "She has something like that—okay. They said to check the screen on the electronic. It's called a glucose monitor. They need to know what it says."

Marlene picked it up, shone a light on it. "It says forty-five."

Vlado repeated it and his eyes widened. "That is very bad, okay, okay. Lewis, did you see tablets in her backpack? They say glucose tablets."

Lewis went through the bag again, found a short plastic cylinder. "This?"

Vlado took it, opened it. "There are two inside, okay. Nora, have you found the Gatorade?" There was a quickness to his words, an undertone of panic that didn't fit the man who seemed cool as a cucumber.

"Here!" Nora gave Marlene a half bottle of Gatorade. "Try this!"

Marlene uncapped it and held it to the girl's lips. "Here you go, sweet girl," she said. "I made you something special."

"But it's sinking. We have to find the leak."

Marlene nodded, smiled. "Oh yes, I know. But you have to drink this, or we can't find the leak. Can you do that?"

Jasmine looked at Marlene and something softened in her eyes. Her lips parted the smallest bit, and Marlene gently and expertly tilted the bottle forward, allowing just a little bit at a time to slide into the girl's mouth. At first it seemed to be working, but then Jasmine's eyes widened and she started choking and spit all the liquid out.

The air was sucked out of the room, and Lewis moaned. Marlene made an animallike sound.

"She's not eating or drinking," Vlado said into the phone.

"They have to come right now—you tell them, Vlado!" Marlene said. "I don't care how much snow is out there, you tell them to come right now."

"Yes, right now, or we will bring her to them," Lewis added.

Vlado nodded. "Okay, yes, we can do that, yes, good. I think you should try that. We are very worried." He let the phone fall from his ear. "Paramedics are on their way. They are going to try and snowshoe in. We need to clear a path."

Nora stood. "Okay, let's go. Marlene, you stay with Jasmine, see if you can get her to drink any of that or take those tablets. The rest of us will start shoveling." Her eyes blazed in the dim glow. "Lewis, you—" She threw her arms around him, squeezed so hard he thought his bones might break. "You are a guardian angel."

She and Vlado were out the door and Lewis put his wet socks and shoes back on before following them, his chest hurting and his goddamn eyes stinging.

CHAPTER
TWENTY-SIX

Nora

The three of them stood at the door, trying to make a path to get past the piles of snow windblown against the entrance so they could work on the walkway. There was more snow than Nora had ever seen fall at once, and it made her frantic, desperately clawing at the cold powder with her hands. Her cotton gloves had already soaked through, but she didn't care; none of them seemed to care how cold or how wet they were. They had only two shovels, so Nora ran to her desk to get a wooden clipboard, which they used as a makeshift shovel. Eventually they worked their way outside, the three of them a quiet team, listening to Marlene cajoling Jasmine into drinking the Gatorade against the soft scrape of the shovels on snow. Marlene had tried to get her to swallow a tablet, but the girl clamped her lips shut and refused to take it. She had been able to get her to take a few sips of Gatorade that stayed down, and it was a weak ray of hope in the dark hours of early morning.

The front-end loader had cleared a tunnel down half of Main Street but not all the way to the library. What if the paramedics couldn't make it in time? She thought of Jasmine taking a book because she had wanted to help her little sister when her mother could not. Nora bit her lip so hard she tasted blood and dug deeper and faster at the snow until her arm muscles screamed and her spine ached and she sweated under her layers.

She felt a hand on her shoulder, and her head popped up from where she'd been trained on the path ahead. Vlado. "They're here."

Circles of light bobbed in the distance, past the plowed portion where Nora could just make out three figures trudging toward them on top of the snow. The sky had begun to lighten, and with shock, Nora realized it must be close to dawn. She waved her arms in their direction. "Here, please hurry! She's here!" Vlado put an arm around her, squeezed, and she didn't shake him off or move away.

It took fifteen or more excruciating minutes for the paramedics to make their way to the library. Lewis and Vlado kept shoveling, and Nora checked on Jasmine, who had lain back down on her blankets. Her heart raced. It couldn't be good for her to go to sleep. Nora found it hard to breathe thinking that they might not be able to get the girl help in time. She felt powerless, like she did so much of the time. She might have lost her brother, but damn it, she would not lose Jasmine.

Marlene sat on the floor next to the girl, talking quietly to her. "They'll be here soon, Jasmine, okay? Then you can tell them all about what a mean, cranky old woman I am."

Nora shoveled harder, working with every bit of strength she had. "They're coming," she called.

"I'm not sure if she's conscious," Marlene croaked and stared down at Jasmine, stroking her tightly woven braids in a protective, maternal gesture. "And I haven't been able to get her to drink anything more, and she hasn't spoken for a while now." Nora went back inside, saw tears on Marlene's face. She fell to her knees beside them and reached for Marlene's hand. "Jasmine?" Marlene said. "Can you wake up, sweetheart? We have people coming who can help you."

Voices and bobbing lights from outside, and then two men and a woman were inside the library with full backpacks and a stretcher, quickly shedding their snowshoes at the door. Vlado and Lewis stood behind them, identical expressions of relief and worry pulling their eyebrows together, and Nora didn't know if the library had ever felt so crowded or if she'd ever been so scared.

The paramedics knelt around Jasmine. Snow had gathered in clumps all over the foyer floor, and Nora's nose ran freely. She wiped it with her coat sleeve, not wanting to take her eyes off Jasmine for even a second. The woman paramedic gently searched around the girl's neck and pulled a necklace with a silver dog tag from under her sweatshirt. Nora noticed a red symbol on the front and remembered her uncle wearing something similar for his pacemaker.

"Type 1 diabetes," the woman said.

They worked quickly, talking to each other, pricking Jasmine's finger, and checking an electronic device, eventually giving her a shot in her stomach. Marlene had moved back to let them work, and the four of them stood side by side, wordless, watching and standing so close their shoulders touched. Nora was pulled back to that morning when she was nine, standing in the cold grass outside her home, watching her brother die and her last words to him tattooed on her heart. *Leave.* She'd spent her entire life trying to make up for that one word, but she never could and now she'd lost him forever.

Her body stiffened. All this time, she'd thought she could save him, but she couldn't. These last few years, Mario had lived largely in her own memory as the boy who wanted to get better. But the truth was that she hadn't known Mario. Not as he was. Anger fluttered against her heart and it surprised her. If Mario was gone, where did that leave her? Alone, like Lewis? Bitter, like Marlene? She pressed a hand to her chest. Where did she go from here?

There was an urgency in the paramedics' voices that pulled her back, and she focused on the girl. "Come on, Jasmine," she whispered, her pulse hammering in her neck. This girl could not die. Not now, not when she hadn't lived the life she deserved. Her hands ached from squeezing them into fists. "Come on, Jasmine," she said again, louder this time.

The sky outside had turned a soft gray, the sun rising behind a thick blanket of clouds, and the light inside the library shifted to a blue with punctures of gold from the lanterns and headlamps. Nora saw Jasmine's eyes move under her lids, and she breathed out.

The woman paramedic turned to Nora and the others. "She should be fine, but we'll take her in as a precaution. There's a number on her medical tag for an Evelyn."

"That's her grandmother," Nora said, and she felt her body slump against Lewis, who leaned back into her.

"Good, we'll call her and let her know all the details."

They loaded Jasmine onto the stretcher, and while they were fixing the snowshoes onto their boots, Jasmine's eyes fluttered open. She stared at the ceiling for a second before twisting her head and looking up at the four of them huddled over top of her. "Hi," she said. "You guys look terrible."

Together they laughed, a relieved but weak whoosh of air, and Jasmine smiled, then closed her eyes, her face slack from what looked to be sheer exhaustion. Lewis threw his thin arms around Nora. It was such a shocking gesture she almost couldn't hug him back. But she did, laughing into his coat, and then she was hugging Marlene and then Vlado, who smelled like snow and pine bark and held her longer than the others.

She went outside, arms crossed against the bitter cold, and watched the paramedics' labored process across the alien landscape of town, staying above the snow, the gurney wobbling awkwardly back and forth until eventually they reached the ambulance, parked with lights flashing on the small tunnel of road that had been plowed.

When the ambulance lights disappeared from view, Nora returned to the library, feeling her bones heavy in her body, and she sank into one of the chairs, head in her hands. The storm was over.

Someone laid a blanket across her shoulders. Marlene. She squeezed Nora's shoulders, and in the thin light of dawn, her eyes looked wet. She squeezed again and looked like she might say something; instead, she nodded and joined Lewis on the floor, who was picking up the scattered items from Jasmine's backpack and returning them to the bag. Marlene slid a book inside, the one the girl had taken, and if Nora hadn't felt drained emotionally and physically, it would have made her smile to think of Marlene as an accomplice.

Nora pulled the blanket tight around her and squeezed her eyes shut. Marlene had lost the love of her life. Vlado, his home country. Lewis had lost everything. Jasmine had almost died. Mario may have died.

But Nora wasn't alone.

CHAPTER
TWENTY-SEVEN

MARLENE

Nora fell asleep almost immediately, with her head leaning back, neck cocked at an odd angle. Marlene winced, thinking about the stiffness that would surely plague her tomorrow. She picked up the blankets from where Jasmine had been just a few minutes earlier and laid one across Nora's lap, another over her shoulders and chest. Nora slept without stirring, but her eyebrows met, making wrinkles in her forehead and a slight frown. Worrying even in her sleep. Marlene touched Nora's hair, smoothed a piece down.

Thinking about Jasmine took all the remaining strength from her legs, and Marlene sank into a chair, hand to her chest. When they'd been out shoveling, she'd tried everything she could think of to get the girl to eat or drink even a little bit, but nothing had worked. Then Jasmine had struggled to talk and had lain down, closing her eyes, and Marlene had wanted to shake her, scream at her, anything to keep the girl from falling asleep. By the time the paramedics had arrived, Marlene was convinced that the girl was beyond help. The idea that someone as bright and warm and lovely and *young* as Jasmine could be gone in an instant, like Charlie, had paralyzed her. If the gun had been in front of her right then, Marlene thought that maybe she would have pulled the trigger this time.

"You're not such a bad person, you know."

Marlene turned her head, startled. Lewis had faded yet again into the background, and she'd forgotten he was still there.

"You're like an old shipwreck, and all your nice is covered in barnacles."

"An old shipwreck, huh?" She tapped her finger on her leg, thinking. "And you're an abandoned mine. Mostly useless, except for a hidden vein of gold."

Lewis slapped his knee and smiled. The sky outside had begun to lighten into a whitish gray, and the light made him real again, turned him back into a pumpkin. His smile was shocking: a missing tooth; the enamel more yellow than white; his skin an unhealthy pallor, dry and worn. Marlene tried not to stare and blinked against a burning in her eyes. In the glare of a new day, he was the man she would have dismissed—a vagrant, a bum, a drug addict. Seeing him for what he was against the backdrop of who he'd been in the dark and during the storm was disorienting. This man with the gray-toned skin, missing teeth, dirty beard, and unkempt hair had saved Jasmine's life.

Marlene said nothing, but it was as if she'd shouted her thoughts at him, because his expression hardened, the warmth leached from his eyes, and he sucked his bottom lip over his top, pulled his collar up around his face.

She wanted to say something to bring back their unexpected camaraderie from the night, but her tongue wouldn't move, and she retreated into herself as well. With the damaged roof in the stacks and the electricity out all night, there wasn't even an echo of heat inside the old building. Marlene shivered inside her coat, wished she could feel her toes. The scrape of Vlado's shovel was loud, and for the first time since the storm had started, Marlene wanted to go home.

An engine sputtered outside, growing loud, then going silent, followed by voices—Vlado and another man. Then the front door opened and her neighbor, Jonah, stood in the doorway, cheeks ruddy, beard covered in frost, and a relieved slant to his eyes. "Marlene! Thank God you're okay."

Marlene stood, surprised at the emotion in his voice. Jonah and his wife, Celia, lived in the next cabin over, about two miles as the crow flies. This past year, Jonah had picked up a second job to support his young family and Celia worked a nighttime shift at a hospital. They were barely holding on, and Charlie had made it his mission to reach out to them, help them in whatever way they'd needed, which had led to Charlie offering to babysit their four- and six-year-olds on occasion. A thing they knew absolutely nothing about, but soon there were smudged fingerprints on windows and juice boxes in the refrigerator. It was their house that Charlie had gone to decorate at Christmas because that's what neighbors do. Marlene had tried to argue with him, saying that some neighbors who were old as the hills weren't meant for scaling ladders in the middle of an icy winter day. And besides, how did he know it was something they even wanted? He'd tilted his head then, and his smile had a hint of loss to it. *If I'd had little kids, I'd want to put lights up for them. All kids love twinkly lights.*

So he'd left, boxes of twinkly lights in the bed of his truck, plus a plastic Santa he'd found on sale, and well, that was that.

"We were so worried," Jonah said.

His concern ruffled Marlene, who felt like a doddering old woman they assumed had wandered off into a storm. She sniffed. "I've been here all night, Jonah, safe and sound." Did she sound too stiff? She hadn't seen Jonah or Celia or the kids since the funeral. She hadn't avoided them—not really, or not intentionally, anyway—but it hurt to be reminded of Charlie driving away with the Santa in his truck.

Remember how the kids called you Marlybean? They adored you.

She shook him off. Imaginary Charlie was wrong. They had adored *him*. "Thanks for checking on me, but you can tell Celia I'm not dead." She cast a glance out the window to Vlado shoveling around the cars. He'd barely made a dent. "Vlado there will get my car shoveled out soon."

Jonah shuffled his snow-covered boots. "The roads up to the cabins are impassable, Marlene, and they will be for the next couple days at least. I've got the snowmobile and I'd be happy to take you home, if you'd like," he said. "The electricity's out everywhere, but at least your cabin has the woodburning stove. You'll be much warmer."

She turned to look at Lewis, but he had returned to his shell, a lump of black wool with legs, and Nora was fast asleep. Marlene wrapped her arms across her chest. The thought of leaving felt strange, like the end of something she knew would be gone forever, and it gave her a start to realize she didn't want it to end. They'd all shared something, been through something together, and for a moment she thought the experience had changed her. But without the insulating dark, the light felt garish and dismal, shattering the illusion that their conversations had been anything more than a way to pass the time.

Why would she stay?

She slipped into Charlie's boots, zipped up her coat, and adjusted her thick hat with the flaps over her head. "Bye, then, Lewis." The lump shifted. "You're a good man—not perfect, but nobody is. I hope . . . well, I hope you get to see your Persie." There was no answer. She turned to Jonah. "No wheelies or racing. I'm old and my hands are too frozen to hold on."

Jonah smiled and opened the door, held his hand out for her to go first. "Cross my heart."

CHAPTER
TWENTY-EIGHT

LEWIS

When the door closed on Marlene, Lewis stirred, pulling his coat from around his face and breathing in cold air that stung his nose. It was so chilly he could see his breath, and quiet, apart from the plows outside and Vlado's shovel. After the night spent with everyone, an unfamiliar feeling surrounded Lewis. When they spoke to him, they had looked him in the eyes. They asked him questions and listened when he answered. He'd felt human. Not a statistic or a nuisance or a problem. Just another human.

And then the girl had gotten ill, and Lewis's hands turned clammy when he thought about her. It had been so close. He covered his eyes with his sleeve and tried to make the girl's slack face, her expressionless eyes, disappear. *She's okay*, he reminded himself. *Jasmine is okay.*

Earlier that morning, after the girl had been taken away by the paramedics, there had been an awkward moment when the four of them stood grouped together in a silence that only minutes before had been comfortable. But with the end of the storm and the beginning of a new day, the ease that had grown overnight had thinned. Broken whatever spell had made him think he had anything in common with these people.

Lewis had helped Marlene put Jasmine's scattered stuff back into her bag, and when it was done Marlene sat in a chair, and they'd had a few words, until the sky brightened and Marlene saw him for what he'd been all along. Suddenly, Lewis had become aware of his own stink. The onion smell that crept out in puffs from his coat, the dirt stuck in the creases of his palms. This wasn't summer camp. Nobody here was his friend and he didn't belong in this world, he told himself. He'd cowered inside his coat, pushed his hands into his pockets, wanting to find something to help him forget, but his pockets were empty.

He waited until Marlene left, and then he stirred, moving his limbs one by one, wiggling his feet. After the paramedics had left, drill sergeant Marlene had ordered him out of his wet socks and shoes. Said after everything, why go and lose his toes now? He stared at the duct tape–knitted socks that Nora had made for him and felt a sting in his eyes. She had a good heart, that woman, and hadn't deserved anything that had happened to her. She was strong, though—like Phyllis, like Heather, like Persie. He wondered if she knew how strong she was.

He gritted his teeth when he pulled his smelly socks back on. They were shockingly cold, a bite of reality against his skin, and he quickly tied up his shoes and stood. He looked around the library; it seemed different to him now. Bleak in the white light of morning, but he didn't want to leave. The thought felt like a jab to the jaw, painful and quick, and there was nothing he could do about it. He searched her desk, finding a pen and note card, then left the knitted bandages and note card beside Nora, and with one last glance around, he left.

Outside, Vlado was still shoveling, and from the looks of it, he'd be at it all day. It was brutally cold and Lewis pulled his collar up against the breeze and began to pick his way through the half-shoveled path. Vlado looked up from his work, eyebrows raised. "Are you leaving?"

Lewis didn't answer. He owed them nothing, and pretending like he did or that they actually cared only made things worse.

"Lewis, wait!"

Lewis kept on walking and had made it down the block before he heard footsteps crunching in the snow behind him.

"Where are you going?" Vlado had run to catch up with him, breathing fast.

Lewis shook his head and couldn't help but marvel at the young man's endurance. He'd only trudged half a block and felt winded and tired by the heavy snow. "I have to go."

"Okay, but wait—here."

Lewis turned, peered up at Vlado.

Vlado took something from his pocket, held it out, and when he saw it, his gut spewed acid. Yesterday, he would have grabbed it out of his hand and run. Today, and after everything that had happened during the night, it felt . . . wrong.

"I don't want your goddamn money," he growled.

Vlado shrugged, smiled. "Then it's a loan."

Lewis wrinkled his forehead. "For what?"

"Use it for a bus ticket, a cab; I don't care, but use it to get to one of these places." He handed Lewis a piece of paper with neat print in blue ink.

"What is that?"

"Rehab places. Most of them are free—with strings attached, of course. You just have to call."

Lewis's chin started to tremble and he covered it with his fist, kept his eyes on Vlado's open palm, the money, and the card. "I told you I already tried rehab. It doesn't work for me." He tried to walk away, but his legs wouldn't move. Why did Vlado care one way or another about a crusty old man like him? And why did the man's offer feel like a punch to the kidneys?

Vlado pulled a book from his pocket, slid the money and note card inside, and held it out.

Lewis swallowed hard. It was a much smaller book than he'd shown Lewis before; this one was a paperback with PROPERTY OF SILVER RIDGE LIBRARY taped to the spine. But the cover looked similar. Of a woman with flowing red hair, holding a flaming torch. Persephone.

"The seasons die, but then they come back to life again." When Vlado spoke, the air puffed in warm clouds from his mouth. "There is no reason you cannot too." He tucked the book between Lewis's arm and side, squeezed his shoulder. "You are the reason Jasmine is alive."

Lewis stared at the ground, shivering in his coat, and listened to Vlado's feet crunch across the snow when he left. If he could, he'd run away as fast as his body would let him, drop the book into the trash, keep the cash and use it to get high. That would take this suffocating feeling away. He moved his fingers, felt the cold saturate his skin and stiffen his joints, and wondered if it would ever be enough.

CHAPTER TWENTY-NINE

NORA

She must have fallen asleep at some point, because when she woke up, a dull light filled the library and her feet were numb. She sat up, tossing the blanket aside, her neck stiff, nose dripping. Her leg jiggled up and down. After so much time spent with everyone—and with Mario probably dead—Nora felt empty inside. The night was over, and she was alone.

"Hello?" She hurried into the stacks. The damage from the tree was bad—a hole in the roof and a soaked carpet—but they had been able to move most of the books, and any that had gotten wet had been laid out to dry. But the room was empty. She touched her chest. Where was everybody? Their sudden absence left her unsettled, like she'd missed the end of a story or forgotten something important. In the foyer, she had picked up the chairs and begun to move them when she noticed the knitted remnants of her duct tape socks on the floor. Her hasty bandages looked much worse in the light. A note card lay on top, along with Lewis's library card: *It's not your fault. Your brother knew that. You're strong. Remember that.*

Her vision blurred and she pressed a hand to her eyes. It meant something coming from Lewis. A truth she knew but couldn't see until now. She was never going to change Mario.

The front door opened and Vlado entered, knocking snow from his shoes and coat. His cheeks and nose were red, making it look like he'd been out in the cold for quite some time. When he saw her, he gave her a tender smile, a recognition of what the night had brought, and a wave of calm washed over her.

"You're awake."

"Where is everybody?"

Vlado took his hat off, and his dark hair stuck out from the static electricity. "Lewis left about an hour ago."

Nora felt a pang. "But where? How could he get anywhere? The roads are still a mess and it's cold out, and he should probably go to the hospital for his feet . . ." She ran out of steam and more words wouldn't come. Lewis was always going to leave. She'd known that from the very beginning, so why did it surprise her now?

"The Methodist shelter is open for the day because of the storm, and it's not too far a walk." Vlado still stood at the door, hat in hand, boots wet and dripping on the mat, like it was her house suddenly and he didn't belong.

She didn't like it and felt uncomfortable, like she'd dreamed everything and nobody remembered but her. She crossed her arms. "What about Marlene?" There was no way the woman could make it up to her house. "Surely those roads are impassable."

"Her neighbor has a snowmobile. Apparently he'd been looking for her this morning, very worried that something happened to her. He came into town and saw part of her car through the snow, offered to give her a ride home."

"So she just left?" Nora's eyes burned.

Vlado seemed to choose his words carefully. "Yes, but she left this for you." He handed her the Mexico travel book along with a piece of paper.

It was from Marlene, and typical of her style, it was short and to the point: *I can't go to Mexico without Charlie. You go. Charlie would have wanted that. Don't be like me or Lewis. Start living before it's too late. —Marlene*

Nora's body trembled. Her chest hurt. The night had taken too much from her, and she wasn't herself. She was exhausted and numb and already making a list of phone numbers in her head to call about Mario. She needed to find out if Lewis was right. "Well, I'd better start shoveling my car out." She pulled on her wet gloves, and goose bumps spread up her arms.

"I've already done that. And your car should be warmed by now too."

She smiled. "Taking keys again. Marlene would not be surprised."

He laughed. "I have a problem, I guess." He glanced out the window. "The roads are passable-ish through town. Where do you live?"

"On the east side, off the emergency routes, so they usually get cleared pretty quickly."

"Good. I'll stick around here and do what I can to patch up around the window until we can get someone out here on Monday. I can't get home just yet, but you should go."

She hesitated. She should stay and help, but her legs were heavy, her mind muddled by how quickly it had all ended. "Um, thank you, Vlado, for that and for, well, you know, everything."

He seemed to want to say something, standing in the door, blocking her exit, but then he stepped to the side with a formal bow of his head. "Drive safe, Nora, and uh, when you start calling around about your brother, I'd like to help." He handed her a slip of paper with his phone number.

For a moment she couldn't move. Friends had offered in the past, like Amanda, but she had quickly learned that when he didn't get better, they stopped wanting to help, couldn't understand why she kept trying for someone who never changed. Maybe it was exhaustion or the storm or the hours spent together, but Nora felt the sincerity in his offer, the kindness in his voice, and instead of saying no, like she'd learned to do, she took the slip, slid it into her pocket, and said, "Thanks, Vlado."

Outside, the snow crunched underfoot and the air stung her ears. Her teeth chattered. The town was a fairy tale of crystal and white, sparkling even in the overcast light. Her car stood out like a sore thumb, blue metal harsh against all the powder, but it was nearly free of snow. She noticed that Vlado's car was still buried beside hers, and her cheeks warmed. It must have taken him hours to do this for her. She slid inside; it was warm, so warm she shivered from the heat, only realizing now how absolutely frozen she'd been for most of the night. Her hands gripped the wheel, and she let her forehead drop to the curved plastic, overcome thinking about Jasmine, and Mario, and all that she'd discovered over the last few hours. Had he overdosed? Or was he still out there somewhere?

In some ways, she was exactly where she'd been before the storm, worrying and unsure about her brother; in other ways, she felt different. She thought of Lewis's note: *It's not your fault.*

He was right; it wasn't her fault. Not the accident or his drug use—on some level she'd always known that. *You're strong.* Was she?

She backed the car out, the wheels climbing over a hard-packed mound of snow to the road. Part of her wanted to drive out to the factory or check the shelters, wanted to do what she would have done before the storm, wanted to hold on to the idea that he was here in Silver Ridge, alive and needing her help.

Instead, she drove home, her eyes bleary and dry, and after she stumbled through the door, she took a hot shower first, then climbed into bed and went to sleep.

~

Sunlight streamed in through her windows, magnified by the whiteness of the snow and blinding her briefly when she opened her eyes. Through the window, the sky was a deep, smooth blue. She turned on her side, tried to close her eyes again, but it was too bright and the events from the night before whirled around her. Jasmine. Her heart raced and she immediately reached for her phone.

There were several messages. A text from Vlado, late last night. Jasmine is doing well and has already left the hospital. Thought you'd want to know.

She sagged into the headboard. Jasmine was okay. She checked her voice mail and noticed one from the night of the storm. A number she didn't recognize, and pressure built in her chest. Was it from Mario? She pressed "Play."

Nora, hi, this is Evelyn, Jasmine's grandmother. She sent me your number, and I'm so worried about her. Can you call me back or have Jasmine call? She's got type 1 diabetes, and she doesn't like to tell people because she thinks it makes her different, but you need to know because she might need your help. Anyway, can you call me, Nora? I would just love to hear her voice and make sure she's okay. Thank you.

She flung the phone onto the bed and tossed the covers to the side. If she hadn't run her battery down listening to the podcast, hoping to get answers about her brother, she would have known what Jasmine needed much sooner. She could have helped Jasmine, spared her the trauma in the first place. She started to pace the bedroom, a tingling frustration creeping through her leg muscles. If not for Lewis, Jasmine might have died. The full force of her own choices hit her hard.

She wasn't an addict, but she had allowed drugs to define her life as though she were.

Her doorbell rang and she jumped. Nobody ever stopped by. She slipped into sweatpants, pulled her tangled hair into a ponytail, and hurried to the door.

Vlado's tall frame blocked the sunlight. He balanced two paper cups in one hand and a brown bag in the other. "Doughnuts and coffee," he said, smiling.

Between Evelyn's message, Vlado's unexpected visit, and the lingering flares of anger in her chest, Nora struggled to get her bearings. "What are you doing here?"

"I left a voice mail." Vlado's forehead wrinkled. "Which you obviously haven't heard. Sorry, but I figured you'd want to start calling around about Mario right away, and so here I am."

"Oh." She stared up at him, stunned at his kindness, thought about his offer to help from the day before. "You were serious yesterday. You'd really do this for me?"

His face softened. "Of course. He's family and he's important to you. I understand that more than you may know. Oh—"

He set the coffee cups on her welcome mat, and she bit her cheek. She should have invited him in by now, but something held her back.

From his pocket, he pulled a small yellow pad. "I called the police yesterday after everyone left to check on the man who overdosed. I spoke with an Officer Santino. No news yet, but I gave them your number to call with anything, if that's okay. Also, the library will be closed until the repairs are done, so I thought we could go into Denver, maybe tomorrow? The roads should be clear enough by then, but I can drive us." When she didn't react, he shifted his weight and looked unsure of himself. "I should have asked first. I'm sorry, Nora; I just want to help."

It wasn't Vlado—or maybe it was, and his kindness was the last drop of water that broke the dam inside her. Her hands were fists, her heart an angry mass that pressed against her ribs. "I missed a call from Evelyn about Jasmine." She spoke between her teeth. "Because I was more worried about Mario."

Vlado reached out as though he wanted to touch or hug her, but she didn't move and his arms fell to his sides. "It wasn't your fault." His voice was steady and calm, like him.

"It was. My whole life has been about Mario, and I've let so many people down because of it." Her voice caught. "Like Jasmine. And this homeless man who overdosed, it might be Mario, it might not." She thought about the podcast and how he'd been sober but never called her. It stung, it hurt, and she knew she was supposed to love him and support him. She knew that his addiction wasn't his fault. She knew he was hurting and in pain. But the night at the library had shifted how she saw herself, and she didn't like it.

"Nora—"

Tears clouded her vision, but she didn't care. Her insides had twisted into knots. "I don't really think the guy by the factory is Mario, Vlado." She scratched at her arms, didn't want to say the other thing that was in her heart. "But it hurts so damn much to know he's alive and sober and doesn't care enough to tell me. Sometimes I think it would be easier if he were dead." It was out, and she couldn't take it back, and she didn't feel better and she hated herself for even thinking it. Vlado touched her arm, and she flinched. "I'm sorry, Vlado, I just can't. Not now." She tried to smile up at him, but her mouth wouldn't move. "Thank you for trying."

She closed the door and returned to her bed, pulling the covers up to block out the sunlight and letting her tears wet the pillow.

CHAPTER THIRTY

MARLENE

Marlene sat at her kitchen table with the barrel of the gun resting on her tongue. The metal was cold, and the taste of iron made her mouth water in a very unpleasant way. The Charlie in her head would not shut up.

Oh, come on, Marly, you can't be serious. You've never been one for histrionics.

Yesterday, after bringing her home, Jonah had loaded her fireplace with wood and set a teapot on top. *Thought you might like some tea later. This has to be better than the library, huh?* He'd pulled his winter hat from his head, held it between his hands like he'd just remembered his manners. Like Marlene cared anymore about something that now seemed so small. She'd wanted to laugh, but back in the cabin, with reminders of what she'd lost all around her, there wasn't space inside her for something that light, so she'd just stared back at him. *Celia snowshoed over this morning and when you weren't here . . . well, uh*—his gaze had drifted to the kitchen table—*we were so worried that something had happened . . .* Jonah had stopped talking, and Marlene noticed that his eyes were shiny. She had stiffened. The man was not going to start blubbering in her living room. She couldn't take it. He breathed in and seemed to regroup, and Marlene had relaxed. *I left a cooler on your porch. Celia loaded it with some food, a few meals—nothing big, just leftovers, but good. You can heat them up with the gas on the stove. I left some matches, just in case.*

Jonah had rocked back and forth on his heels, and if Marlene were a more sensitive kind of woman, she would have said something to put him at ease. She knew how highly he and Celia had thought of Charlie and that his death had been hard on more people than just her. Charlie had been that kind of person. She held no bitterness for the young man and his family, none at all. She just didn't have space inside her for others. So she had tried to make her face softer. *Thank you, Jonah.* She gestured toward the kitchen table. *Had to scare off a cougar the other night.* Jonah breathed out, nodded. They all understood wildlife. *I'll be just fine.*

He'd seemed relieved, and with a promise to check in on her the next day, he left.

This morning she'd stood in the middle of her living room, feeling unsure what to do with herself. Charlie had replaced the old windows—the thin single-pane ones that let the air flow right on through—with newer energy-efficient double-paned ones. The cabin warmed quickly, toasted by the burning pine that crackled in the old stove fireplace, yet she felt cold and empty and wished the night at the library hadn't ended quite so soon. With an entire day stretching ahead of her, she didn't know what to do with herself. She could settle onto the couch, the soft one that Charlie had bought for her last year when she'd mentioned that the bed felt hard as nails at night when her joints were screaming in pain. *Try the couch when it gets bad,* he'd told her. So she had and it had helped.

She could curl up on the sofa with her tea and a *Reader's Digest* and read about the new list of top-ten foods that may or may not give her cancer. Or she could go back to bed, try to nap for a few hours under the thick down comforter Charlie had brought home one frigid winter evening to replace the old thin quilt she'd had for decades. *No sense freezing our tushes off for history's sake.* She'd smiled to herself. Before Charlie, she hadn't thought much about comfort. She'd spent so much of her life caring for her father, then her mother, and then just herself that the idea of doing something just because or for comfort didn't register. Her life was order and predictability, and she didn't think it would ever be much more than that.

Before Charlie, she'd kept to herself, watched her news programs, read her magazines, and figured life was as good as it would ever get. And she was okay with that. She didn't understand this generation of young people who thought life was supposed to be easy. The ones who complained about Wi-Fi and social media and had the attention span of a gnat.

Oh, Marly, stop acting like an old woman.

"I am an old woman," she argued to the empty room.

You don't have to act like one. Start living.

The light in the cabin was the thin kind of white that comes after a storm. The kind that had nothing left to promise. Her feet wouldn't move, and her eyes kept trailing to the kitchen and the table and the gun on the table that called her name. So she'd moved like a puppet with its strings controlled by someone else and slid into one of the dining chairs. It was colder in the kitchen, away from the fire, and her legs protested, light pain tickling her thighs.

She rubbed her fists up and down the length of them and thought about Jasmine. Was she alone at the hospital or had her grandmother been able to get there? She couldn't bear the thought of the girl alone; then again, if anyone could make friends with the staff, it was Jasmine. Not surprisingly, Marlene hadn't made friends with the nurses. She didn't need to. They'd been there to do a job, and she'd been there to watch her husband die.

Now here she was, sitting at her kitchen table in the last minutes of her life, *Reader's Digest* open to "Seven Warning Signs You Might Be Depressed," gun in her mouth, her free hand tapping the tabletop with her fingers. Her finger brushed the trigger, and it sent goose bumps prickling her skin, and the metal touching her tongue became too much and she started to gag. She took the gun out, laid it on the table, and let her head rest on the smooth wood surface. Who was she kidding? If she'd wanted to kill herself, she would have already done it.

Oh, Marly.

"Shut up," she told the empty kitchen, and picked up the magazine and hurled it across the room. It landed in a heap by the closet door in the hallway, the one Charlie opened his first time here and discovered her paintings. She pushed herself up from the table; her knees popped. The day she'd come home from the hospital, she destroyed every single painting, throwing them outside and slashing each one open with a kitchen knife. Except for one. That one she'd put back in the closet. The door hinges creaked open, and light from the kitchen spilled into the dark and dusty interior. The painting lay behind a mop bucket, against the wall and beside a handful of blank canvases and an old set of paints.

It was light in her hands, longer than it was tall. Maybe not her best work, the edges roughed out, but the subject was what she'd been focused on: Charlie. Except Charlie had insisted that the real subject had been herself. She studied her image in the paint, and maybe it was lack of sleep or the cold that lingered in her bones or the night spent with four strangers, but right then she saw what Charlie had seen. In the painting, she was leaning against the diner counter with a lazy smile on her face, relaxed, comfortable, content—a glimmer of the young girl she'd once been who'd loved to paint. A girl who had dreams. She thought of Nora and Jasmine, how they cared for others over themselves, echoes of herself. And Lewis, who was too afraid to care for anyone, least of all himself. Even Vlado, who let guilt and expectation keep him from getting a degree he loved. They'd all had something in common, and their night together suddenly took on a significance she hadn't expected.

Weak sunlight poked through the clouds, sifting into the cabin like delicate strokes of watercolor. The gun looked garish, ugly, and cold in the light. She felt a chill. What had she been thinking? She leaned into the closet and reached for a blank canvas, an old easel, and the paints, brushed a cobweb from her hair, and returned to the table.

I knew you had it in you, Marly.

Suddenly she had an idea, and it was so out of character and also exactly right that she laughed out loud and picked up her phone to make a call.

And then she started to paint.

She heard his laughter in the whine of the teakettle, the pop of the fire, the creak of the old wood floors, and in the saltiness of tears that ran unchecked down her face.

CHAPTER THIRTY-ONE

LEWIS

With the snow and freezing temperatures, the Methodist shelter had stayed open for another day. Lewis had been given a pillow and a blanket, and he'd walked quickly to a corner of the small fellowship hall and huddled against the wall. This was familiar, this was the life he had chosen, but his thoughts kept flipping back to the library, and it made Lewis feel the canyon between what he could have been and what he'd become, and he didn't like it one goddamn bit.

He tried to drown out the noise of the men's voices around him. The book pressed against his side, hidden away under his layers. It both scared him and unburied a tiny seed of hope. Part of him wanted to blast it out of him, obliterate it beyond recognition, because hope was useless and it only ever did more harm than good. But then he thought of Persie with her bright smile, doing well in school, working at a job, loved and cared for by her mother. The sharp edge of the book poked into his stomach, and he thought for just a brief moment that maybe, just maybe, he could do the right thing.

He'd helped Jasmine, hadn't he? That was a good thing and Lewis couldn't remember the last time he'd done a good thing. He thought of the relief he'd felt when Jasmine opened her eyes and he knew she'd be okay. It had almost brought him to his knees. He thought of Nora wasting her life living for someone else. Had Heather done the same? He thought of Marlene and her Charlie, Vlado and his degree. They'd all lost something, but only Lewis had lost everything because of it. The floor bit into his side and his feet ached. Marlene had said he wasn't invisible. Jasmine had said Persie knew he had come to Silver Ridge. Vlado had given him enough for a bus ticket.

His thoughts went all the way back to the beginning. To the boy who couldn't stand up to his father. To the kid who fired on innocent people. To the man who couldn't look himself in the mirror. It woke the beast that slept inside his veins, that made all his doubts—everything that scared him, everything he hated about himself—rise up. His hands trembled, his head hurt, and his body cried out for the numbness that Vlado's money could buy. Lewis scrunched his eyes shut and brought his knees to his chest, asking himself the questions he could never answer:

Was Persie enough?

Was he enough?

CHAPTER THIRTY-TWO

NORA

It had been a week since the storm, and the library was still closed for repairs from the tree damage and a roof replacement. The roof had been in terrible condition, and they'd been lucky it hadn't given way under all that snow. Nora should have been at work, helping to manage the repairs, but thankfully Vlado had volunteered to be at the library all week, even calling a cousin of his who was able to start work on fixing the roof immediately.

She sat on her couch, watching the wind kick against the bare branches outside, jerking them back and forth like puppet limbs. She and Vlado had only spoken by text since he'd stopped by. It had been unfair of her to push him away like that, but when her anger cooled, it left her despondent and regretful of how she'd felt and what she'd said about Mario.

An endless series of renovation shows paraded across the screen of her television. But Nora wasn't watching. Her heart hung suspended in her chest, a solid rock that knocked against her insides. She reached forward, flicked open the lid of a pizza box, and pulled out a cold piece.

She took a bite, threw the rest back in the box, and closed her eyes, thinking, as she often had, about the night at the library.

They'd all let something control their lives. And for Nora it had been her fear that if she didn't hold on tight enough, fight hard enough, sacrifice enough, she'd lose Mario. Yet none of it had mattered. Mario's battles were his own.

Since the storm, Nora had ignored calls and texts from everyone. Except for Evelyn, whom she'd immediately called back. Her face still burned with shame. She'd apologized profusely, making sure the woman knew that Lewis had been the one to understand what was happening with Jasmine. That Lewis had saved her life. But Evelyn had just laughed and said that God had put everyone there together for a reason and she believed they all had a part in Jasmine surviving. Nora had been so touched she couldn't speak. But it had given rise to that anger again, the one that had begun to feel like a friend, camped beside her and stoking the embers.

After some time, she'd listened to the podcast episodes again, hoping to find the answer to what had happened to him there. With each episode, Mario had grown a little more confident, a little more secure, and it came through in the deep timbre of his voice, a natural ease in his interviews, his laughter that became more and more frequent with each episode. Like he was shedding the weight of his addiction one sandbag at a time. She was happy for him.

Her phone rang, and when she saw the screen, her heart skipped a beat. The police. She'd been here too many times to count. Sleepless nights, thinking he was dead. Days filled with dread that the next phone call would confirm her worst fears, and her heart ached knowing that Lewis's family had probably experienced the same.

"Hello?"

"Ms. Martinez?" A woman's voice.

"Yes, did you find out what happened?"

"No, ma'am. I'm very sorry. If that was your brother, his remains were already cremated. We had quite a surge after the storm—quite a few, uh, unclaimed bodies—and we had to make room. I'm so sorry."

Nora ended the call and pressed a hand to her chest, pained to think of Mario or Lewis or anyone ending up as an unclaimed body.

A firm knock on her door made her jump, followed by a voice she knew all too well. "Hello, Nora!" Marlene sounding exactly like Marlene, her words clipped by an undercurrent of annoyance. "It's Marlene and it's cold out here, and I have a lasagna that just came out of the oven and needs to be eaten now." There was a pause, and then in a softer voice: "I also wanted to make sure you're okay. I wasn't okay after Charlie died, not for a long time, so I understand, you know."

Her words brought to mind the time at the hospital with Charlie. The room had been filled with the kind of flowers people send to hospitals and funerals. The kind that smelled like astringent and death. It had clung to her nose then in the way it had stuck to her memories of her parents' funeral. Mario had held her hand the entire service and halfway through pulled her into his lap. He'd been in a wheelchair then, his face a mess of bruises, cut lip, a cast on one arm, his leg gone. But he'd let her sob into his shoulder, held her tight, and told her that everything would be okay.

The memory faded and she pressed a palm against her eyes. He'd been only sixteen, too young to hold up under so much loss.

She opened the door. Marlene stared up at her, her hat with the flaps smushed down on her head, the tip of her nose red from the cold. She held a glass pan with a lid and looked Nora up and down. "You look pretty good in the sunlight."

Nora smiled. "Thanks," she said. "So do you."

Marlene held out the pan along with a paper shopping bag. "There's bread and a salad in there too." A wrinkle formed between her eyes, and for a second Nora thought the woman looked unsure of herself. "Are you going to take me up on my offer?"

"What offer?"

"Tulum, Nora. I want you to go." She frowned. "The airline tickets and the cabana are all paid for because these days people don't believe in refunding for death or the end of the world or . . . well, you get my point. It would be a waste, and I think it's perfect for you. You have a year to use it, but I think you should go tomorrow. You're young and you should do something fun. You deserve some fun."

Nora cocked her head, gave Marlene a look. "What about you?"

Something flickered in her eyes. "Well, now, sometimes a dog is just too old to learn new tricks."

"Marlene—"

She held up a hand. "No arguments. When I decide something, it's a done deal. Here." She handed her a card. "It's our travel agent. She'll get you all set up. Oh, I almost forgot." She dug in her purse and pulled out a small school picture of Jasmine. Her smile was wide, eyes a beautiful deep brown. So different from the girl carried out on a stretcher. "Evelyn gave that to me for you. She wanted each of us to have one."

Nora took it, palm pressed against her chest, and smiled. "She's beautiful."

"Inside and out, that girl."

Nora stood in the door, her arms loaded with the pan of lasagna, the bag of salad and bread, the business card clasped in one hand, the picture of Jasmine in the other, touched by the kindness of Marlene's gesture. "Thank you, Marlene," she said.

She tightened her scarf. "It's what neighbors do," she said gruffly, and had turned to leave when Nora did something totally out of character herself.

"Do you want to stay for dinner?"

Marlene stopped and smiled. "Not this time. I'm meeting Jasmine's grandmother at the diner." Her sigh reflected the old Marlene. "The woman thinks we're all angels or messengers or God's ambassadors or some such business. Oh, Charlie would have had a field day with that. But I can stay for coffee, if you're offering."

Nora was relieved. Marlene's company was like a warm summer breeze, and it was exactly what she needed right now. She made the coffee while Marlene settled at her kitchen table, thumbing through a stack of magazines Nora kept in a bowl in the center. Nora joined her with two mugs of coffee, noticing that Marlene's overalls were stained with splotches of color. Paint, it looked like, on her fingertips, sprinkled in her hair, and dusting her face.

Marlene held up a small magazine, a triumphant smile on her face. "I knew there was a reason I liked you!" she said.

It was the *Reader's Digest* Nora's aunt had given her a subscription for years ago, and it still came every month. She sipped her coffee. "I like that little magazine."

Marlene flipped through it. "Because it's full of perfectly useless information and really bad jokes. See here." She perched a pair of reading glasses on her nose. "This article says that I could live longer if I eat kale."

"And that's good information to have."

Marlene squinted at her over the glasses. "Yes, but the problem is that I hate kale."

Nora laughed. "Me too."

"Do you like spinach?"

"I don't have anything against it."

"Me neither. Guess we'll have to take our chances with that, then."

Nora laughed and one side of Marlene's mouth perked up. "How do you go on, Marlene?" The question came out unexpectedly; she wanted to grab it out of the air and stuff it back in. Heat pricked her face. "I'm so sorry, that was rude. I didn't mean it—"

"Don't backpedal, Nora. If there's one thing I can't stand, it's people who don't speak their minds."

When Nora was younger, she'd learned to stuff whatever was on her mind so deep inside it disappeared. She'd realized how easily her thoughts could affect the people she loved. Like Mario when she told him to leave and then he overdosed because of it, or her aunt and uncle when she told them she'd never give up on Mario like they had. But ever since the storm, Nora found it harder and harder to keep things locked inside.

"And to answer your question," Marlene continued, "I don't know. I haven't figured that out just yet."

She said it simply and with the same firm way she always had of speaking, but Nora heard it catch in her throat, and she looked up from her coffee. Marlene looked the same—lips pressed firm, her gaze implacable—but there was a softness in the creases around her mouth, a slight movement in her chin, and Nora's heart ached for what Marlene had lost. For what they'd both lost.

"He was a good man," Nora said.

She nodded. "Too good. If he'd been more selfish, he'd never have been up on that ladder." Marlene looked out the window over her sink, and in the glow from outside, Nora noticed the soft gray blue of her eyes. "But that's not the man I married, so if it wasn't the Christmas decorations, it would have been something else." She turned a page of the magazine. "Well, now, this article tells me that I should do yoga for back pain. Hah! Namaste."

"How did you and Charlie meet?" Nora had met Charlie and Marlene after they'd been married for five years, which had surprised her at the time because they'd moved the way a couple does when they've been married for decades. Symbiotic. Like how a flock of birds flies across the sky—coordinated and confident that where one is, so are the others.

Marlene's eyes grew a brighter shade of blue. "The first time we met, I was only nineteen." She fluffed her thin hair and Nora laughed. "I was pretty back then—well, pretty enough. And Charlie was young, with those thick, black-framed glasses that were popular for men. He was traveling through Silver Ridge one day and stopped into the diner. He ordered an apple pie, warmed, with the ice cream in a bowl and coffee with cream and sugar."

Nora lifted her eyebrows. "You remember that?"

"Oh, I never forgot him. He started up a conversation, of course; you know Charlie."

Nora smiled.

"And he stayed for a second cup of coffee, and then when my shift was over, he bought me a cup too. We talked for hours."

"Why didn't you see each other again?"

"Oh, we were supposed to. He was coming back through town the next month." She sipped her coffee. "But then my father started to get really ill, and I had to leave the diner. No hospice around to take care of him in those days." Her mouth tightened. "Not that we could have afforded it anyway."

Nora touched a hand to her chest. "That must have been hard."

"Well, yes, it was."

Her face clouded, and Nora wondered if she should change the conversation.

"And no cell phones like everyone has these days to tell him where I lived. I was fifty-eight years old when he came back through town the next time. Too old to fall in love. But Charlie, well, the old sap said he'd never forgotten me." The wrinkles in her cheeks smoothed, and her smile was that of someone much younger. "I guess you could say he swept this old lady off her feet."

"I think it's beautiful."

"It was."

"But have you ever just wanted to give up?" A voice inside her screamed that it was the wrong thing to say, but she crossed her arms and muzzled it because sometimes it felt good to say exactly what she meant.

"I do. Every day." Marlene tapped her finger on the table. "The morning of the storm, well, the reason I came into the library is that I'd thought about killing myself, even held the gun to my head."

Nora shivered.

"But then I just couldn't. So I came to the library because I didn't want to be alone. And then I was surrounded by all of you, and I realized I wasn't the only one alone, not by a long shot." She sipped her coffee. "That snowstorm was the best thing that could have happened to me."

Tears pricked Nora's eyes to think of Marlene in such pain. She touched her arm briefly, and the woman smiled.

"Figured it was better to say it out loud so someone else could hear how foolish it sounds."

They sat a little while longer in silence, and Nora didn't mind. It was nice to be around someone who understood. "You know that you're covered in paint?" she said after a bit.

Marlene laughed, an easy sound that Nora was still getting used to. She guessed that Charlie must have always seen this side of Marlene. "I'm painting again."

"Walls or pictures?"

"Pictures. I wanted to go to school for it, even dreamed of having my paintings in an art show one day." Her face brightened. "Now I'm just doing it for me, and it makes me happy." She stood, took her mug over to the counter. "Thank you for the coffee."

They walked to the door, and Nora had to fight the urge to hug the woman. Marlene had changed, but that might be too big of a leap for now. "Thank you," she said simply. "For coming here and for the lasagna and everything."

Marlene's eyes were kind. "Charlie used to say that you reminded him of me because of your stubborn single-mindedness." She paused and her cheeks wobbled. "But you're more like him."

Nora felt a tightening in her chest. "How?"

"Because he believed in purpose, too, and he was always looking for it." She cleared her throat. "Maybe you've just been looking in the wrong places, Nora."

She watched Marlene drive away, still smiling from her visit. Marlene had been . . . *nice*, and her company had made Nora feel content, connected to someone. She laughed to herself. Connected to Marlene! Of all people. She thought of Aunt Sophie. Her aunt had tried to reach out to Nora, still tried, even when Nora pushed her away because she thought she had to choose between Mario and her family. She pressed a palm against her eyes. They'd never asked her to choose.

A few days ago, she'd downloaded another picture of her twin cousins with their mom at a university football game and added it to the wall. Her aunt had the same kind smile that gently lined her eyes, but her hair was shorter than Nora remembered, cut to her chin.

In the beginning Mario had been the one to hold Nora when she cried at night, until he grew distant, finding his escape in the pills, and one night when she was crying into her pillow, trying not to wake her cousins, her aunt slipped into the room. Nora's back was to the door. The mattress dipped down; her aunt's arms were thin but solid, and she held tight to Nora while she cried, rocking her gently, humming a song Nora didn't know, until she fell asleep.

Nora wiped her face dry and stood. She'd let their relationship wither by not calling her family back or visiting when they invited her, and eventually the calls stopped, although her aunt sent a Christmas card every year and always called on her birthday. She'd thought they'd picked a side when they decided to let Mario go. She hadn't thought she had a choice. But they had loved her, and they had loved Mario, too, she never doubted that; they just couldn't help him.

Had she been the one to draw the line? She thought about Mario getting sober and hosting a podcast without telling her and felt a flicker of anger. Or had he?

She opened her phone contacts and pushed the number. Her knees bounced up and down, and her heart beat fast. What if it was too late? What if she'd hurt them too much with her silence? What if—

"Hello?" The same rich tone, the same welcoming inflection, and Nora remembered extra pats of butter on brown sugar oatmeal, homemade chocolate cake for her birthdays, hugs when she needed it, helping her cut out a thousand paper bubbles for a science fair display.

She breathed in. "Hi, Aunt Sophie, it's Nora."

CHAPTER THIRTY-THREE

NORA

Nora drove into town on roads empty of cars, under a sky so blue it turned the white of the remaining piles of snow into a brightness that stung her eyes. Since the storm, the weather had turned drastically, warming up to nearly above-average spring temperatures. The heated air next to the cool powder was a mountain disparity that happened at some point every spring but was magnified this year by the amount of snow still left over from the big storm. In town, a few younger children were sledding down the small hill by the courthouse in snow pants and T-shirts. She smiled at the sight and pulled into a spot in front of the library.

The library was finally opening up today after being closed for nearly two weeks for the repairs. It had felt odd getting ready and driving in to work with no to-do list of volunteer activities running in her head, no sandwiches or drinks in a cooler in her car, no plans to stop at the shelter after work—just a plan to drive to work and see how the day went. She'd had to push away the little girl inside who argued that she didn't deserve to be happy when Mario was hurting or dead. But

Nora thought about Marlene and how she was moving forward without Charlie, and she admitted to herself that maybe she deserved to do the same.

She turned the car off and hesitated. A form huddled just beside the door to the library, puffy brown coat, scarf, and a hat pulled low. Nora felt a twinge. The door opened and Vlado appeared. He waved like he'd been waiting for her, and her stomach did a little flip-flop that didn't entirely surprise her. She got out of the car.

"Welcome back!" he called, and spread out his arms. "The library has missed you."

The form beside the door shifted, and as Nora climbed the stairs, she recognized the person and sucked in her bottom lip; the last time she'd seen Nonnie, she'd been on her way to transitional housing. What had happened?

"Hi, Nonnie," she said and couldn't keep the disappointment out of her voice. "I thought you were . . . is everything all right?"

Nonnie pushed to her feet, and Nora noticed that her gray hair had been brushed until it was soft and her coat was clean, if a little threadbare. "Why wouldn't it be? I'm not camping out. I'm here to use the computer to email my sister, but Vlado wouldn't let me in until you got here." She glared up at him.

Vlado smiled and it creased the skin around his eyes in a pleasant, relaxed way. "The library doesn't open until eight, Nonnie. But it is eight now and our librarian is here, so come in!"

Nora followed them and froze just inside the door. The smell of books, weathered stone, and old carpet hit her with a familiarity that tapped against her chest. Like coming home. Vlado turned and smiled, and she noticed his brown hair, wavy and thick, and how it fell just over one eye in a sexy kind of way, his firm jaw, full lips, and her stomach did the flip-flop thing again. She still hadn't apologized for how she'd acted the morning he'd stopped at her house. A text or phone call seemed too impersonal but now, standing so close to him, she was suddenly unsure of herself, so she dropped her eyes and hurried to her desk.

She sat down in her chair and looked up to find Vlado had followed her and stood above her, his eyes a hazel green against his hair. "Here. This is for you." He handed her a package—a present, she guessed, based on the pink wrapping paper. "It's from Jasmine's grandmother. She keeps dropping little gifts off; last week it was hot coffee for me." He held his hands out, palms up. "Evelyn says she's forever grateful to the strangers who saved her granddaughter's life."

"It was a group effort, wasn't it?" she said, and Vlado's eyebrow lifted with his smile.

"It was."

She opened the package to find a knitted scarf and a card with a delicate script: *Thank you for taking care of Jasmine. She is so precious to us and you saved her life. It's only a scarf, but Jasmine said it was a perfect gift because knitting was your thing.*

"Oh, that's so nice." Her eyes started to burn, and she bit her lip. She'd had coffee with Evelyn and Jasmine last week, and the woman was as kind and forgiving as her granddaughter. Neither of them thought anything about her missed voice mail, and Jasmine never mentioned how Nora had burned her battery listening to the podcast. But Nora hadn't forgotten. It still bothered her and perhaps fueled her decision to take so much time off from the library when she should have been in, helping to manage the repairs.

"We all got one."

Her head shot up. "Lewis?"

Vlado's eyes clouded. "I still have his."

He didn't say more but he didn't need to. Nobody had seen or heard from Lewis. Of course Lewis was not in Silver Ridge. What did she think? That one night in the library would solve everyone's problems? "Vlado, I-I'm sorry about the other day at my house." She rolled her shoulders. "That was so rude of me, and what I said about Mario—well, I didn't mean it."

He stopped her when he put his hand over hers. "I'm just happy to see you back where you're needed."

She nodded, touched, and began to go through a pile of books.

"Nora?"

"Mm-hmm?"

"Are you okay?"

She opened a book on her desk and breathed in. "Yes and no."

At first, he didn't say anything, and she regretted almost immediately being so candid. Then he leaned down, and she inhaled fresh laundry. "I have something to show you," he said and straightened. "Come with me."

His long legs made it to the basement door before her, and she wondered what could be down there. "Oh no, was there flooding from all the snow?" She hadn't even thought about that. There wasn't much there, but she had recently moved in a secondhand couch and a few other things she'd been collecting for the teen hangout room. It would set her back a bit if they'd been damaged.

He turned on the light, and from her position on the stairs, the floor looked fine. Other than smelling like a basement in an old building, nothing seemed amiss—until she reached the bottom and looked around, and her hand flew to her mouth.

"Oh," was all she could say because her throat closed over the words. The room had been cleared, boxes stacked in the back on new shelves, and in the middle stood the couch with a new slipcover, plus two deep armchairs, also with slipcovers, and a few brass lamps and dark-wood end tables.

"My grandmother was getting rid of furniture, so she decided to donate a few things." Vlado stood just behind her. Nora heard a touch of pride in his voice.

Lights had been strung in the exposed ceiling studs so that it had the effect of stars and also made the space warm and inviting. A Bluetooth speaker was on one of the end tables, and a huge colorful rug extended under the furniture, adding brightness and fun to the whole setup despite the shadowed basement corners. Empty metal bookshelves—the old ones Nora had retired and stored down here some time ago—stood like bookends on either side of the space.

"I thought you'd prefer to stock the shelves yourself," he said.

"It's the hangout space for the kids," she said.

"Do you like it?"

"You did this?"

"Jasmine talked about being new and feeling different, and it sounded like she needed a place where she felt like she belonged, and, well, I just knew how much you'd wanted to do this for the kids. Since the library was closed, I had some free time."

She stood with her arms folded and felt the heat of Vlado behind her, heard him shuffling his feet on the concrete floor.

"Are you upset?"

She shook her head. "No, I love it." The kindness of the gesture overwhelmed her, bringing to the surface emotions that simmered inside her, and it was almost too much for her to handle.

"Nora, I'm so sorry about your brother."

She turned to look up at him and tried to pretend she was fine, tried to push him away like she had everyone else for so long. But she couldn't speak. They stared at each other for a few moments, and then, slowly and gently, Vlado took her in his arms and held her.

She rested her head against his chest, relaxed into him, and closed her eyes, listening to the steady thump of his heart. When had she last been hugged? Vlado's body felt safe and warm and exactly right, and for a moment, she wished it would never end.

He released her to meet her eyes. "Have coffee with me after work?"

She almost said no, but that was the old her. "Okay." From upstairs came the sound of footsteps. She wanted to tell him how deeply she was touched, but all she could say was, "Thank you."

He smiled. "Let's get to work." And they hurried back upstairs.

The day flew by with a visit from Johanna and Marlene, who had resumed her Spanish lessons, followed by a story-time group Nora hosted for toddlers and moms. It was one of her favorites, and today was especially exciting when one little girl threw up all over another little girl and story time ended in all the kids crying. On her way out, Marlene had passed by Nora on her knees, cleaning up the stain, and stopped, smiling. *See how much you're needed here?*

At the end of the day, Nora was in the nonfiction stacks, shelving books, when Vlado appeared with his coat on, hat pulled low on his head, handsome in a way that made it hard to pick out why but easy to spot. "Ready for that coffee?" In his arms was a small cardboard box. Inside was the weather radio along with a picture of him with his arm around a white-haired woman in a Denver Nuggets basketball jersey, a Rapids calendar, and a Shakespeare bobblehead. Her cheeks warmed with shame. She knew hardly anything about Vlado because she'd never asked.

"You like sports and you study English?"

He shrugged. "I'm full of enigmas."

She pointed at the picture. "Grandmother?"

"Nana, yes, and a diehard Nuggets fan."

"And she makes the best *hibanca*."

He laughed. "Gibanica, yes."

She glanced again at the box. "Are you leaving?"

Vlado just smiled and put the box in his car. "C'mon, let's go have that coffee, and we can talk."

Her legs felt heavy. For a moment, she'd imagined that their night together during the storm had meant something more to him. Did it surprise her that he was leaving? He had bigger things to pursue. Could she blame him for wanting to move on?

They walked to the diner in silence, her throat tight the entire time. The diner was light and bright, and they took the same booth Nora used to sit in before school.

Jasmine appeared—carafe in one hand, two white mugs in the other—her smile wide.

Nora brightened, always happy to see the young girl so animated and full of life. "Hi, Jasmine." She stood to hug her.

"You're wearing Grandma's scarf! Hold up, let me get a picture for her." She slid her phone from her pocket and snapped a photo. "She'll love that." She poured coffee into their mugs. "You know"—Jasmine ducked her head—"I've never, uh, actually said sorry for all of that."

"Sorry for what?"

"For letting myself get so bad. I don't like to tell people about my diabetes." She set down a plastic container of small creamers. "I don't know, I just already feel weird as the new girl, and it just makes me more weird, you know?"

Nora thought about being the only high school girl with a brother as an addict. "I get it. I felt that way sometimes because of Mario."

Jasmine's face clouded. "Yeah, I'm really sorry about that. Are you okay?"

"I will be."

She set the carafe on the table between them. "My grandmother loves you—well, she loves *all* of you, and she wants to have everyone over for dinner." She rolled her eyes. "There might be medals or something, I don't know."

"As long as she's making her famous jerk chicken," Vlado said, and Jasmine laughed before moving on to serve another table.

Nora watched the girl work. "I used to come here a lot when I was a teenager."

"Did you know Marlene then?"

She played with the sugar packets, making a stack of the pink ones next to a stack of the white ones. "No, I kept to myself, head in a book. Big surprise, I know."

"I was twelve when we moved to the States, and kids didn't know what to do with me," Vlado said. There was a light stubble on his cheeks, and when he smiled, it creased the skin around his mouth in a pleasant way. "I was too tall, with a funny accent and lunches that smelled weird. I was an easy target and, as you know, a bit of a pacifist. I used to hide in the library after school." In the bright diner lights, his eyes were a really striking shade of a golden brown flecked with green. Nora wondered how she'd never noticed how beautiful they were before now. "It was a safe place for me, so when I saw the job listing here, I thought it sounded like a good fit."

She laughed then; she couldn't help it. "A pacifist security guard?"

He laughed. "I see that now. But I was also avoiding committing to what I really wanted. Our night in the library made me realize that there was no time like now to go for it. My dad will understand . . ." He shrugged. "Eventually."

"You're really leaving." Her stomach churned. She wanted to say more—wanted to tell him to stay, wanted to tell him she'd miss him—but after years of pushing everyone away, she was out of practice.

"I am. I would have told you earlier, but I wanted to tell you in person."

She poured a sugar packet into her coffee, then another, even though she preferred it black, but it gave her something to do with her hands. Long ago, she'd accepted that she'd be alone, but now, just when she was ready to make room for someone else in her life, it was slipping away.

"I've tidied up my desk, left a few instructions for the new guy. I think he starts sometime next week. This one's a theater major." His eyebrows raised and he smiled. "Be nice to him. Not sure he's cut out for the job, but I don't really think you need a guard anyway."

She'd forgotten what it felt like to have normal conversations that weren't about the library or homelessness or addiction. "The library will miss you."

He reached across the table and took her hands in his. "I'll miss you."

Jasmine passed by their booth, paused, and grinned when she saw them holding hands across the table. "I knew it. I totally shipped you two." She walked away, still grinning.

Vlado's mouth twitched. "I have no idea what that means."

Nora laughed. "Me either."

"But I can guess. Denver's not that far. Can I take you out sometime?"

Nora pulled her hands away and leaned back in her seat. There had been very few times in her life when she'd felt truly happy, and when she had—with her aunt and uncle, in college with Amanda—it had come at Mario's expense. It hurt to think that this time it wouldn't affect her brother at all, but it was also a feeling she'd never had before. Like she was free to do what she wanted.

Vlado's hands curled back into themselves, and his face was guarded, like he expected her to turn him down.

But Mario was gone, had been gone from her life for years, really. So what did she want? Her body felt like it hardly touched the seat when she looked at Vlado. "I'd love that."

~

When she got home, Nora went to the kitchen and preheated the oven to warm Marlene's lasagna from the other night. A lighthearted feeling spread through her body when she thought of Vlado. She giggled, but her quiet apartment absorbed the sound, reminded her that she was alone. And she didn't want to be alone.

Something occurred to her then—a realization that was so obvious but had eluded her for years. She didn't have to be alone if she didn't want to.

She grabbed her phone and texted Amanda. Hey A! Want to come over for lasagna and salad? And a Netflix binge?

There was no reply for several minutes, and Nora scratched her thigh, tapped the floor with her foot. She couldn't remember the last time she'd initiated plans with Amanda. She'd been such a crappy friend. Was it too late? Her phone dinged.

Oh, hell yeah. I'll bring the red wine and I've got a whole slideshow from my trip to Vietnam that I can't wait to show you.

Nora breathed out a laugh. Perfect.

With the lasagna in the oven, Nora sat on the floor, waiting for Amanda and studying her wall of photos. There was one of her in Mario's arms when she was a baby; another with her aunt at a waterpark when she was seven, wet hair in her face, head thrown back midlaugh. And in a small space right before her bedroom door was the school picture of Jasmine. She smiled at the girl's photo. It looked right at home on her wall of pictures.

CHAPTER THIRTY-FOUR

MARLENE

September

She parked Charlie's car in one of the slanted spots on Main Street. She liked driving his car now because he'd left his sunglasses in a cup holder, like he'd just taken them off to run inside for something. She turned the car off and touched the mirrored lenses. They were a cheap pair he'd had to buy at a gas station when they drove down to Santa Fe last year. He'd forgotten his at home.

She looked out the window. The aspens were about to hit their peak color, so the town was busier than normal with the leaf lookers from the city hoping to catch a glimpse of gold. Marlene snorted. This lot was a week too early.

The car door creaked when it opened, sounding the way she imagined her bones did when she moved, and Marlene stood on the sidewalk with her purse over her shoulder. She'd gotten a call from the bookstore in town that her order had come in, the invitations were ready to be picked up, and she was meeting Johanna for coffee to discuss how things were progressing with the art show. She'd been painting almost nonstop since the storm. It was something she'd always wanted to do, and she'd figured that life was too damn short to wait a minute longer.

"Hello, Marlene!" Johanna's upbeat voice carried from down the sidewalk.

She smiled. "Hi, Johanna." Johanna was on the local arts council board and the perfect person to help her pull together the event Marlene had been preparing for since last spring. She was nervous and excited and wishing with all her heart that Charlie could be here to see it.

I see it.

She gave the air a swat. *Oh, shut up, you old man. You're dead, remember?* He wasn't there, but she didn't mind carrying his voice in her head. It reminded her of who she was now.

Johanna stopped in front of her, holding a box. She had silver hair that she wore short and cut close to her head, and her skin was a wrinkled pink that, like Marlene's, had once been smooth and elastic. But that was a long time ago, even longer for Johanna, who had to be a good fifteen years older than Marlene.

They sat outside a coffee hut, paper cups in hand. Johanna wore beaded earrings that hung down in a line and a silver-and-turquoise necklace looped over her light cotton wrap. She had a clipboard and was ticking off items on a list. "I have a handful of volunteers to help with setup and teardown, although other than the easels, it's not much. I'll have a cash box on hand for sales and a separate box for donations, and"—her smile lines deepened—"I showed the board your paintings. I'm impressed, Marlene. None of us had any idea you had such a delicateness to you. You are truly an inspired artist."

Marlene laughed. Johanna was growing on her. People were growing on her. "Thank you."

"And this is your first show? That's incredible!"

"Well, yes, it is, isn't it?" Marlene's stomach even did a youthful jump in response. "And Nora and the others haven't seen any of the paintings, right?" She'd been storing them at the arts council building after running out of room in her small cabin.

Johanna crossed her heart. "Not a thing. I can't believe it's tomorrow. Oh, and I have something I wanted to ask you."

Johanna held out a book, and Marlene had to work to keep her smile from melting into a grimace. The woman was relentless about her Book Club for Old Biddies, or some such ridiculous name. She'd been asking her ever since Charlie died, and Marlene had suspected it had to do with her being a widow. Like it had bonded them in some way, opened up membership in a secret club.

"*Pride and Prejudice*," Johanna said. "We've decided we need a little bit of a love story this month, and who doesn't like Mr. Darcy?"

Marlene stopped herself from raising a hand.

"And we're taking a page from the library's playbook and gathering at my house to watch the movie after our discussion." Her voice thinned at the end of the sentence, the way it did for older vocal cords. Like there just wasn't enough juice in there to make it to the finish line.

It softened Marlene even more toward the woman.

"The used section at the bookstore has copies for fifty cents," Johanna said, smiling.

Up until this point, Marlene had never wanted to be part of Johanna's lonely hearts club, but now . . . well, maybe she was different. Maybe she did want to bond with other women who'd lost someone they loved. Besides, she'd already planned to stop at the bookstore today.

"You should go now before the leaf lookers start crowding the shops with their pumpkin-spiced-up coffees and walking around like they own the town." Johanna rolled her eyes, and Marlene smiled at the youthful gesture. "So, will you join our little book club?"

"Yes," she said, and it felt so good to say it—another feather in her cap for developing a social life. A breeze rustled the aspen leaves, making them sound like paper bells, and in them she heard Charlie's delighted laugh. "I'd love that."

~

She headed straight for the diner from the bookstore, wishing she could run but settling for a slow stroll because it was all her body could do. She hoped Jasmine was working today. A bubbling laughter rose up, and she could hear Charlie laughing along with her. She felt free-spirited in a way she'd always wished she could have been when she was younger.

The diner was busy today with leaf lookers waiting outside for a table, disappointed—no doubt—that all they'd seen was green. They milled around outside: overdressed couples or small families with cranky kids, a few in bike wear like they'd just competed in the Olympics.

Marlene was headed straight toward the door when she noticed a figure sitting on a bench across the street. Her body felt weightless and she laughed some more, loud enough that a few of the city folk shot her worried glances. She ignored them and crossed the street. He wore a gray jacket that had a tailored look to it, with big pockets and a nice collar, and between his hands, he rolled a brown tweed flat hat, the kind Charlie always favored. She knew him immediately, even if he had been hardly more than a broken voice in the dark of the library. The bright morning light played inside the lines of his face, giving them unflattering depth. She imagined it did the same to her. He jiggled his knee up and down, eyes trained on the diner, and he didn't even notice her approaching.

"The hero has returned," she said.

He jerked upward, staring at her for a second too long, like he didn't recognize her.

She stuck out her hand. "Marlene. I suppose the last time we met, you'd just overdosed and I was rather, well, rude."

"I know who you are," he said, and his voice was thick, gravelly, but he took her hand and they shook. "Lewis."

She narrowed her eyes. "You seem different, Lewis. Are you sober?"

His forehead wrinkled and it showed his eyes, bright blue and clear. "And you are still as outspoken and rude as ever, Marlene."

He patted the bench and she joined him, thankful to take the weight off her feet. They sat for a few minutes in silence, watching people pass by, the sun warm and the air that perfect fall temperature between hot and cool. Marlene breathed in a leathery musk, realized it came from Lewis. "You smell much better this time."

He chuckled. "And you are exactly the same—maybe a bit nicer."

She leaned into the bench. "Thank you for noticing. I'm working on it."

He crossed an ankle over the opposite knee. They both sat staring at the diner, Marlene looking for Jasmine, and Lewis, she suspected, watching the girl behind the counter with the purple-and-pink hair and a bright smile. "She looks a little bit like you," she said.

He grunted. "You think?"

Marlene tilted her head, watched the girl expertly load a huge round tray with plates of pancakes, bacon, and syrup, and thought about her own days working here. Back when it was all shiny linoleum and polished chrome. It seemed ages ago now. "Well, she's got better hair, but there's something about her eyes that make me think of you."

Lewis rubbed his bald head, laughed.

The silence between them was comfortable, but, Marlene supposed, they had spent a night together in the dark, divulging their deepest secrets, so why shouldn't it be? His knee jiggled up and down, and Marlene noticed that he kept sliding one hand in and out of his pocket.

She touched her bag. "I have something to give to Jasmine."

He looked down, shook his head. "What's that?"

"It's my way of apologizing."

He raised his eyebrows, nodded, like it made perfect sense to him too. "You have changed, Marlene."

She smiled. "I have—oh, and I have something for you too." She pulled an invitation out of her bag, held it out.

Lewis picked a small pair of reading glasses from his shirt pocket and slid them on. It gave him the look of a distinguished grandfather. Marlene liked it.

He raised one eyebrow and looked at her over his glasses. "An art show tomorrow night, huh? Your own?"

"Well, I kept thinking about Vlado's Sissypants fellow and his boulder, and I guess you weren't the only one stuck in some kind of purgatory. You might not realize this because of my youthful disposition, but I'm old like you, Lewis."

Lewis laughed.

"And I figured, what the hell do I have to lose?" She glanced at the diner, then pointed to the invitation. "I hope you can come. Everyone would love to see you. Bring Persie."

Lewis pocketed the flyer but didn't say anything.

Marlene stood. "Well, Lewis, it's nice to see you sober and all cleaned up. It looks good on you."

The edge of his mouth ticked upward. "Thank you, Marlene. And I hope you can keep up with this nice act. It's sure to fool everybody."

She laughed and turned to go, hesitated. "Would you like to come inside for a cup of coffee?"

His knee jiggled harder. "No, I think I'll stay here awhile and enjoy the weather."

"Suit yourself. But it was nice to see you, Lewis."

"You too, Marlene."

She left him sitting on the bench, wondering if she should have said more or grabbed his arm and pulled him inside. Then again, she understood needing to do something on your own. And if Lewis was going to get better, he needed to figure out how to do it himself. The crowd outside the diner had dwindled, and Marlene approached the hostess stand.

The young hostess smiled, pulled a menu. "One?" she said.

"Yes. Can you seat me in Jasmine's section?"

The hostess frowned, checked her seating chart. "Uh, sure, okay."

Marlene sat down. A restless energy rushed through her muscles, and she stretched her feet out, squeezed her legs to ease it.

"Marlene?" Jasmine stood by her table, carafe of coffee in one hand, a white, glossy mug in the other. Her smile was genuine but also guarded, and Marlene couldn't blame her. "Coffee?"

"Yes, thank you."

Jasmine poured the black liquid into the mug, ending with just enough room for cream should Marlene want it.

"Good pour," Marlene said.

Jasmine gave her a look. "Um, thanks?"

Marlene laughed. "Have I ever told you that I used to work here back when it was the newest restaurant in town?"

"Wow, really?" The girl had a genuine warmth about her that Marlene admired.

"Really. I'm that old."

Jasmine's smile showed her teeth, pearly white and straight. Today she wore her hair out of braids, curly and pulled into two puff balls on top of her head. Her eyebrows met in a look of concern, and her eyes flicked toward the windows behind Marlene. "I never got to say goodbye to Lewis after the storm."

"Well, you did leave in quite the dramatic fashion."

Jasmine laughed. "Yeah, not the coolest way to leave the library." She jerked her head at the window. "He's out there."

Marlene turned to see Lewis still on the bench, still with one leg jiggling, one hand in his pocket. "Oh, yes, I spoke with him earlier. He's sober now." She looked toward the girl with the pink-and-purple hair. "Does Persie know he's here?"

"Yeah, she knows. She's always known it was him, but this is the first time he's been here since the storm."

Marlene thought of Nora and how if she were Persie, she would have already run outside and spoon-fed him coffee and pie and done whatever it took to sober him up.

"Why hasn't she ever said anything to him?"

Jasmine looked at Persie, who laughed with a customer at the bar, and Marlene noticed how the girl glanced Lewis's way and her smile faded briefly. But then she seemed to shake it off and returned to happily chatting with the customer.

"She says that he'll come in when he's ready to be her granddad."

"Wise girl."

"Yep." Jasmine sighed. "Would you like to order?"

Marlene shook her head. "Just the coffee today." She slid an invitation onto the table. "And I wanted to give you this."

"Your own art show—that's awesome. Can I bring Grandma?"

"Bring your whole family."

She pulled the gift from her bag, suddenly nervous. It had been months since the storm. Was it too personal? Something they shared in the dark of that night but that should have been left there, not brought out into the light? "Actually, I have something for you."

"You do?"

Marlene nearly snatched it from the table, sure she'd done the wrong thing, but then Jasmine set the carafe on the table and sank into a chair. She unwrapped it and held it out in front of her, holding it delicately like it might break. Her face softened and her eyes grew shiny. "It's the book. It's the exact one. Did you find this?"

Marlene nodded. She had never been one to believe in any kind of preordained nonsense, preferring the likelihood of coincidence and randomness and the happy accidents that sometimes brought two worlds or two people together. Like the snowstorm stranding them together and Nora spying Lewis outside, then Lewis saving Jasmine's life because of a stripper he once knew. Like Marlene meeting Charlie. Random. Coincidence. Happy accidents.

But ever since that night, Marlene wanted to find the book that Jasmine so desperately wanted for her sister. And she was not about to leave that up to happy accidents. She'd called every bookstore she could find, used and new, finally pestering the local owner to help. He'd located a copy in a tiny bookstore in the northernmost part of Maine and—for a very hefty fee, she might add—he'd had it shipped here.

"For me?"

She nodded again.

"Oh, wow, thank you. That's just so . . ." Jasmine smiled wide. "*Nice* of you."

Marlene felt a warmth spread across her chest. "Well, it's a new direction for me."

Jasmine giggled and flipped open the cover, and her lips spread into a wider grin. "Oh, there it is. See, look at those two, all naked and posing like that. I mean, what is that all about?"

Together they looked through the book, Jasmine pointing to pictures that she remembered, and they both laughed at the ridiculous nature of many of the drawings. She had to leave a couple of times to serve her few remaining customers, but the diner had emptied of most people and there seemed to be a relaxed atmosphere among the staff. When they got to the end of the book, Jasmine closed the cover and held it to her chest. A wet line traced her cheek. "Thank you, Marlene. For this and for everything, you know?" She checked her watch. "I should get back to work, but, hey—" She shrugged, for the first time seeming unsure of herself, and then threw her arms around Marlene. At first, Marlene stiffened. Charlie had been the last person to hug her with such exuberant affection. Her mother never hugged her. Jasmine smelled like fryer grease and roses, and a tiny remaining iceberg melted inside Marlene.

She blinked hard, slid her arms around the girl, and hugged her back.

CHAPTER THIRTY-FIVE

Lewis

Her hair was purple now, with pink on the roots, and she moved around the diner gracefully, like a dancer. Did she take dance? He didn't know. The last time he'd seen her had been months ago, right before the storm that changed everything. That's how he'd thought of it in the months that had followed. What he told himself when the withdrawal pains were worse than anything he'd ever experienced in his life. That night had changed him in a way he didn't think was possible. It didn't make anything easier. It hadn't changed his need to get high or to escape. Afterward, he wanted to get high so bad he felt it in his veins, humming his name, calling to him until his throat was so dry he couldn't swallow, and getting high was the water he needed. He wanted it so goddamn much he nearly gave up. But something had made him stronger after that night. Was it seeing Nora give up everything to wait for her brother? Was it seeing how much her brother's addiction still hurt her? Had Lewis fooled himself into thinking that he could live however he wanted as long as it was away from the people he loved? That it would somehow hurt them less?

He'd spent that first night after the storm in a shelter in Silver Ridge, his whole body shaking, and then he'd done what Vlado had suggested. He got on a bus and returned to Denver, found a center that would help someone like him detox, then found a place that would allow him to stay as long as he followed the rules. And he followed the rules. Even if doing so left him curled into the fetal position in bed when his need had a voice that sang to him at night. Made his hands shake, his head hurt, and his body ache.

He watched Marlene walk into the diner and sit down. Saw Jasmine pour her coffee, smile at the old woman like she was happy to see her. Lewis shook his head. It had been a surprise to see Marlene, yet he found that he had grown to enjoy her dry remarks. The old woman was like a sour candy. Sour but surprisingly sweet enough to make you want to have another.

Persie was talking to a customer at the bar. She'd just graduated high school, and from what Jasmine had said that night at the library, she was one of the smartest in her class. Was she going to college? If she did, he imagined her becoming a doctor or a lawyer and living her life in a beautiful house with comfortable beds and a stocked pantry. Or was she just going to start working straightaway? He didn't care. There was no shame in being a hard worker and bringing money in. Whichever path she chose, he would be proud of.

Tears filled his eyes and he let them. It was part of the cost of being sober, he supposed, this emotion that punched him in the chest when he least expected it. On the bus to work. Or sorting mail at his job. Or in the middle of the night, when the need to get high was a poltergeist in the corner of his room, beckoning him.

His hand slid into his pocket, and he rubbed his finger along the object. He kept it there to remind himself of what he could accomplish. Of what he could be if he kept moving forward. But it scared him, too, because the responsibility to stay sober sat on his back like a monkey, nearly as demanding—if not more so—than his need to escape. Because as each day piled onto the next, he got higher off the ground, had more to lose, much farther to fall.

A breeze flitted through the aspen leaves, brushed across his face, and he breathed in the earthy smell of nature not encumbered by exhaust or fumes. He put his hat on top of his head, pulled it low, and pushed his palms flat against his thighs to stand. He'd been sitting so long he swayed when he got to his feet and had to grab the back of the bench to keep from stumbling to the side. "Old-man legs," he grumbled to himself, waiting until his feet felt firm on the sidewalk. He brushed at his jacket, pulled it down to straighten out the creases, and crossed the street.

When he got to the door, he stood, rooted to the spot. He couldn't get his lungs to work right, and his chest hurt from the effort. He'd never made it this far, and up close, Persie looked so much younger, a hint of the baby he remembered in the roundness of her cheeks. He worked his jaw, tried to keep his chin from shaking, but damn if it didn't have a mind of its own. A man pulled open the door, letting his wife out first, then stood there holding it, hand out, eyebrows raised. Lewis tensed, started to back away. He wasn't welcomed inside restaurants. But the man smiled. "Coming in?"

Lewis scrambled forward, walking awkwardly to accommodate the stiffness that plagued his hips. Too many years sleeping on concrete, and now that he had a bed, his body hurt like hell. The bitter scent of coffee mixed with fryer grease and a buttery smell like pie dough. A girl stood at the hostess stand. "Would you like a table?"

His back itched like everyone in the room was staring at him, and Lewis remembered that he still wore his hat. He grabbed it from off his head, held it between his hands, and looked at the floor when he spoke. "I'll sit at the counter." He thought he sounded gruff; he didn't mean to, but it was hard to change his habits, and it was taking time to get used to interacting with people again.

He settled quickly onto a barstool, perched his elbows on the counter, and hunched over a menu. His heart beat so fast he was sure that everyone in the diner could hear it. A cup of coffee, filled to the brim slid into view, followed by four packs of sugar. "Mom said you always liked your coffee sweet."

He froze, and for a second he thought he might just turn around and run, leave before he looked at her, get out before it was too late. Her voice was lilting and youthful, and it plucked at his heart, made it sing and hurt at the same time. He tried to pick up the mug, hoping the coffee could settle him, but his hands shook and the coffee splashed across the plastic menu. "Oh, damn it," he growled and tried to sop it up with the thin napkins from the dispenser.

"I got it." Her voice again, and a cloth appeared and quickly wiped up the mess. "There's a woman who comes in here every Thursday, and nearly every Thursday she knocks her Diet Coke over with her purse when she gets up to leave. I'm not kidding. Every. Thursday." Her voice shook, like she was nervous, and the idea that she might be poked at his heart. He looked up and he couldn't breathe because she was so god-damn beautiful, and she looked a lot like Heather, a little like Phyllis, and even a tiny bit like him. Marlene was right; it was in her eyes. But mostly she just looked like Persie.

She smiled and he noticed something in the crease above her nostril, glinting in the light. An earring in her nose. Huh. She refilled his cup and he saw that her fingernails were painted black with pink tips. He didn't know what kind of style that was, but he liked it and thought it seemed to fit her well. He cleared his throat and slid his hand into his pocket. Before, his choice was always between Persie and drugs. Between Persie and the chance to disappear from what scared him. Between Persie and forgetting. "I'm your pop, but you can call me Lewis since—oh, well, or whatever you want."

She smiled and he felt a lump grow in his throat because her smile was untroubled and beautiful and kind. "Hi, Pop," she said. "I'm Persephone, but you can call me Persie or whatever you'd like."

His entire body relaxed and he smiled, not caring that it showed two missing teeth or how it made his old skin scrunch up around his eyes. "I like Persie."

"Great, me too. I have no idea what my mom was thinking naming me that anyway. Would you like a piece of cobbler?"

He nodded.

She left and returned a minute later with apple cobbler, the ice cream already melting into a creamy lake.

"I have something to give you." From his pocket he pulled the dark-blue coin and set it on the counter, used the tip of his finger to push it close. "Um, this is a coin and it means—"

She picked it up and her eyes were soft. "It means you've been sober for six months. I've read about these. That's amazing!"

"Yeah, that's right."

"But why are you giving it to me?"

He tried to sit up tall, but it wasn't easy on the stool so he stood, pressed his hat against his heart. "I'm giving that to you, Persie, because . . ." He wasn't sure but he thought his voice was too loud, that it carried too far. "It's my promise to you that I'm going to stay sober, because . . ." His chin started to wobble and his voice shook, and he hated it because there was nothing more pathetic than an old man crying. But he'd come this far and he was not going to stop now. "Because you deserve better." He added one more piece, something he'd learned from Nora. "But if for some reason I can't do it, then it's my own GD fault, and you just have to let me go, okay?"

She was nodding, and crying, he noticed, big tears that came down her face in black streams from her thick eye makeup. Jasmine stood by the cash register, pretending to punch buttons, but he knew she was listening because she glanced his way and gave him a thumbs-up. Marlene had stood, her purse strung over her shoulder like she was leaving, but she had stopped and openly stared at Lewis and Persie, laughing, and it wasn't mean; it was joyful, and it was a sound that Lewis never thought he'd hear from the old woman.

"Okay, Pop," Persie said.

He sat back down, took a bite of the cobbler and a sip of the coffee, and watched Persie slide the coin into her own pocket. He felt lighter without it.

CHAPTER
THIRTY-SIX

Nora

Saturday. Her day off. Vlado would be here soon, and Nora was hurrying around the apartment, turning on her new lamps that gave the
room a cozy glow, lighting a candle that made everything smell like
apple pie, and fluffing the pillows she'd bought to go with the new
slipcover on her couch. She opened an app on her phone for the local
public radio station, and music floated from a Bluetooth speaker in the
kitchen. The program featured local bands, and this one filled her apartment with moody lyrics and acoustic guitar. She checked her reflection
in the mirror: her cheeks were pink, hair in thick waves down her back.
Her body felt light; thinking of Vlado made her happy. She smiled at
her reflection.

She pulled out ingredients to make cookies so she had something
to do with her hands that wasn't fussing with her hair or straightening
the slipcover for the thousandth time. They had been dating since last
March, and while the distance made it challenging at times, it hadn't
dampened her desire to see him whenever she could. Today they were
going to dinner at Jasmine's house, a quasi-monthly tradition that

included Marlene and a card game or two. But tonight was special because after dinner, they were all heading to the library for Marlene's art show. Marlene had been somewhat mysterious about the show, giving very little clues about what she'd painted. Nora had no idea what to expect, but she was looking forward to it.

Her phone buzzed. Is McSteamy there yet?

Nora smiled. Not yet.

A selfie popped up of Amanda standing on a paddleboard with flat blue water surrounding her. Tell him hello from Perth!

The music ended, replaced by the host. Nora was only half listening, placing round balls of cookie dough onto a baking sheet. "Up next is Mario Martinez, host of the new podcast *Life on the Street* and our new weekend host."

The dough dropped from her fingers, and she had to place a hand on the counter to keep from sinking to the floor. He was alive? She sat down at the kitchen table. Had she heard that right? She opened her phone, looked up the number of the station, and started making calls.

~

Nora was glad Vlado had offered to drive her to Denver because she would not have trusted herself to stay on the road. She was boiling with anger, anticipation, and nerves that had set her hands shaking. Outside, the mountains gave way to the flatter land surrounding Denver, and they were soon on roads clogged with cars and trucks and semis, busy even on a Saturday.

Vlado had not said a word for the entire fifty-five-minute drive to the city, and Nora was grateful for the silence. His voice startled her when he did speak. "We're here."

She looked up. They were in front of a beige three-story building. The kind with windows that are too small and a bland architectural style straight from the seventies. "This is the radio station?"

He nodded.

Her fingers grasped the door handle but she couldn't move, and her stomach churned, suddenly queasy. She thought of the last time she'd seen her brother. The way he had looked at her, his eyes dull like he'd been stripped of everything. She felt Vlado's hand on her shoulder, lightly touching her back, and she couldn't help but lean into him, his presence solid, reassuring. But the fact that he was here, witnessing this, gnawed an old wound open inside her. With Mario back in her life, would Vlado still want to be part of hers? She knew what it looked like with Mario in it, and Vlado deserved better. "I don't know if I can do this," she whispered.

Vlado tipped up her chin and looked her straight in the eyes, calm as always. "You came for answers, right? He's moved on with his life. Maybe you need to see that so you can do the same. Do you want me to come inside with you?" he asked with a slightly protective clip to his words that felt new, or maybe it had been there all along.

She shook her head. "I think I need to do this on my own."

He pressed his lips against hers, hand gently touching the back of her head, and she softened into him. He pulled back but just enough to look in her eyes with an intensity she'd never seen in him before. "Okay, but you're not alone, Nora. Haven't you figured that out yet?"

Their eyes locked for a few seconds before he released her. With a deep breath, she opened the door, stepping out into the warm city afternoon, the rumble of buses and hum of cars loud in her ears. Nothing like her quiet mountain town. The lobby of the radio station was empty of people, except for a broad-shouldered security guard at the reception desk with black hair dipped in blue and a name tag that read Josie. "Can I help you?" she asked, looking up from her book.

Nora was about to answer when her brother's voice drifted from speakers hidden somewhere in the lobby. "This is 93.2, and I'm Mario Martinez. The Rockies are scoreless in the top of the fourth against the Giants . . ."

274

She listened to her brother's rich voice echo through the lobby with the weather, news, and sports, and it was all so normal that her legs turned to toothpicks and she had to sit down in a rubbery leather seat. "Is this live?" she asked the guard, who had returned to her book.

"Um-hmm. This is Mario. He's the new guy, but he's real good. Probably make it off weekends before long."

Mario's voice was more professional sounding than his podcast, but still raw in a way that made listening to him feel like listening to a friend tell a story. He had launched into what sounded like a prerecorded segment very similar to *Tales from the Flip*, talking to people from all walks of life, sharing their stories, painting everyone as people first, then sometimes sharing that this person was homeless or that person had battled addiction or mental illness. It was good, and as Nora listened she felt her pulse slow, nerves settle, and she relaxed. He was not dead. Mario was alive. Mario was sober.

Again.

The show ended. Nora shifted her weight, unsure if she should stay or leave, unsure if she wanted to see him at all. She kneaded her thighs, remembered the look in his eyes when she screamed at him to get better. Hurt and betrayed. Exactly how she felt now. She folded her arms, indecision flitting through her muscles. Mario was exactly where she'd always wanted him to be. What more did she need from him? Her feet planted firmly to the floor. Answers. After all this time, didn't she deserve at least that?

The elevator doors opened, and for the first time in years, she was staring at her brother. He looked nothing like the broken man she remembered, but a ghost of him flickered in his eyes, and when he saw her, he went a shade paler than his normal bronzed color.

"Nora," he whispered.

For a moment, she wanted to run. She didn't want to hear the truth. What if it hurt even worse? She swallowed but found she couldn't speak.

"Um, how—uh . . ." He glanced at the security guard, who stared at them openly over her book, not trying to hide her interest. His curls had grown out into loose waves that fell to his ears, and his trimmed beard had gray highlights. He looked so much like the pictures of their dad that Nora felt her eyes well.

"I heard an ad for your show."

"Oh."

She struggled to equate this man in front of her with the brother she'd known for most of her life, with the picture she'd kept in her head all these years of the struggling kid, the emotional addict, the guy who couldn't keep his life together no matter how much she begged him to try or gave him money to help or a place to crash. "I thought you were dead, Mario."

It hit her square in the chest. She didn't know this man at all. He had sobered up, but it had been on his own terms and away from her. Away from the one person in the world who reminded him of the pain he was always trying to outrun. She could see it in his eyes. The way they clouded over, like her very presence could take him back to the night he drove their car off a cliff and the years of guilt that came afterward.

"I should have emailed, or not come at all, I—"

He dropped his bag and hurried to her in his halting gait, and then his arms were around her, pulling her to him.

He smelled clean and good, his body solid and real. She rested her head against his chest. They stood frozen like that; she cried, he rubbed circles on her back, and for those few minutes it was how it should have always been.

He squeezed once, released her, and took a step back, and Nora felt the space between them in her heart. His expression changed.

"Nora." His voice was warm but guarded. "I should have called. I'm sorry."

"But you didn't."

"No, I didn't."

"Why?" She hated how she sounded, like a petulant child, but she felt vulnerable and terribly exposed. She took a deep breath and said exactly what she was thinking. The way Marlene had taught her. "Why the hell didn't you call me? At least to let me know you were okay? I was so worried, so scared for you. How could you do that to me?"

His eyes hardened the tiniest bit, like he was lifting up a shield. He glanced at Josie, who had put her book down to stare openly at them. When she noticed Nora had stopped talking, she sucked in one side of her cheek. "Well, if y'all are going to have this very sweet emotional reunion right in front of me, I'm sorry, but I'm gonna listen. If it's privacy you want, go find a spot in that corner over there, way away from my desk."

"Sorry, Josie," Mario said and picked up his bag. Nora followed him to the corner, where they each took a seat.

"I don't understand." She didn't shift her gaze, or move at all, just put her hands in her lap and waited because after all this time, she deserved an answer. She'd pictured so many reunions but none like this, yet here he was and the idea that her brother had not succumbed to his demons—the fact that he was right here, healthy and alive—burned inside her. It was what she'd always wanted. To be a family again.

"Nora," he said. "There's not a day—" His hands had started to shake, and he ran his fingers through his hair, looked around at the empty lobby and at the security guard, who sat with her book open but her eyes still on them. "I know you don't understand and you shouldn't have to." He looked at his hands, opened and closed them. "I killed them. I took everything from you, Nora." His face twisted. "I relive the crash every night. I've played it over and over in my head, tried to figure what I could have done differently. But it doesn't matter because I can't take it back. I can't make anything better." He spoke quietly and controlled, but Nora saw his jaw tighten, his neck muscles bulge like he struggled to keep his feelings leashed, and it touched on an old nerve.

She reached out, put her hand on top of his. "You were just a kid, Mario. I've never blamed you." She'd find a job in Denver, move closer to him. Vlado already lived here, so why not? She and Mario could meet for breakfast, bike together the way they used to, hang out. They could make up for years of lost time. But even as she thought it, the images quickly dimmed. It wasn't what he wanted, and she realized, it wasn't what she wanted. Not anymore.

He hung his head. "You never have, but I've blamed myself. And the drugs, they just . . . they let me stop thinking. They helped me to forget."

"But now you're doing so well." She was trying to take it all in, how he carried the guilt like a cross. Sadness for his constant pain lodged itself like an arrow inside her heart.

"I am doing well, really well, but every day is a struggle, Nora." He spoke through his teeth when he said, "Every. Single. Day."

She reached out, wanting to touch him, but he flinched and her hands hung useless in the space between them. "Why couldn't you let me help you?" The question flayed her. She'd thought he needed her, but she'd been so wrong.

He wiped a hand along his jaw. "I won't put you through another failure."

"But you haven't failed."

"Not yet. But one thing I've learned is to trust the process, and it's day by day by day." She wanted to hold him, she wanted to tell him she could help, that together they could beat anything. But that was the old her, and it had never helped.

Maybe it was having known Lewis that shifted everything for her, because in that moment, it felt like the clouds above her dissipated and she understood. This wasn't her battle, it wasn't her fight, and it wasn't her place to make sure he stayed sober. And that was okay. It was okay for her to let him survive on his own. And it was okay for her to live her own life while he did. "I've put so much pressure on you, haven't I?"

"I know you meant well, Nora. I never doubted that. But I have to do this by myself and for myself. If I try to do it for anyone else, I just—I can't."

She touched his hand and his fingers opened. They sat together in the lobby with the radio show playing in the background, holding hands, and Nora felt as sure as she had that Thanksgiving when she was nine. "I'm proud of you, Mario."

He smiled and it showed the lines around his eyes.

"Mom and Dad would have been proud of you too." She squeezed his hand and stood, smiling back and hoping it masked the hurt. "I'm still at the library in Silver Ridge, so if you ever want to stop by"—her breaking voice belied the strength in her words—"I'll be there."

He sagged into the seat, and the worry lines in his forehead eased, as though a heavy weight had fallen from his shoulders. Then he rose to his feet and hugged her, and she melted into him, his smell familiar in a way that hurt, his arms strong around her. "Thank you," he whispered into her hair.

She turned to go, hesitated; her chest ached from everything she wanted to say but wouldn't. "Aunt Sophie always thought you had a perfect voice for radio. She was right. You're really good." She slung her purse over her shoulder and smiled. "See you around, Mario."

"Love you, Peaches."

"Always." She walked out the glass doors, keeping her back straight and hurrying across the small plaza to a metered spot in front where Vlado had parked. With stinging eyes, she climbed inside and buckled her seat belt.

"How did it go?"

Her bottom lip trembled. "I let him go."

Vlado put his hand on her thigh, palm up. She slid her fingers through his, and the feel of his skin against hers was enough to remind her of everything that waited for her in Silver Ridge.

"Home?" he said.

She checked her watch. They'd missed dinner at Jasmine's house. "The library. I don't want to miss Marlene's art show."

He started the car and began to drive. The city disappeared outside and the mountains rose up from the earth. Vlado held her hand but didn't say a word all the way back to Silver Ridge, and for that she was grateful.

CHAPTER THIRTY-SEVEN

NORA

Vlado pulled up to the library and shut the car off. Nora stared at the building, glowing in the September dusk. On the drive from Denver, the sky had turned heavy and gray, with scattered snowflakes drifting in the air. There was an early winter storm forecast for the foothills. Nothing like last spring but quite a measurable amount for so early in the fall. Despite the weather, the library was busy with people coming in and out, carrying canvases of all sizes. Johanna stood by the door, directing everyone inside.

Her heart hurt but it had been the right thing to let Mario go. Something she should have done a long time ago. Someone knocked on her window. Marlene. She rolled down the window.

"To truly appreciate an art show, one has to come inside to see the paintings," Marlene said, and in a softer voice: "Vlado called to tell me about Mario. You did a very brave thing, Nora."

"Thank you," she whispered.

"I saw a friend of ours yesterday who did a very brave thing too."

"Who?"

Jasmine appeared beside Marlene, smiling. "Lewis! He's sober and he actually came into the diner and talked to Persie. Can you believe it?"

Nora's heart pushed against her chest. Lewis had done it. She got out of the car, and Vlado joined her.

"My grandma saved you some jerk chicken and a piece of her strawberry shortcake," Jasmine said. "You're invited for lunch tomorrow." She rolled her eyes. "She might just feed you all and give you gifts for the rest of your lives. Bet you wish you hadn't saved my life now."

Marlene smiled. "Not in a million lifetimes."

Nora's shoulders lifted; their presence reminded her of everything she'd gained, everything they'd all gained since the storm. And it was exactly what she needed. Together, they walked inside. It was warm and bustling with people setting up Marlene's artwork. She pointed to the stacks, where canvases leaned against the walls, perched on easels. "Those are all yours?"

Marlene stood a little taller and she looked stronger, too, like her body didn't have as much of a say in how she felt. "I call it *A Night at the Library*."

Nora felt something burst open inside her, and she laughed and it felt like a release, a return to normal, but a normal she'd never known she was missing until right now.

Vlado picked up a couple of canvases to take them into the back. "And how fortuitous that there's another winter storm to celebrate it."

"Happy accidents," Marlene said.

"If she sells anything," Jasmine said, "she's donating all her money to an addiction and rehab place."

Marlene's eyes opened wider. "'If'?"

Jasmine smiled. "Oh, don't worry, Grandma will buy a ton."

Johanna poked her head around the corner. "It's all set up. Come and see."

When Nora entered the stacks, she didn't know where to look first. Most of the paintings were layers of black and blue and gray paint, giving the impression of an endless velvet darkness. A soft glow punctured the shadows and illuminated faces, and each face told a story.

Immediately she was drawn back to the night of the storm—the cold, the uncertainty, and the warmth that had come from their little circle. There was one of Jasmine with her overstuffed backpack pressed to her chest, dark eyes defiant and angry, a lift in her chin that showed her strength, a softness around her mouth that showed her kindness. One of Lewis, his face heavily lined, shadows under his eyes but a determination in the lift of his shoulders, standing by a ruined library wall and passing a snow-covered book to someone beyond the canvas. One that made her laugh of Vlado, his starched security shirt taut around his torso, with long blond hair that tumbled in waves over his shoulders and down his back, standing waist deep in a calm sea.

"Um, Marlene?" she said.

Vlado was smiling. "Galene, the goddess of calm seas. You did some research, Marlene."

Marlene sniffed. "Turns out your Geek mythology is pretty interesting."

"Greek," he said.

Marlene tapped him on the shoulder. "I thought she fit you best."

"Goddess of calm seas. It's perfect," Nora said. "It's what draws people to you."

Vlado touched her back. "'People'?"

She smiled. "And me."

The paintings were beautiful and real—some funny, some piercing—and it brought the entire night back. There were others, too, of Silver Ridge, that highlighted the beauty of the mountains, the thickness of the forests, but didn't hide the forms that hung out on park benches or stood in line for food at the church. The entire collection was a beautiful tribute to the people who called their town home.

"You've been watching, Marlene," she said.

"It's what Charlie loved about me, I suppose."

"Me too." She said it before she had time to think, but it was true. Marlene had been her friend when she'd needed one the most.

Marlene made a noise in her throat but didn't respond. Instead, she took Nora by the shoulders and turned her so that she was face-to-face with her painted self. Hers was nothing like the others. It was painted in loud, expressive colors with too many images to process at once. She was in the center, at her desk with a book open in front of her, and in a clockwork procession around her was everyone: Jasmine, Vlado, Lewis, even Marlene.

"Your book was right after all," Vlado said.

"What book?"

Jasmine piped up from behind her. "The manuscript."

"Oh yes, the magical manuscript that told you that your life had purpose. It was almost right," Marlene said. "But it had one thing wrong."

Nora turned to look at her. "What?"

"Your purpose isn't to save the world, Nora, or to save Lewis or me, or Mario for that matter. It never was."

"Then what is it?" She could barely get the words out because her throat had closed over a lump.

Marlene touched her face. "To be you."

"I'm not sure I know who that is," Nora whispered.

Marlene just smiled and laughed. "Nobody does. That's why we have each other."

Nora breathed in. That night had changed everybody. Vlado lifted one side of his mouth and looked at Nora in a way that she felt from her toes up. Marlene was right. Amanda had been right. Her aunt and uncle had been right. And whatever Mario's path, it was time, Nora supposed, that she started living for herself.

She wiped her eyes dry. Despite the snow, the library had started to fill up, and people held glasses of wine and studied Marlene's paintings.

Nora found one of Charlie and Marlene that had been tucked away in a far corner.

"Marlene, do you still have those tickets to Tulum?"

"Good until next May."

"Can I take Charlie's place with you?"

Marlene stared at her for a minute, her face blank; then she smiled and blinked several times. "He would have loved that."

AUTHOR'S NOTE

The creative pull to write a story often comes from moments of quiet or when I'm listening or learning about someone or something else.

I listen to podcasts. They are my audiobook equivalent. And one of my favorites is *This American Life*. So it was on a snowy mountain day (much like in the book) when I was listening to the December 28, 2018, episode called "The Room of Requirement" that I first heard about the Brautigan Library. It's a different kind of library that offers unique and interesting stories from aspiring writers and was inspired by the twentieth-century American author Richard Brautigan and his fictional library where all manuscripts had a home.

As a writer, I was immediately drawn to the idea of a library for all. The podcast interviewed the curator and librarian, John F. Barber, faculty member of the Creative Media and Digital Culture program at Washington State University Vancouver. Mr. Barber developed and curates American Dust, an online resource about Richard Brautigan. Barber published two books, *Richard Brautigan: An Annotated Bibliography* and *Richard Brautigan: Essays on the Writings and Life*, and several essays about Brautigan.

In the interview, Mr. Barber described a few of the volumes housed at the library, including one of its most prolific contributors, Albert Helzner, who contributed sixteen philosophical manuscripts to the library. Mr. Helzner was a chemical engineer by day—with a US patent published in the professional journal *Chemical Engineering*—and a chess enthusiast who won a Massachusetts Class A chess championship, and by night he was a philosopher who wrote deeply thought-provoking pieces.

As I listened to the episode, I started to get creative butterflies dancing inside, the ones I've learned to listen to because they mean an idea wants to grow. I immediately connected to the writings of Mr. Helzner and could feel the passion in his thinking and in the observations he shared through his manuscripts. He questioned the simple interactions between people and strangers, and his writings shed light on an individual's unique experiences that had led them to any particular moment in time. In one manuscript, he spoke directly to a newborn baby born on October 6, 1990, and asked himself questions like *How did the birth of that baby come about?* and *What is the long-range effect of this particular birth?*

I reached out to Mr. Barber, anxious to know more about the library and Mr. Helzner in particular. Sadly, Mr. Helzner passed in 2016, but I was put in touch with his lovely and very talented daughter, Ronnee-Sue Helzner, who enthusiastically and kindly shared so much of her father and his writings with me. He was a truly special man who had an impact on all who knew him, and I was grateful that our worlds overlapped because of the podcast.

Inspired by Mr. Helzner's writings, I considered how our experiences affect our interactions and perceptions of people and strangers, and those butterflies kept dancing when I linked my thoughts with another idea about people experiencing homelessness and our public libraries. It didn't take long before the idea grew into a small town, a snowstorm, and five strangers stranded at a library.

ACKNOWLEDGMENTS

So much work and effort goes into writing a book, and not just from the writer. It's a team effort, and with each book, my gratitude for the team grows deeper. Thank you to Chris Werner, for taking on yet another of my stories and working so diligently with me to mine all I could from this one. To Jessica Faust, for being the greatest agent ever and working with me to shape this writing thing into a career. To the miracle worker Tiffany Yates Martin, for going all in with every single editing pass and enthusiastically and skillfully guiding my characters and story to places I couldn't see in the beginning. And to the Lake Union crew who work their magic every step of the way: Gabe Dumpit, Nicole Burns-Ascue, Rachel Norfleet, Kellie Osborne, and everyone else who had a part in putting this book into the hands of readers.

To Mr. Albert Helzner, for seeing the world in a way that inspired me to come up with a character like Nora. And for sharing your unique perspective with readers like me. I wish I could have met you, but I'm forever grateful to have heard about your work in the first place. The world needs more inquisitive minds like yours.

To Ronnee-Sue Helzner, for sharing your father's work with me and for the many emails back and forth helping me to gain a deeper understanding of his work and perspective when world circumstances kept me from traveling to the Brautigan Library to read them myself. I love when research and writing bring me into someone else's orbit. I enjoyed getting to know you and your father and now count you as a friend and look forward to staying in touch.

To John Barber, for your continued work curating the Brautigan Library. I'm forever happy to know there's a place that collects, preserves, and curates unpublished manuscripts from aspiring writers. Everyone has a story to share.

To the brilliant folks behind *This American Life*. Thank you for bringing your listeners interesting stories and perspectives every week. Your show is a constant companion while I fold laundry, clean the kitchen, and walk the dog, and I always take something new away.

To my family: Ella, Keira, and Sawyer, Mom and Dad, Sean, you have all made space in each of our relationships for me to burrow away in a hole with a bunch of characters for months on end. I'm immeasurably lucky to have your love and enthusiastic support. I love you back with all my heart.

And to my early readers, who always see my book when it's half-dressed and still wearing its retainer; Sara Miller, my talented author-friend, who also happens to be a kick-ass editor; Taryn Young, my dear friend who has read nearly every word I've ever written and still volunteers to read more; and my critique partners, Mary Johnson and Elizabeth Richards, whose feedback I can't do without.

BOOK CLUB QUESTIONS

1. We live in a world filled with many different kinds of people, and often, before we get to know someone, we allow stereotypes to inform our view of others. This book is about getting to know a person by learning her story first. What preconceived notions did others have about Nora? About each other? How did that affect how they related to one another at the beginning of the story?

2. As a reader, what preconceived ideas did you bring to the story from your own experiences? How did that lens affect the story for you? Did anything change for you as you got to know the characters?

3. The night at the library was a pivotal turning point for each character. What prompted the shift for each of them?

4. How did Nora, Marlene, and Lewis change as the story progressed? Did you find their growth believable? Why or why not?

5. Addiction is a fact of life for many people, whether indirectly, like Nora, or directly, like Mario and Lewis. Nora felt like her brother's sobriety was partly her responsibility. How did that affect her life and choices? Could you

relate to her? Why or why not? Did you find her shift at the end of the book believable?

6. Without power, it is very dark throughout the night at the library. How did the dark play a role in the characters' interactions?

7. Lewis is a homeless addict with PTSD who ended up living on the streets. His odor and dirty clothes are mentioned often, yet despite his physical appearance, everyone grows to understand him and see him as the person he once was and is. Did you find this plausible? How often does appearance play a role in how we judge others? How can we learn the stories of others in our own lives?

8. Did the ending satisfy you or leave you with lingering questions? Was there anything that frustrated or spoke to you about the characters or story?

9. Many libraries and librarians witness the tragic effects of homelessness and addiction firsthand and have had to come up with creative solutions for serving this marginalized population while also keeping the libraries a safe space for everyone. Has your community experienced these challenges? Have you?

10. The Silver Ridge Library was based on what famous libraries? How many of these libraries were once scattered across the US? Extra points for knowing this without an internet search. ☺

ABOUT THE AUTHOR

Photo © 2020 Eric Weber

Melissa Payne is the bestselling, award-winning author of *The Secrets of Lost Stones* and *Memories in the Drift*. For as long as she can remember, Melissa has been telling stories in one form or another—from high school newspaper articles to a graduate thesis to blogging about marriage and motherhood. But she first learned the real importance of storytelling when she worked for a residential and day treatment center for abused and neglected children. There she wrote speeches and letters to raise funds for the children. The truth in those stories was piercing and painful and written to invoke a call to action in the reader: to give, to help, to make a difference. Melissa's love of writing and sharing stories in all forms has endured. She lives in the foothills of the Rocky Mountains with her husband and three children, a friendly mutt, a very loud cat, and the occasional bear. For more information, visit www.melissapayneauthor.com.